Singing with Angels

DILLON ORR

WESTBOW
PRESS®
A DIVISION OF THOMAS NELSON
& ZONDERVAN

WestBow Press books may be ordered through booksellers or by contacting:

WestBow Press
A Division of Thomas Nelson & Zondervan
1663 Liberty Drive
Bloomington, IN 47403
www.westbowpress.com
1 (866) 928-1240

ISBN: 978-1-9736-9498-4 (sc)
ISBN: 978-1-9736-9499-1 (e)

Print information available on the last page.

WestBow Press rev. date: 6/22/2020

Contents

John

It was another average Sunday morning. John William and his parents had breakfast and are now getting ready for church. It's eighty degrees in the small town of Bruce, Alabama, but as soon as they step a foot into the church, they will be freezing. It's too cold when the weather is hot and too hot during the winter.

Before leaving his room after getting dressed, he looked in the mirror. He was wearing a plain white button-down shirt with blue jeans and had on his fifty-dollar pair of church shoes. He stood there six feet three and had his red hair combed. *I don't look too bad.* He thought to himself. *Maybe today the Lord will give me the sign that I need.*

For the past two years, John has been trying to find out what his gift is. He knows he is good at something, but doesn't know what it is. He tried drawing; painting, commentating, and he even tried being a clown. None of them worked. With only a couple of months left of high school, he is running out of ideas. Both of his parents have faith in him though and have been praying that he will find out what God wants him to do.

"Let's go, son." His dad yelled from downstairs.

"Yes, sir!" John yelled back.

Please, God. Lead me the way.

He walked downstairs where his parents were waiting on him. His parents' names are Mary and Michael. They've been together since they were teenagers, and not once had a single fight. They got married shortly after high school and a year later John was born. They both go to church, pray every night, and help anyone as much as they can.

Mary is wearing a long blue dress and has her dark red hair in a ponytail. While some mothers and wives stay at home, her husband lets her work once John went to school. She is now a manager at a beauty salon.

You would think she would be too tired to cook supper after work, but most of the time she still will have the energy needed to do so.

Michael is around John's height and has black hair. Usually, Michael and his son wear the same thing on Sundays, but this time Michael is wearing different church clothes. He has on a red polo shirt and black jeans. He owns his own business called 'William's Hardware Store'. Not only does he sell hardware supplies, but he also fixes things, like lawnmowers, after work, for a little extra cash.

Some people would say John is lucky to have parents like his. The truth is, though, he isn't lucky. God blessed this family. He gave them John, and gave his dad his very own business, and let his mom become a manager. God wanted them to do these things. However, He hasn't given John a clue of what He wants him to do.

John's parents said to him to be patient, and he has been. Sometimes it's tough, though. Waiting for a sign and never knowing when he will get it. Will he know a year from now or will he find out today? Only God knows. "I have a feeling that today will be the day that will change my life forever."

The three of them got into the truck and drove toward the church. The truck was a black Toyota Tacoma and one day it's going to be John's truck. He knows this because his dad told him he can have it once he graduated. John heard his parents talking about some guy drinking.

"Yea, he got arrested again the other day." His dad said in a disappointed tone. "I don't know why people would want to waste their lives away by drinking all the time."

"Maybe you should try to get him to come to church one day," Mary replied.

"I've tried sweetie, but he always refuses. It's worse that he's doing that stuff around his daughter. Maybe I can see if he will let her come with us one day."

"I heard the mother does drugs. Lily told me last week she saw her buying drugs from some odd-looking guy."

"How did she know it was drugs?"

"Well, she said that's what it looked like. Lily loves to watch them cop shows."

I'm not sure who they are talking about, but I feel sorry for them. Why would people want to destroy themselves with alcohol and drugs? They could be doing something with their lives. Instead, they would rather let the devil take away a piece of their life, a little at a time. I'll pray for them. Usually, it's one person out of each family that goes down the dark path. Like with my family, my cousin was doing meth. We didn't find out until he passed away from an overdose. He never really talked to any of us. Every time we would mention church, he would mock us. He said if there was a God, then why hasn't He made him rich! Sometimes he would tell us he had a meeting and didn't have the time for church. I guess that meeting was getting a fix. Yea, every family has someone who goes down the wrong path. Sometimes it's not just one member. Sometimes it's most of the family, and the one that is trying to walk on the righteous path keeps getting blocked off by their family.

Looking out the window, John could tell that he and his dad will go fishing after church. They have always gone fishing after church when the weather is warm enough. It's been that way as far back as John could remember. The only way they wouldn't go fishing is if it was to rain. From the way the sky looks, it won't be raining. The sun is shining brightly, and there isn't a cloud in the sky.

He always has loved going fishing with his dad. It's his favorite thing to do with him. They do stuff together like jogging, watching sports on TV, and fixing up lawnmowers. His dad doesn't make him help either, John always volunteers. All this stuff they do together, and fishing is his favorite. The warm air makes him feel relaxed, with a small cool breeze coming by now and then. They would throw the small fish back into the water and keep the big ones to bring home and cook. They never bring alcohol to drink while fishing, they always drink sweet tea or some sodas. Of course, they never wanted to bring alcohol while they fished. As a matter of fact, they don't allow alcohol in their home. His parents told him he can drink at the age of twenty-one if he wanted to, but he said no. He had seen what that stuff does to people. Sure, he could drink responsibly, but that doesn't mean that one day he'll just change his mind and get drunk. Besides, drinking doesn't make you an adult. That stuff is just a waste of time and money.

He overheard his parent's conversation again. This time they were discussing on why, whoever the person was, drinks.

"Maybe he was abused as a child," Mary said.

"Or maybe he was never disciplined." Replied Michael.

"Thankfully, our son is."

"Yea, thankfully."

Michael looked at the rear-view mirror to see what John was doing. He was just staring out the window. What he didn't know was that John was listening. They thought just because they had <u>Mercy Me</u> playing loud on the radio that he wasn't listening. He was though. Well, sort of. Now he was thinking of all the times that his dad whooped him with a belt for getting into trouble.

I remember when I was younger, and I talked back to not just my dad, but my mom too. Boy, I never did that again. Some people would whoop their kids for being in a fight, but not mine. At least, not because of the situation I was in.

It was about two years ago, and it was during recess. I heard what sounded like an argument. So, I went over to the side of the building where the noise was coming from and saw a girl and her, what I'm guessing was her boyfriend, arguing. They looked older so they must have been in a higher grade than I. Anyway, I saw him slap her and I ran over and tackled the guy. Next thing I knew, we both were in the principal's office with busted lips and me with a broken nose. Both of us had three days of suspension. At first, it upset my dad that I was in a fight. But on our way out of the school, the girl that got hit stopped us and thanked me. She told me I was one of the good guys. I told my dad how the fight started, and she stood there agreeing with me. My dad went from being mad at me to being proud of me.

They were now at the church and his dad parked the truck and they got out. It was your average looking church. White with a cross on the top of the roof. The church has been here since the construction of the town. At least that's what the preacher said. Since this is such a small town, there was only one church.

Alright. John thought to himself. *Let's go worship the Lord.*

Katherine

Katherine Lee woke up sweating from the morning heat again. This happens every spring and summer. Her parents would rather use the money on drugs and alcohol, then to buy an air conditioner. It was early Sunday morning and this time she wasn't woken up by her parents yelling at each other. *Either they're passed out or they aren't home.* She thought to herself.

She got up and tried to decide on which dirty clothes she should wear today since they don't have a washer or dryer. She usually wears the same dirty clothes repeatedly. Sometimes if the weather isn't too bad, she would go down to the pond or creek and wash a couple of clothes if possible. Well, she wouldn't really wash them since they don't have any soap. *What should I do today?*

Today she wore her red button-down shirt and blue jeans with her white sandals. Her clothes are a little tight since she hasn't had any new clothes in two years. After putting on a different pair of clothes, she looked into the broken mirror on the wall. Her black hair was a mess and tangled up. *For once I wish I could brush it, so it could look nice.* The only two things that grew were her hair and herself. She is five foot five with bright blue eyes.

I finished reading the book I borrowed from the library, so I guess I can return it and get a new one. Oh, wait! It's Sunday, they are closed today. The owner goes to that church on Sundays. Maybe this time I'll go. I've always heard that church is a good place to go to. I've never been myself so I'm not sure if that's true or not. All I know is that people go there to talk about some guy named Jesus. He is supposed to be this really nice guy that helped many people a long time ago. Wish He was still around. He could help me out some. Oh well, soon I'll be done with high school and then I can get out of here and be free.

No more yelling. No more fighting. She raised her shirt up and showed herself in the mirror. *No more bruises.* Her back was bruised from where her dad would hit her with a belt. *He only does it when he gets in trouble from work, which happens a lot because he is always drunk at work. Just a couple of more months and I'll be free.*

Before she graduates though, it would be nice if someone would ask her to the prom. *It's at the end of the month and no one has asked her yet.* A tear ran down her cheek, but she wiped it away. *I never even had a boyfriend.*

Katherine heard a door slam and her dad yelled.

"Get up woman and make yourself useful!" he shouted.

Katherine's dad was about six foot with brown hair. His voice was as deep as you could imagine, and he had a beard as thick as a bush since as long as she could remember, Kenny, which is her dad's name, was always drunk. He's drunk most of the time unless he's asleep. He never stays at one job either. He would work at one place until the manager would get tired of him, and then he'll get a new job somewhere else. No one knows how he is still getting jobs.

He must have found a liquor store that was open. She thought to herself. *He ran out last night.* Her body shook as she knew after he yells at her mom, he will come in her room next. Her mom probably was lying on the couch again. *Get a hold of yourself.*

"How about you make yourself useful for once, you drunk!" her mom yelled back.

Her mom was probably asleep before her dad came home. Sarah Lee was her mother's name. She had black hair and was about Katherine's height. Just like Kenny, she too had an addiction. Hers were drugs, though. Katherine doesn't know what kind, but she could tell that her mom is always on something and it's never alcohol. Sarah never had a beer or a bottle of liquor in her hand, but she always seems like she's out of her head. That or she's usually asleep on the couch.

"I'm the one who works!" Kenny screamed back.

"Yeah and use up all the money on booze!"

"Well, I wouldn't have to use it on booze if I had a real wife! You know the kind that doesn't take my money and spend it on garbage for a fix!"

"I don't know why I put up with you! You're not even a real man!"

After Sarah said that, Katherine heard crashing noises and more yelling. Tears rolled down her face as she shook even more. *Why do they have to be my parents? What did they even see in each other? I'm tired of those two doing this every other day. My heart hurts again.*

She doesn't know much about her parents' childhoods. They dropped out in twelfth grade and got married a year later. At first, Katherine thought it was for love, but how can that be? They yell and fight with each other all the time. *Why don't they leave each other? That might stop all of this chaos and anger.*

Then she remembered about that church building. *Maybe I can find that Jesus person over there and ask Him for help. I heard people say He was around a long time ago. Maybe He came back to visit. I just know I can't stay here while they are awake. I don't have time to grab some clothes and go to the creek. The library is closed. Church is the only option, and it's supposed to be a good place. I know I can't handle this today and if my back gets hit anymore, I'll bleed.*

"How about you leave me alone and go bother your good-for-nothing daughter!" Sarah yelled.

Katherine panicked and opened her bedroom window. Climbing out, she heard her dad screaming for her.

"Katherine!"

No. No. No. No. She looked back and saw him kick the door open.

"Oh, no you don't!"

Katherine jumped out and ran. As she ran, she could hear her dad yelling at her to come back. *No, I can't take anymore. Not today, anyway. Just leave me alone for once. I have to find that Jesus guy. I know He can help. Please be at that church. Please.*

After she thought she was safe, Katherine slowed down and started to walk. She was burning up in her room, but it feels decent outside. The warm air felt nice against her face. She stopped and stared at the sky. The sky was bluer than the water in the lake. She then closed her eyes and took a long deep breath. *Fresh air. Clean, warm, fresh air. Better than the air back at the house.*

Katherine wiped her tears away and went back to walking. *I don't even know what a church looks like. I've only heard people talk about it. I never actually knew where it is or what it looks like. I guess I'll know when I see it. For such a small town, you think I would know. Of course, I don't live in the actual town. I just lie right outside.*

She and her parents have always lived outside of town. Her dad said it's because he doesn't like people. Sometimes she wished they lived in town, so everyone could hear her mom and dad. She also wished that someone would stop by and just talk to her. Kenny doesn't want any company though. Besides, who would want to come to her house. It's old, worn out, and smelly. Most of the paint is off on the outside and there are, what seems like, an endless pile of beer bottles in the yard.

I wonder what dad is doing now I ran off. Is he hitting mom, or did he pass out? Hopefully, he'll be asleep by the time I get back. I'll be able to sleep peacefully. Man, how long have I been walking? It's only about a mile from the house to town, and I ran a good bit. Oh, here it is.

When she got into town, she searched for what she would think will be the church. So far, she only saw the usual; a grocery store, a bank, some houses, and the school, so nothing out of the ordinary. The towns' people seemed nice though. They were saying "Hey," "How are you?" or "Good morning!" none of them yelled at her or gave her a dirty look.

Maybe I should ask where the church is. No. then I'll look stupid and would be embarrassed. Oh, man! I bet I look a mess! I sure hope that no one can smell me. This stinks. Literally!

"You there!" some woman yelled.

She was wearing a flower looking dress and had black glasses.

"Aren't you Kenny Lee's daughter?"

"Yes, ma'am," Katherine replied as she looked down.

"Well, what are you doing here in town? I never see you around."

"I got tired of being around the house."

"Oh, well. I could use the help with this flower shop. My name is Holly by the way."

"I'm Katherine."

"Nice to meet you, Katherine."

She knows my dad and is still talking to me? I can't believe it. It's nice to talk to someone other than a teacher. Someone who doesn't yell at me or tells me I'm a mistake. Actually, I'm a little surprised that she hasn't told me I smell. She must know where our house is and what it looks like.

"You go to school Katherine?" Holly asked.

"Yes, ma'am. I graduate this year."

"Well, how about you help me out after school hours? I'll pay you. A girl your age should have a part-time job after school."

"Really? Thank you!"

A huge smile formed on Katherine's face and she gave Holly a tight hug. Katherine's back was in extreme pain from hugging so hard, but she didn't mind. She now has a small part-time job. She might can even buy a dress for the prom.

"Can you start today?" Holly asked while trying to catch her breath.

Katherine let go and stared at Holly. *Oh man, I almost forgot! I got to find that church building!*

"Actually, I'm kind of in a hurry. I'm trying to find someone, and they're supposed to be at the church."

"Oh well, that's ok. You can start on Monday after school. You better hurry if you don't want to miss them. Church should end any minute now."

Katherine took off without saying goodbye to Holly. She heard Holly saying she'll see her tomorrow. *Oh no, I forgot to ask her where the church is and what it looks like! I don't have time to go back though. She said church is about to end. I have to hurry. I have to trust my gut on what it looks like.*

She finally stopped in front of a white building with an unusual plus sign on top. *Could this be it? There's something inside of me saying this is it. I'm kind of nervous. I mean, what if that Jesus guy isn't even here? There's only one way to find out, and that's just to walk right in. Okay, here I go.* Katherine took a long deep breath and went inside.

A Great Sunday

Katherine walked into the church and everyone, even the pastor looked at her. She stood there, staring back at them. After about a second or two, everyone turned their head back to the pastor as he went back to preaching. She sat down on the last bench of the left side of the church. There were ten brown wooden benches on each side, and they filled most of them with people. The walls were white and two of them had Jesus on a cross on them. Where the pastor was, a giant cross stood behind him.

Ok, now that I'm here, where is Jesus? Katherine thought to herself. *Let me see. That lady wearing the huge glasses isn't Him; at least I don't think so. Jesus sounds like a man's name. What about the bald guy? No, that doesn't seem right. Maybe He's the guy in the front that's talking loud! No, that can't be Him either, because he's talking about Jesus.*

She looked around some more, trying to find Jesus. *What about these ornaments with that guy on that odd-looking plus sign? Could that be Jesus? Hmm. I'm not sure. I mean, it feels like that could be Him, but I'm not sure. He must be popular here.*

How come I don't feel that nervous being in here? You would think I would since I'm in a place I never been in. Especially with many people in it. This is a little strange to me. I actually feel comfortable and calm. I feel safe. Maybe I'll come here from now on, instead of the library. I can't explain it, but I'm calm here. Hopefully, this place is open every day and not just Sundays.

Maybe I should try to get my dad and mom to come here. Then Jesus can talk to the two. Help them get their lives straight and convince them to be better parents. Of course, the opposite will happen, and dad will get mad at me. First, he'll yell at me and then he'll get the belt. While he's doing that, he will cuss at me. Never mind. I'll just keep my mouth shut.

"Let us pray." The pastor said.

Pray? What pray? Why does everyone have their heads down? The guy in the front is still talking, but he has his head down as well. Is he talking to himself or to his dad? He keeps saying Father, so he must be talking to his dad. But why isn't he looking at him instead of the floor?

Everyone said 'amen' and then began to leave. *What just happened? Where is everyone going?* While people were leaving, she saw a boy from her school walking towards her. *I guess Jesus isn't coming today.*

───

Today the pastor was preaching about signs and gifts. Not the gifts you would get on Christmas, but the kind that makes you good at something. Some people would call them talents, but John calls them gifts.

"God has given each and every one of you a gift." Pastor Bill said. "Some of you already know what your gifts are. Some of you haven't found it yet, but I'm telling you that you will find it. Look for the signs that God will give you. Whatever that gift may be, God wants you to use it."

I know He wants me to use it. John thought. *I don't know what it is yet. I wish I did, though. Whatever it is, I know that God has a reason for me to wait to see what it is. I don't care what my gift is; I know that I'll put it to good use.*

Suddenly, the doors opened, and a random girl walked in. It was Katherine Lee from school. *Oh wow, what is she doing here? I never knew she liked church. Man, it got quiet in here suddenly. Even Pastor Bill stopped preaching. This is so rude of us to be just staring at her.*

Everyone went back to listening to the pastor as he continued preaching. This time he talked about Jesus. John heard his parents whispering about Katherine.

"Isn't that Kenny and Sarah Lee's daughter?" Mary whispered.

"Yeah, I think so." His dad whispered back.

"What is she doing in church? I've never seen her here, and why is she alone?"

"Well dear, you know what her parents are like. I mean, they mock Christians. They think we're crazy or something."

"Maybe their kid wanted to see if we really are insane."

"Or maybe she wanted to find out what Christianity is all about. She probably doesn't believe her parents and wants to see who God really is."

"Either way, she looks like a mess. At least, she should wear some decent clothes."

"That's rude, Mary."

I don't know what my mom is talking about. I think Katherine looks beautiful. Her clothes are fine. I don't know why, but just by thinking about her makes my heart race. Ever since I saw her the first time in school, I've always wanted to ask her out, but never could find the courage to do it. I mean, it's not just because she's gorgeous. She's smart too, and not always trying to show off. Maybe I should ask her to come fishing with us. I mean, I know it's a dad and son kind of thing, but something tells me I should ask. Does she even like to fish? I don't even know. I'll ask her after church. Great, now I'm sweating.

Pastor Bill closed out with a prayer and then everyone started walking out. *Alright, John. Just get up and ask her if she would want to come fishing. Maybe I should ask dad if it's ok first. What if he says no?*

"Hey, dad," John said, facing his dad. "Is it ok if Katherine joins us? I mean, I know it's our thing, but she looks upset or something."

"Uh ..." Michael said, sounding surprised. "Oh, why not? I guess it wouldn't hurt. Go invite her."

"Thanks, dad."

John walked over to where Katherine was sitting and took a deep breath. His hands were trembling, and his heart raced. *Calm yourself down. Everything will be fine.*

"Hey, Katherine," John said to her, smiling.

"H-Hey." She said back, all nervous.

"I didn't know you come to church. How long have you been coming here?"

"Today."

"Oh. Well, that's good. Um. I was wondering if you would like to go fishing with me and my dad. If you don't want to then I guess I understand."

"Fishing?"

"Yeah, fishing. You know, catching fish with a pole and a line?"

"You really want me to come?"

"Well, you seem kind of upset about something and I figured that fishing would help you feel better. It always has helped me feel better whenever I'm upset."

"Oh. Well, sure, I guess."

John sighed with relief. His heart calmed down and he made a huge grin.

"Really? Great! You can ride with me and my parents. We have to drop my mom off at the house first. Where are your parents?"

Katherine's eyes shifted away and took a deep breath.

"They um … they don't want to come."

"Oh, ok. My parents are waiting. Come on."

⬯

They dropped Mary off back at the William's house. The drive there was pretty quiet. Michael and Mary didn't ask any questions to Katherine. *They must not like me.* She thought to herself. *Either that or they know who my mom and dad are. They must think I'm like my parents. I'm not like them though.*

After Mary got out of the truck, they drove towards the pond. Katherine felt embarrassed. She knew they didn't know she sometimes washes her clothes in the pond, but it still made her feel ashamed. *I sure hope they will never find out. Then they'll think I'm disgusting.*

She turned her head and stared at John, who was looking out the window. He was biting his nails as if he was nervous. *Why did he ask me to go with them? We're not friends that I know of. He never really spoke to me in school, and he never asked me to hang out with him before. So why now? It can't be because I'm pretty. Because I'm not. I smell, my clothes are always dirty, and I never have makeup on. He could just be trying to be nice. He doesn't have a reason though. I would ask, but that would be rude.*

They got to the pond and sat everything up. The chairs were a couple of feet away from the water, and the cooler was between the chairs. They only had two chairs, but John volunteered to stand, and let Katherine have his chair. They got the poles ready and tossed the lines.

"We got chips and stuff in the truck if you're hungry," John told Katherine. "There're sodas and bottles of water in the cooler as well."

After hearing him mentioning food, her stomach growled. The only time she gets to eat is when she's at school. Sometimes, if she's lucky enough, she'll find a piece of ham in the fridge at the house.

"Chips sounds nice." She said.

"I'll bring you a sandwich too."

"Thank you."

He is so nice. He's also very handsome. I can't explain what has all happened today. First, I got an after-school job at a flower shop. Then, I got asked to go fishing with a cute and kind guy. I enjoy it, but this feels strange. I've never been treated like this before.

The air still felt nice, and the pond looked so clear. There wasn't a cloud in the sky, and you could hear the birds chirping nearby. *It's so calm here. I've never hung out with such kind people. Oh man, I feel like I'm going to cry. Keep yourself together, girl. You don't want them to see you cry. Take a deep breath and enjoy the rest of the day.*

"So, Katherine." John's dad said. "Have you ever been fishing before?"

"No, sir." She replied sadly.

Her dad never took her fishing before. Her dad did nothing with her. No watching movies, no doing projects together. Nothing.

"Oh. Well, how about I teach you?"

He went over to her and taught everything he knew about fishing.

For the rest of the day, she had a great time. She caught two small fish and threw one of them back. The other one, the guys kept cooking later on. She laughed with them, made jokes, and drank sodas. They did all of this until the sun went down.

"Well, it's time to go," John told Katherine.

"Wait." She blurted.

"What is it?"

"Can we watch the sunset? Please?"

John smiled at her and sat down right next to her.

"Sure."

The sky went from blue to orange with a hint of pink. There are two parts of the day that Katherine loves. When it's dark out and when the sky is full of stars, shining bright. And right before it gets dark; when the sky is at its most beautiful. Watching the sunset makes her feel good. Kind of like giving her hope that tomorrow will be a better day.

John and his dad are taking Katherine home after a good day of fishing.

"I had fun today," John told Katherine as he smiled at her.

I did have fun today. He thought to himself. *This was one of the best Sundays that I've ever had. Church and then fishing with the most beautiful girl I have ever seen. She's also the kindest. None of the other girls in school are as nice as her. I also never felt nervous around her. Should I ask her to the prom? No. Not yet. It's too soon. I mean, I just started hanging out with her. Oh, I know. I can ask her to join us for dinner tomorrow night!*

"Me too," Katherine replied.

"That's good. Um. I was wondering if you would like to join us for dinner tomorrow night. If that's alright with my parents, that is."

"That's fine with me," Michael said, keeping his eyes on the road. "Got to ask your mother too."

"I-I guess," Katherine mumbled. "I've never been asked to eat at someone's house before."

"Really?" John asked, sounding shocked.

"Yeah."

"Well, there's a first time for everything. My mom can cook really well. What time can I pick you up?"

"Oh. Well, I got a job today at the flower shop and I told the woman I'll start tomorrow after school."

"That's fine. She closes at around seven. I can pick you up at closing. After supper, we usually play games."

"What kind of games?"

"Cards, board games, sometimes we'll make up our own games. Then we close the night with a reading from the Bible and a prayer."

"Oh."

"Will your folks be fine with you coming over?" Michael asked."

"They won't care."

"Well, here we are."

Michael pulled up about halfway to her house. John got out and went to the other side, opening the door for Katherine.

"Thank you."

"Goodnight," John said as he looked into her eyes.

He breathed heavily and felt butterflies in his stomach. After she walked off, he got back into the truck.

"Well, today was a good Sunday," Michael said.

"No, dad. Today was a great Sunday."

Dinner

It was Monday afternoon and Katherine was working at the flower shop. She was wearing almost the same clothes as yesterday, but this time the shirt was a different color. Just like every other school day, the kids were staring at her with a strange look. The kind of look that knows something smells. She got so upset she ended up crying during lunch in the girl's bathroom and even more on the way to work. *I can't wait till I get paid so I can finally buy myself some deodorant. Then everyone in school will stop staring at me.*

John told her that morning that his mom is also fine with her coming for dinner. *I'm not sure if I should be glad or scared. I mean, I'm glad that there are people who want me around, but what if they smell me? They will never want me to be around them again. What am I going to do? I need to get a grip and try to stay calm before I end up messing up some of these flowers.*

"You're doing an excellent job, Katherine," Holly said as she walked by Katherine. "Keep it up."

Katherine hasn't really done much so far; a snip here, a snip there, and making sure that all the flowers get plenty of water. It's easy to do, but she thought there would be more to do. *Since I'm new, I guess it's smart to have me start off by doing this. After a while, she'll probably make me help the customers and stuff. Hopefully, she will teach me about flowers. I know nothing about them except that they're pretty. They also need plenty of sun.*

It was another warm day, and the sky was once again clear and blue. *Another beautiful day.* She took a deep breath, inhaling the warm air. Part of the work involved being outside to take care of the flowers. It was better than being inside. She felt freer being outside. It made her feel more relaxed.

With an hour away from being closing time, she couldn't help think about John. The most handsome and kindest guy and human being she has ever met. Thinking about him made her feel warm inside. *What is wrong with me? Why do I feel this way? When I think about him, I grin as if I am a circus clown. However, thinking about him makes me happy. I haven't been happy for a long time. As a matter of fact, I don't think I've ever been happy before.*

Her back was aching from working a lot with the flowers. The huge bruises on her back were also the reason why she was in pain. She had to sit down and take a breather. If her parents were awake when she came home last night, she knew what would have happened. Her mom would stick a needle in her arm and acting as if she was high and mighty, talking down on her own daughter. She would say Katherine is a mistake and she should have had an abortion. Then she would pass out on the couch like she always does.

Then it would be her dad's turn. He would lose his balance as he walked toward Katherine. Her body would shake with fear and would start crying. He would yell at her and call her trash and cuss her out. Finally, he would put more bruises on her, until he thought it was enough. Thankfully, both were asleep.

When she got home last night, she had so much fun from fishing that she actually walked through the front door. Usually, she would climb through her bedroom window to get inside. This time was different, though. This time she didn't care. Instead of a beating and being yelled at, her mom was already unconscious on the couch. Her dad was also asleep. He was in his bedroom, snoring.

She got in bed and laid there until she fell asleep. That night, she fell asleep with a smile on her face. It was also the first time she hadn't fallen asleep while crying.

"Alright, Katherine," Holly said in the distance. "It's about closing time."

Already? That was fast. I hope she didn't see me sitting here and think I'm lazy. I can't get fired on my first day. This is my first job and I want to keep it for a while. At least, until I have enough money to get out of town.

"Yes, ma'am," Katherine said back.

"Well, thank you for helping me out today. I sure appreciate it."

"You're welcome. I've enjoyed it."

"Well good. I'll see you on Wednesday."

"Yes, ma'am."

Holly locked the front door and took a deep breath.

"Another long day. Do you need a ride home?"

"Oh, no ma'am. I'm waiting for someone to pick me up."

"A boy?"

Holly gave Katherine a smile and nudged her.

"John William, from school. I'm eating at his parents tonight."

"That's nice. He's a good kid."

"I think that's him and his dad now."

Katherine pointed to the truck that pulled up.

"Good luck."

"Thanks."

I'm going to need it.

John was getting ready to pick up Katherine at the flower shop on Monday afternoon. He wore a red polo shirt with blue jeans. He even gelled his hair. *I don't know why I'm acting like it's a date. She's just having dinner with us. Oh, no. I'm having butterflies again.*

John has been having butterflies since that morning. He was so nervous that he couldn't eat breakfast. At one time, he thought he would puke in the middle of class. *I'm sure glad I got through the day. I better head downstairs. It's ten minutes till seven. The flower shop is about to close.*

"Are you ready son?" Michael yelled from downstairs.

"I'm on my way down, dad." He yelled back.

John went downstairs where his dad was waiting for him. Michael would not let his son drive the truck just yet. He believed John doesn't have a reason to.

"I hope she'll like my meatloaf," Mary told them from the kitchen.

"I'm sure she will, darling," Michael said back. "Let's go, son."

They walked out and went to the truck. The air was comfortable, and the sky was clear as usual. John thought about his discussion with his parents last night. His mother did most of the talking.

"I'm not sure if I want you to be around that girl, John," Mary said with a concerned look.

"What's wrong with Katherine?" John asked.

"For one, her parents are terrible people. One drink and there's talk that the mother does drugs. Second, I don't think she bathes. I could smell her in the truck."

"Mom. Just because her parents do that stuff, doesn't mean that she does it too. If she smelled, I couldn't tell. Her folks probably don't buy her cleaning supplies. She told me she got a job at the flower shop, so tomorrow, she'll smell like flowers."

He formed a small grin after saying that.

"Yea, well, I don't think she believes in God. I mean, if she did, she would have been coming to church for a while."

"I know that mom. Don't you think I should help her with that? When someone doesn't believe in God or doesn't even know who He is, comes around, shouldn't we help them?"

"The boy has a point, Mary," Michael said, agreeing with John.

"I think, no I know, that she can be saved. Please, mom. She needs our help. She needs to know who Jesus is. Is that not important?"

His mom smiled and put her hand on one of his cheeks.

"Of course, it is, son. Look at you, becoming a man."

"Well, sweetie, he's started becoming a man a long time ago."

"Yeah well, he will always be my baby boy."

"Come on, mom. You're embarrassing me."

They all chuckled, and his mom agreed to let Katherine join them for dinner. He thanked and hugged them good night and went to bed. Now he and his dad were on their way to get Katherine at the flower shop. John kept taking deep breaths, trying to calm himself down.

"Nervous are we?" his dad said, grinning.

"A little," John said with a shaky voice.

"It'll be alright, son. Actually, I wanted to talk to you before we pick her up."

"Sure. What's up?"

"This will be the first time you would have brought a girl over for dinner. I will be honest about this. I thought this moment would have happened a long, long time ago. However, I am happy that you waited. That means you waited for the right one to come along."

"Dad, she isn't my girlfriend," John said with a nervous laugh. "I mean, she's pretty and all, but I know nothing about her. Just what her parents are sort of like."

"Well, maybe that'll change after tonight. As a matter of fact, I was thinking of letting you take the truck this weekend. Maybe you can take her out to eat or something. You can work some at the store after school to earn money."

"Wow, really? You mean like a date?"

"Yes. Plus, instead of us trapping her, you can talk to her about Jesus. That way, she won't feel cornered like a defenseless animal. You two can talk about it alone. I'm sure she would feel more comfortable that way."

"I guess you're right."

"I know I'm right."

"With the home she is living in, I just know she's in trouble, and alone, and cold. Not cold as in, shivering in the snow. I'm talking about cold as in, not feeling safe. Feeling alone and being surrounded by the darkness. She needs to know who died for her. She needs to be saved, dad."

"I know, son. I'm proud of you."

Michael took a deep breath like he was trying to hold himself back from crying.

"Are you going to cry?"

"No."

"Yes, you are! I can tell. I've never seen you cry before. Well, unless we watched 'Where the Red Fern Grows'. You cried like a baby."

"Keep on, and I'll smash your face in your mom's meatloaf tonight."

They both laughed as they stopped in front of the flower shop.

⬭

The food smelled delicious. On her plate were meatloaf, mashed potatoes, and green beans. Katherine inhaled the smell and thought she would drool. She never had this kind of food at her house before. It even smelled better than the school's food.

Across from her was John and at the two ends were his parents. All three of them smiled at her and were being so polite. Katherine returned the favor and remembered her manners. She didn't pick up her manners from her parents. Growing up, she knew she wanted other people to treat her the way they would want to be treated. That's with respect and kindness. Not hatred and bitterness.

John was looking just as handsome as he did yesterday. *Why do I feel all weird in my stomach?* She thought to herself as she tried to stop her leg from shaking under the table. *It's just dinner. Not a date. Besides, why would he want to date me? I smell.*

The Williams held hands, and Mary and Michael reached out to hold hers. Curious, she took theirs and watched them bow their heads. *What are they doing? They're bowing their heads and talking to someone called Father. No one is here but us. Why won't they open their eyes? Mary's the one who cooked the food, so why are they thanking this Father guy? I say 'they', but John's dad is the one doing all the talking. Is he doing the talking for them? Why do we need to hold each other's hands? I'm starving.*

"Amen," Michael said.

"Amen." John and his mom said, after Michael.

"Alright let's eat," Michael said.

Everyone dug in. *Finally.* The first bite Katherine took was the meatloaf. *Oh, wow! This taste incredible! Why can't the school cook like this?* She then shoved the food in her mouth, a spoon full at a time.

"Slow down, Katherine," Mary said. "You'll end up choking yourself."

"I'm sorry," Katherine said, after swallowing a mouthful of food. "This food is amazing."

"Well, thank you. So, what are your plans after graduation?"

"Save up money and leave Bruce. Try to find myself and find my destiny."

"Oh. That sounds nice."

Mary then looked toward her son, like she was trying to give him a sign to say something.

"How was work?" John asked as she looked straight toward Katherine.

"I-It was good." She responded in a quiet tone. "I like it there. Holly is nice."

"You smell like flowers."

"Thanks."

I smell like flowers? Yes! I don't stink! Man, that's a relief. Why did I sound nervous when I answered him? She took a big gulp of sweet tea and continued eating. After drinking milk and pond water, sweet tea was refreshing.

This would be a perfect time to ask when Jesus is coming to town. I'm kind of afraid to ask though. What if they look at me as if I'm stupid? Maybe I'll just wait. Hmm. I could just ask John at school. That way his folks won't be there and make me feel uncomfortable.

After dinner, the Williams and Katherine played a couple of games. First, they placed Phase Ten. Since Katherine never played it before, John had to teach her. For a beginner, she did pretty well. She won with a breeze. After that, they played goldfish. Katherine had to be taught to play it. Michael ended up winning that game.

I'm having so much fun! It stinks that I have to go back to my house. Right then, her laughing smile went to a depressed frown. *Home. I don't want to go back home. Yelling. Fighting. Mom and dad. Hopefully, they both will be asleep when I come home. Wish tonight didn't have to end.*

"Are you alright?" John asked, looking worried.

"Yeah, I just remembered that I have to get home."

"Oh. Sure."

John and Michael and she got in the truck and went to her house.

"Katherine. I was wondering if you and I could hang out tomorrow after school? If you're not working, that is."

"Really? Sure, I would love too."

"Great."

This is perfect! I can ask him about Jesus after school. Unless his parents come along. Then it will have to wait.

"I wished you could have stayed for Bible Study."

"Yeah."

What's Bible Study? Some kind of group thing? It doesn't sound like it would be for school. I would ask, but he'll just think I'm dumb. Oh, I just thought of something. What if he's going to ask me to the prom tomorrow? I would be excited, but that probably won't happen. Great. I'm back at my house.

John opened the truck door and told her good night.

"Good night." She said back.

Then she went to bed.

Friendship

It was a sunny Tuesday afternoon and school had just ended. Katherine was waiting for John on the sidewalk. Her and John are going to hang out and talk. *I wonder what he wants to talk about.* She thought. *Maybe it's the way I smell.* She let out a long sigh and tapped her leg with one of her hands. *Either way, I need to talk to him about Jesus and where I can find Him.*

Katherine looked around as kids continued to leave the school grounds. The school wasn't as big as a city school. There are only around fifty students, and that's including elementary and Kindergarten. The buildings were made of bricks, with each having their own sign: Kindergarten, Elementary, and High School. The town school doesn't have enough students for any sports teams, so they never have pep rallies.

"Man, it's warm today." She said out loud.

It's been hot for the past month. I don't think we even had any rain in the past month. Actually, I don't think we even had any cloudy weather at all in a while. I bet the farmers are having it rough with the crops.

Hmm. I've read in some books that the weather represents a sign sometimes, like rain, for example. If there is a drought that would mean life for someone is hard for them or getting harder. That they're in a rough patch. Then when it rains, that's like a sign for peace. Like a taste of freedom. I wish I knew what that feeling was like. I want a break from mom and dad. I need to think of something else before I start crying and I don't want John to see me crying. What book did I read that from? Oh wait, I don't think it was a book. I think it was from the newspapers a few days ago.

She spotted John walking out of the school and coming toward her. He waved and gave her a big smile. She waved back with a small grin. *What if rain doesn't have to be a sign of peace? What if it could be a person? Could John be my peace? Could he be my rain? No. He can't be. Even though I feel safe around him, I don't feel like I'm at peace.*

"Hey, Katherine," John said to her.

"Hey," She replied.

"I know a great place where we can talk in peace. It's quiet and the best place in town."

"O-Oh. Alright."

"Alright, let's go."

Best place in town? He's not taking me out to eat, is he? No, it can't be dinner. He said a quiet place. What on earth could it be? The pond? Well, I guess that'll be fine. I trust him. I'm not just saying that because he's handsome either.

"How was your day?" he asked.

"It was fine. School was school. So, you know. I learned things."

John chuckled and said, "Yeah, me too."

"So where are we going?"

"You'll see. Don't worry, it's a safe place, and it's public, so you don't have to feel scared."

"I'm not scared."

I am a little nervous though. Where could we possibly be going? She could hear birds chirping in the distance. *I love the sound of birds chirping. The sound is so calm and peaceful. Wherever we're going, it definitely must be a safe place. Oh, hey, there's that church building.*

As they got closer to the church, Katherine felt warm inside. Something was telling her to go inside. *I can't explain it, but I feel so calm when I was there. I felt safe. It felt right being in there. Maybe I can ask John to see if we can go in.*

"Well, here we are."

He stopped in front of the church and turned to Katherine.

"Really? I was just about to ask you if we could go in. This place is always open?"

"Oh yeah. Twenty-four seven."

"Can I tell you something weird?"

"Sure. Go ahead."

"When I was in there, in the church, I felt something. I felt warm, calm, and safe. Like there was someone watching me. Making sure I wouldn't get hurt."

John put his hand on her shoulder and smiled.

"That's not weird at all."

"R-Really?"

"Yes, really. That's how you should feel in there. That's a great feeling, isn't it?"

Katherine thought for a second. *Is it a great feeling? I mean, I don't feel scared or feel like I'm in danger of any sort.*

"I-I'm not sure. I think so."

"Katherine, I brought you here to talk to you about Jesus."

Jesus!? Are you serious?

"Wow, really? I was about to ask you about Him. I heard people talking about Him in church and was wondering if I could talk to Him. You know where He is?"

"You don't know who Jesus really is, do you?"

"No."

"Well, today I'm going to tell you. Come on. Let's go inside."

This is it. I will finally get some answers. They then walked into the church.

―

The church was quiet, and the air was a little cool. While Katherine sat in the front row, John stood in front of the cross. He closed his eyes and bowed his head. Then he prayed.

"Dear Father, please help me today as I explain to Katherine about You, my Lord. She needs to know about You, about Jesus. Please, I pray that she opens her heart, mind, and soul to You. She needs You. In Jesus' name, I pray, Amen."

He sat down next to Katherine, who was looking confused.

"Katherine," He said as he looked into her eyes. "Have you ever wondered about how we got here? What I mean by that, is do you know how we were created? How we wake up every day, how the sun shines every morning, how the stars shine in the night sky."

She looked at the cross at the front and took a deep breath.

"I don't know." She mumbled. "I mean, I have wondered how everything exists or what could be beyond the stars. That big bang theory doesn't seem right. The stars, planets, everything, couldn't have come from a small ball of light that just exploded randomly. It had to come from somewhere."

"God created us."

"God?"

"Yes. God."

"Is that some kind of science thing?"

"No. God is our Creator. He's our Father."

"So, when you do that praying thing, that's who you are talking to?"

"Yes. When we pray, we are talking to God. Of course, you don't have to close your eyes to talk to Him. You could take a walk and still talk to Him. No matter who you are, or where you are, He will always listen to you. You're His child."

"His child?"

"Yes. You, me, everyone. We are all His children. We come to church to worship Him and to learn. He loves everyone. I believe the reason you came to church Sunday, was God wanting you to know who He is. I believe He wants me to tell you about Him."

"I can't explain it, but this feels right. My heart feels warm. When I was here Sunday and right now too, I just feel so peaceful. Almost like I am being protected and being watched. Like I am welcomed."

"That's God, Katherine. He wants you to open up and let Him in."

"What can you tell me about Him?"

John told her about the Old Testament. About Moses, David and Adam and Eve. He also talked to her about Jonah and anything else that he could tell her. They talked for a good hour and with every question she asked, he answered the best way he could.

"I don't understand though." She said. "How does God and all of this have to do anything with Jesus?"

"When God first created man and woman, all things were wonderful and perfect. Then one day sin entered their lives and God had to separate Himself from man because God hates sin. As man continued on with his evil ways, this made God sad. The Godship is made up of the Father, and the Son, and the Holy Spirit. God loves us so much, even as sinners. He came up with a way to forgive us of our transgressions. A perfect Sacrifice had to be shed."

Tears ran down his cheeks and looked at the cross. After a few seconds, John took a deep breath and wiped his tears away. He stared at Katherine and took her hand as he continued.

"God had a Son named Jesus. He sent Jesus to this Earth to be our Sacrifice for our transgressions. Jesus is the only man ever born of a virgin and the only man ever resurrected and not having to die again. This man named Jesus is fully God and fully man. The Bible says anyone that calls on the name of Jesus, and believes in his heart that Jesus is the son of God, will be saved."

Katherine sat there, soaking all of it in. Her eyes kept shifting from

John to the cross. He kept waiting for her to say something. After what felt like hours, she finally spoke.

"What else can you tell me?" She asked.

Her voice was quiet. John told her all that he knew about Heaven and Hell. About Jesus dying on the cross. He told her that when Jesus returns, the saved will go to Heaven. He told her about Satan ruling Earth for a few years. John could tell that she was either nervous or scared by what he told her.

"Is this one of those religions, like Buddhism or something?"

"Some people call it a religion. I call it the truth. I have faith. Since I've been saved and known Jesus, I've felt great. I know that no matter what happens, God will be there for me. These bodies are only temporary. Heaven and Hell are forever. I believe God sent you to this church, so you will find the truth. You will find peace. I believe He wanted me to tell you all of this. I will not force you to believe. That's your choice. I just hope you make the right one."

"I'm not sure what to believe, John. I mean, I'm not sure if I even fully understand all of this."

"That's alright. If you ever have questions, you can talk to me. You could talk to our Pastor if you would be more comfortable. He preaches to us about the Word of God and helps us understand it more. He's the guy that was talking in the front up there."

Katherine pointed to the figure on the wall that had Jesus on a cross. "Is this Him?"

"Yes. He was beaten and had a crown of thorns put on His head. Then He carried His own cross, which He was later nailed onto. He died for you, me, everyone."

"If it's alright with you, I'm just going to sit here for a while."

"That's fine."

An hour passed by with silence. One person came in and prayed. They didn't talk to John or Katherine. Eventually, they left, and John and Katherine were alone again. Katherine didn't take her eyes off of the cross in front of the room.

Does she believe? He thought to himself. *Is she trying to understand it all? What is she going to do or say next?* He looked at his watch and it was now six o'clock.

"Can you walk me home?" she said.

"Sure."

What does this mean?

She stopped in the middle of the aisle and looked back at the cross.

"I want to believe," Katherine said. "When you told me about God and Jesus, I felt warm inside. A good feeling. It was also a new feeling. What you told me feels right, and it seemed like I found what I was looking for. So much is going on, John. Before I met you, I didn't have any friends. Not one. Now I have you and Holly. She's my boss, but she's my friend as well. At least, I think she is. You said I will find peace. As of right now, I do feel a little peaceful. Not completely, though. Thank you, John. Thank you for talking to me."

"You're welcome. Don't forget that you can talk to me about anything. I will always listen. You can also talk to God."

"Thanks. Come on, let's go."

Katherine thought about what John said. About God and Jesus. They were discussing it at the church for a couple of hours and John is now walking her home. The weather got a little cooler, and the sun was setting. Katherine smacked one or two mosquitos that were on her. She decided that she would not let him take her to the door. Her parents might be awake.

It was quiet most of the way to her house. Mainly because she kept thinking about Jesus. The only noises she heard were cars passing by and crickets chirping. She took a deep breath as her back began to hurt.

Could all of that be true? She questioned herself. *I had a feeling that we weren't made out of thin air. We had to come from somewhere or someone. Someone had to create us, and His name is God. He has a Son named Jesus, who died on a cross for our sins. That's what the lower-case 't' means at the church. It's a cross, and Jesus died on it for us.*

John told me I will find peace through Christ, which is Jesus. I want to believe that, but I don't know. This is all so much. It feels like it's right, and it's the truth. When he told me about God, I suddenly had a warm feeling. A safe feeling. To be honest, I don't think that's enough words to describe it.

"Well, we're here," Katherine said.

"Yep," John replied. "I had a good time."

"Yeah, I think I did too."

"Do you mind if I walk you to the door?"

Katherine looked toward the house as her hand trembled.

"Uh. Actually, there're a few holes in the driveway and I don't want you to end up hurting yourself."

"Oh, I'll be fine." He said as he chuckled.

"I'm sure that your mom and dad are wondering where you are. I-I'll see you in school tomorrow."

"Uh. Yeah, sure."

"Goodnight, John. Thank you for walking me home."

"No problem. Goodnight."

Katherine made sure that John walked away before she walked toward the house. The lights were off, but of course, they are always off. She has a lot of thinking to do. *Maybe I should ask John out. Not just so it'll be a date; he could talk to me more about God. I don't know. What if he says no?*

She stood at the front door for a few minutes, hoping to not hear any noise in the house. Silence. She didn't hear a peep from her mom and dad. The door creaked when she opened it, but no one got up to see what the noise was. After closing the door as quietly as she could, she tiptoed to her room. She then sat down and looked up.

"Hey, God," She said in a whispering tone. "John told me about You. I-I don't know what's happening around me, but John told me I could talk to You and that You always listen. I'm not sure how all of this works. I'm not even sure if I understand or believe."

Katherine cried.

"I-I don't know if you're really there or not, but if you are, please listen … I'm tired. I'm tired of hurting, I'm tired of being scared about coming home, and I'm tired of crying. Every day my back aches. Every day I'm scared of coming home to a beating. I cry myself to sleep almost every night.

"Why? Why are these people, my parents? When will there be a change? When will I stop having bruises on me? When will I have peace? When will I have my rain? If you can hear me. Please, help me."

Just like every other night, Katherine cried herself to sleep.

Butterflies

John was helping his dad at the hardware store after school. Until he could find out his gift, he has to make a bit of money. John usually stocked shelves and helped customers if he could. Every now and then he would sweep and mop the floors after closing. John never really spends the money he earns. For a while, he would only help his dad fix engines and stuff like that. Since Katherine came to dinner Monday, Michael has been giving John some extra work in the store. For the past year, John would barely be in the store. Since Monday night, he has been in the store, after school, a lot. Well, unless he gave the 'talk' to Katherine about Jesus.

He could work an hour before and after closing last night. Now it's nine o'clock and Michael will be closing the store in about an hour. It's been warm outside, but it's even hotter in the store. Of course, John's been working his tail off to earn some cash. It's a good thing that the school has a study hall because if not, he would be up late at night doing his homework.

Katherine is in the same study hall class as I'm in. How come she didn't come say, hey? Maybe she's shy or something. I could ask myself the same question though. I could have got up and gone to the table where she was at. Why didn't I? Oh yeah, that's right. My stomach was feeling weird.

Ever since he's been talking to Katherine, his stomach has been acting funny. It only acts up when he's near her. He knew exactly what the problem was, the butterflies. Everyone gets them. Especially when they talk to someone they like.

Do I like her? He asked himself. *She's pretty, kind, and fun to talk to. That means nothing though. I prefer something deeper. Oh, who am I kidding? She has a good and warm heart. The only problem is, she never heard of God or Jesus. Well, she hasn't before I told her.*

Even though she didn't know about God, I can't stop thinking about her. She's the first thing I think about when I wake up, and the last thing I think about when I fall asleep. Why can't I get her out of my head? I barely know her.

Could I be falling for her? No. We just met. We just started talking to each other. Why is it then, that when I think of her, my heart feels warm? She makes me smile. I even had a dream about her. We were having a picnic near the pond. The sun was shining as always, and we were having an amazing time. We talked and laughed. Then I woke up. I don't remember what was so funny in the dream.

He took a deep breath and continued stocking the shelves. *Should I talk to dad about this? Should I pray about it? What do I need to do?*

"John." He heard his dad say.

John jumped from being startled and faced his dad, who had a concerned look on his face.

"Uh. What's up dad?" he asked Michael.

"You alright, son?"

"Y-Yeah. I'm fine. Why do you ask?"

"Well, you got the wrenches where the screwdrivers are supposed to be and the bolts where the nails are meant to be."

"Oh. Sorry."

Oh man, what have I done? I can't believe I messed up the shelves. Have I really been thinking of Katherine that much that I can't put stuff where they go?

"I'll put them back in the right places."

"First, tell me what's on your mind. Is it school?"

"No, sir."

"Is it Katherine?"

John blushed a little and looked away from his dad.

"A little."

"Can't get her out of your mind, huh?"

"No, sir. No matter what I do, I can't seem to block her out of my head. It's like she made a home there."

"Sounds to me that you like her."

"I don't know her that much though, dad. Plus, she didn't know about God until I told her about Him yesterday. What do I do?"

"Ask her out on a date."

"What? Are you serious?"

"Of course, I am. Go on a date with her. Maybe then she'll get out of your head."

"What if she doesn't?"

"Well then son, you must want to keep thinking about her."

"I-I don't know if I want to or not."

"You could be falling in love with her."

"What? How do you know?"

"I don't. I'm not your heart."

"My heart?"

"If you still feel warm inside after you take her out, then that's your heart. It's telling you she's the one."

"Did you feel that way about mom?"

"Son, I still feel that way. My heart has never felt cold around her. There was never a time where it stopped feeling warm around her, or when I think about her. Take Katherine out on a date. After that, then you'll know what to do."

"Thanks, dad."

"Anytime. Now, fix the shelves Mr. Daydream."

John fixed the mess he made until closing. Then, he swept and mopped while his dad put the money in the safe. *So, I have to ask her out, huh? I guess I must fight past the butterflies in my stomach and build up the courage to ask her in study hall tomorrow. Now, I only have one question. What if she says no?*

When he woke up, the first thing that popped in his head was Katherine. He brushed his teeth and put on some clean clothes. His mind was so focused on her that he put his shirt on backward. It wasn't until he went downstairs that his mom pointed it out. Michael moved his mouth with the words 'good luck' and then left to go to work.

This morning, his mom cooked scrambled eggs, waffles, and toast. Even though John's stomach was feeling uneasy, he ate breakfast so his mom wouldn't suspect anything. He knew if his mom found out what was wrong with him, she would speech up a storm. She wouldn't be upset or anything. She would just be excited that her son will ask a girl out on a date for the first time. After eating, he grabbed his backpack and got on the bus.

The town only had one school bus since the school was so small. Most of the kids either walk from home or have their parents drive them. Usually, John would walk, but his stomach was too nervous. It was early in the morning, and he already had the butterflies. Even though he kept practicing on asking her out, one question kept running through his mind. *What if she says no?*

John was in school and about to go into study hall. He practiced how he would ask Katherine out. Should he sound confident, a showoff, or tough? He stayed up until one in the morning last night, thinking of how to ask her. After overthinking everything, he finally passed out and had a good sleep.

He walked into the classroom and saw Katherine sitting alone at a table. There was talk that the school would turn the room into a library. They finally just left it as a study hall, so the students can do their homework. *Well, here I go. Oh man, my stomach feels so weird. I'm just going to sit down next to her.*

John took a deep breath and went to the table that Katherine was sitting at. When he sat down next to her, Katherine gave him a surprised look.

"W-What are you doing?" she asked nervously.

"Well, we're friends, aren't we? Plus, I kind of wanted to ask you something."

He was getting so nervous that he began to sweat.

"Oh, alright. W-What is it?"

John gulped and stared at her. Her eyes were shining like diamonds as she looked at him, clueless. *Calm down, John. Yes, she's gorgeous and sweet, but she's just a human. She's just a girl. A girl that makes my heart feel warm and that stays inside my mind nonstop. I don't think asking her is what is making me nervous. It's wondering what her response will be, that's making me go crazy.*

"Uh. K-Katherine. Would you like to go out with me on a d-date this weekend?"

Katherine's jaw dropped and then she covered up her mouth with her hands. She couldn't believe it. *Come on, say something. The anticipation is killing me. Please say yes.* John thought.

"Y-Yes. I would love to."

"Really? Great! I'll pick you up at your house on Saturday, around seven o'clock. Is that okay?"

"Yeah, that's fine. Seven in the afternoon, right?"

John chuckled a little and said, "Yeah."

They talked for the rest of study hall and helped each other with their homework. When Katherine said yes, he felt a ton of stress falling off of him. Even though she said yes, John still had the butterflies. Now, he's worried about their first date.

First Date

It was Saturday morning and Katherine was working at the flower shop with Holly. She didn't need an alarm clock to get up early. Her dad started a new job today, and he had to be up early. He was practically skimming cabinets and raising his voice at Sarah to make him a lunch. Katherine made herself stay awake after he woke her up with his slamming and yelling.

She hasn't forgotten her conversation with God a few days ago. It's been a couple of days since she cried herself to sleep. As a matter of fact, her dad has been staying away from her with his belt. Now she thought God heard what she had said. Something inside her felt different. Not in a bad way but in a good way. She knew being in church felt right and that all that John told her felt like it's the truth. It's not that she doesn't believe John, it's just that what he told her was so much at once.

Something tells me I should get one of those bibles. Katherine thought to herself. *Maybe I'll understand all of this more after I read some of it. At least I hope so. I can ask John where I can get one at. I will not take one from church. That'll be stealing. If I mentioned God to my folks, they'll yell at me and stuff. They made fun of people who believed in Jesus yesterday. Some guys stopped by and wanted to talk to my parents about God. Instead of letting them in, my parents said Jesus was a joke and a waste of time. They said if God is real, then why hasn't He given them a mansion. Then Kenny slammed the door in their faces. I wanted to talk to the people, but I was too worried that my dad would see me with them. I didn't want to get hit.*

Today Holly taught Katherine on how to use the cash register. At first, Katherine was a little slow. After an hour or two, she got the hang of it. It was like she's always been a cashier. She was excellent at counting change. Math was her best subject in school. The flower shop was busy today, she figured, because it was the weekend.

Saturdays are usually date days for most people, and today will be my first one. I've never been on a date before. I know though that I have to dress nice. Maybe I can find clothes I can wear tonight. Something that isn't too dirty.

"So, Katherine," Holly said randomly. "What are your plans for tonight?"

Plans. I actually have plans for tonight. I'm going on a date. I can't believe it myself.

"A-actually, I'm going on a date tonight."

"Oh, really? Wow! That's great. Going out to eat?"

"Yes, ma'am."

"Do you have anything nice to wear tonight?"

"No, ma'am."

"Oh, well, you need something nice to wear for a date. How about I pay you today? So you can get yourself some nice clothes."

"Really? Thank you!"

"Also, I'll let you get off early so you will have time to go shopping and get the right one you need."

"Oh wow, thank you so much!"

"No problem hon."

Katherine worked until three o'clock and left to go clothes shopping. Luckily, Bruce has a small clothing store that she can get to. She looked around for a few minutes until one worker came to her.

"May I help you?" the worker asked.

"Oh, uh. I-I'm looking for a dress for a date tonight."

"Well, I can show you what we have, and you can try them on in our dressing room in the back."

"Thank you."

The woman measured Katherine to see what size she needed and handed her a few dresses. After spending a few minutes trying them on, she decided to buy the light blue one. She left the store and counted how much money she had left and went to the market and bought a stick of deodorant. Finally, she won't smell bad.

She snuck into her room from the window to avoid her mom. Her dad was at work, she thought, work or out drinking. Her mom was passed out on the couch again or watching T.V. Either way, Katherine didn't want to find out. *I don't want any negativity before I see John tonight.*

She put deodorant on and then changed into the dress. For once, in a long time, she had something that was not tight on her. As she looked at herself in the mirror, she cried. It wasn't a sad cry though. It was more of a happy cry. She looked beautiful.

I don't believe it. I look nice and I don't smell for once. Well, I don't stink as bad. Hopefully, John will think I look nice. So much has happened this week. I made a friend, got asked out on a date, and I found out about Jesus. After all these years, I'm finally starting to be happy.

Katherine heard a truck pull up and a few seconds later she heard her dad.

"Man, I need a drink!" he yelled.

Kenny always thought he needed a drink. No matter where he was at or who he was with, he always wanted a drink.

"I'm trying to sleep here!" Sarah yelled at him.

"Oh, hush woman."

"Don't tell me what to do!"

"I just did!"

"Well, I don't have to listen to you now do I you loser!"

"You're nothing but a waste of time!"

Katherine heard a door slam and then heard the truck driving off. *He must have left to go to a bar.*

She snuck out the window to avoid her mom. *Seven o'clock needs to hurry.* Katherine walked up to the highway and stood there. The air felt warm like it has the past month. It was still a while until John would pick her up, but she didn't care. All that matters is that she's out of the house and will have a good time tonight. She stood there until John came.

Tonight will be John's first date ever. He's never been so nervous in his life. He's already been to the bathroom twice from a stomachache. These butterflies have never been so bad. Tonight, he will wear a short sleeve, blue button-down shirt, and blue jeans. He combed his hair and sprayed cologne on himself. Hopefully, after tonight, the butterflies in his stomach will fly away.

When he told his parents that Katherine said yes, they got excited themselves. Well, Mary was more excited. She kept telling him to be a gentleman and be romantic. She even went to take a picture of him to put in the photo book. Michael, however, told John to treat Katherine right and to just be himself.

John's body trembled as he walked downstairs. *Get a grip, man.* He thought to himself. *You don't want to go to the bathroom all night, do you? Stay calm and everything will be alright. Listen to dad and just be yourself. Everything will be fine.* He got downstairs and both of his folks were standing there staring.

"You alright son?" Michael asked, grinning.

"Uh, yes, sir. Why do you ask?"

"Well, it's just that you're sweating as if you ran five miles."

"Oh man. Really?"

"You will be fine." Michael chuckled.

Will I be alright? I'm not even sure if I can do this. My heart is racing. All it is is dinner with an amazing and beautiful girl. You would think the first girl I ask out would be a Christian. Instead, I ask out one that doesn't even know who Jesus is. I've never felt like this with any of the girls in school though. None of them gives me butterflies.

Mary took a picture of John with her phone and smiled.

"My boy's first date!" she said excitedly.

"Calm down, hun," Michael told her.

"Well, I can't help it! You should be more excited."

"I am excited, but you are making the boy more nervous than a chihuahua."

"I will print this picture the next time we go to Wal-Mart."

Michael rolled his eyes and chuckled. He put his hand on John's shoulder and gave him a serious look. John figured that this would be one of those dad and son moments where his dad gave him the serious talk. *He's not going to talk about kissing or something, is he?*

Michael handed John the keys to the Toyota and then patted John on the back. For about a minute, everyone was quiet. Mary stopped being weird. John began to breathe hard and looked back and forth at his parents, waiting for one to say something.

"Take good care of the truck," his dad said.

"I will."

"It's Saturday and some people tend to drink and drive on Saturday nights."

"Some do it every day," Mary mumbled.

"Don't be out too late, you hear?"

"Yes, sir."

"Alright. Now go have a nice night."

Before John could walk out the front door, his mom called him to come back. He went back to the kitchen and looked at her.

"John," she said in a soft voice. "Out of all the girls that go to church, why did you pick the girl that doesn't? Why pick the one that's from a bad family? A family who drinks and does drugs?"

John stood there for a while and thought about it. Finally, he gave his mom an answer.

"To be honest, I'm not even sure why I want to go out with her. She gives me a warm feeling inside." He smiled at his dad when he said that. "None of the other girls make me feel warm inside. None of them give me butterflies. I think about Katherine nonstop. Plus, just because she comes from a bad family, doesn't mean she's like them. She's not like them."

"How do you know for sure?"

"It's just a feeling. Besides, she needs me. She needs us. Katherine is still trying to understand about God and she needs us to be there for her."

Mary sighed and said, "Alright. I guess you're right."

She hugged John and let him leave. The air felt perfect outside as he walked to the truck. *Oh, no! I forgot about the gift!* He ran back inside and grabbed the present he got for her. *I can't believe I almost forgot. I hope she likes it.*

He got in the truck and drove to Katherine's house. Tonight, he took her to the country restaurant that's in town. Besides that, there's only a Sonic. John thought of going out on a picnic, but he figured that's a second date kind of thing. *A second date. Will there even be a second date? So much has happened this week. I found a girl I like; I told her about Jesus, dad is letting me drive the truck by myself, and I'm going on my first date. All of this started when Katherine ran into the church during the sermon. Again, I ask myself, will there be a second date? I guess I should ask her that at the end of this date. Of course, do I even want a second date after this? I think I do.* John picked up Katherine and he couldn't believe how gorgeous she looked. John was looking handsome as ever and he was by himself when he picked Katherine up at her house

They were quiet most of the way to the restaurant. She was too nervous to bring up a conversation. She was starving, but being around John made her stomach feel weird, like she would vomit from being so nervous. Katherine wanted to tell him he looked nice, but she never got the courage to do so.

For a Saturday night, the restaurant wasn't that packed. There were only two or three vehicles in the parking lot and that's not including the employees. John heard Katherine's stomach growling on the way there. It was about as loud as a motorcycle.

"Wow, you must be ready to eat." He told her.

"Yeah, I'm starving."

They didn't say much on the way there. John figured it was the butterflies. *She must have them, too. Maybe after we have food in our bellies, we'll feel better. What do you talk about on a date? Especially on the first one.*

John ordered catfish with a side of french fries and macaroni and cheese. He loved their sweet tea; it was better than his mom's. He never told his mom that. Katherine ordered a cheeseburger with fries. She liked Mary's sweet tea, so she had theirs to drink. While waiting for the food, John couldn't stop staring at Katherine.

"I-Is there something on my face?" Katherine asked nervously.

"Oh, no. I'm sorry. You're just so beautiful, I couldn't help myself."

Katherine blushed and said, "Thank you."

"How was your day?"

"Fine. Actually, it was exciting."

"Really? What happened?"

"Well, I went dress shopping. This is my first date. I never had one before."

"Same here. I guess we both are excited about tonight."

"Yeah. Y-You, look handsome."

John grinned and said, "Thanks."

I can't believe this is her first date. I mean, as beautiful and nice as she is, I figured she would have at least one date before. Well, I guess that's a good thing. We both are new to this and can share the experience together. My stomach feels a little better now.

"It's pretty in here." She said as she looked around.

"It was your average country restaurant. On the walls were pictures of famous people from Alabama and paintings of animals."

"Yeah, it's nice in here." He replied.

"Smells good in here too."

John smiled and said, "The food is good. Oh, I forgot something in the truck. I'll be right back."

"O-Okay."

He went outside and grabbed the present out of the truck. When he came back to the table, their food was there.

"What's that?" she asked.

"I kind of bought you something."

He then handed her the gift.

Date night has been wonderful, so far. *What's wrong with me?* She thought. *Why can't I make myself talk to him? Am I that nervous? My stomach feels weird too. It growled like it's hungry, but at the same time, it feels sick. Maybe I'll feel better after I eat. How does this even work? I think the guy usually pays for dinner.*

The first thing that Katherine noticed when they got to the restaurant was the smell. She could smell the food from the parking lot. *The food smells wonderful! I have never been to a restaurant before, but so far, I like it.*

They went inside and ordered their food. She had a tough time deciding on what she wanted because she has had little of what was on the menu. Finally, she went with the cheeseburger and fries. While waiting for the food, they talked about how this is both of their first dates and John told her she's beautiful.

He thinks I'm beautiful? Wow! I feel like I'm going to cry. Hold the tears back, Katherine. Be strong. While he went to grab something from the truck, she let out a few tears. No one has called her beautiful before. She wiped her tears away quickly before John came back. When he came back, he handed her a present. *A present? W-Why did he get me a present?*

The wrapping paper was blue with a red bow on it.

"Why did you buy me something?" she asked.

"Well, I figured that you could use it." He replied to her as he smiled.

"I didn't get you anything though."

"Oh, that's alright. This is something you need in your life."

She ripped the paper off and couldn't believe what it was. It was a book that said The Holy Bible.

"I-I was literally going to ask you where I could get one of these at. What does NKJV mean?" She asked as she pointed to the edge of the Bible.

"New King James Version. It's easier to read than the original version. At least, it's easier for me to read."

"T-Thank you. Thank you so much."

"No problem. Now the Old Testament is before Jesus came. So, if you want to read about Jesus first, then read the New Testament."

"Alright. Um. Do you want to pray before we eat?"

"Yes, I do."

They prayed and ate their food. The two were at the restaurant for about an hour. They talked about their favorite colors, favorite animals, and many other things. Katherine even mentioned about her talking to God a few days ago. *Maybe now, I can understand Jesus more. All that He's done and maybe I'll learn more about Him.*

"John, I'm having a wonderful time."

"Me too."

They smiled at the same time and talked a few more minutes before leaving the restaurant. John paid for both of them.

"You know," John said before they got in the truck. "I'm happy that you ran into church on that Sunday. I've had such an amazing time tonight. When you had dinner at my parent's house, I had a great time too."

"Me too."

"I was wondering if you would like to go on another date with me. Next weekend if that's alright."

He wants to go out on another date with me? I can't believe it! He must really like me!

"I would love to, John."

After she agreed to go on another dare, all the feelings that were in her stomach went away. Her face formed the largest smile she had ever made in her life. She's never been so happy in her life. As soon as they got in the truck, that smile went away. Katherine remembered that she will be going back home soon.

"John, I don't want tonight to end."

"Why not?"

He started up the truck and drove toward her house.

"Because I'm having such a nice time with you. I don't want all of this goodness to end."

"Katherine, goodness doesn't start with me or ends with me. Goodness begins with God, and that never ends."

"Yeah."

"Are you okay? What's wrong?"

"Nothing."

"I can tell that something is wrong. You can talk to me."

"I'm fine."

John sighed and had a worried look on his face. Katherine stared out the window, trying to hold back more tears. *I don't want this to end. I don't want to go back home. That house is filled with so much darkness.*

"Well, I'm here and I will always be here for you. No matter where I am or what I'm doing. I don't care if it's late at night. You can always talk to me."

"And God?"

"And God."

It was quiet on the rest of the way to Katherine's house. John pulled into the driveway and opened the truck door for her.

"Can I walk you to the door?"

"No. I uh ... I don't want my folks to embarrass me."

He chuckled as he said, "Parents are supposed to-"

"Just, please don't come to the door," She snapped.

"O-Okay. Sorry."

"No. I'm sorry. I can't tell you why, but I can't have my parents seeing you."

"Is anyone even home? I don't see a vehicle anywhere."

"Yeah, my mom is. She's always home."

"Alright. Can I at least give you a hug?"

"Of course."

She hugged him and watched him drove off.

Katherine II

After John drove off, Katherine stood in the driveway for a good thirty minutes. She didn't want to climb through the window to get into her room anymore. However, she also didn't want to go through the front door. Her parents haven't seen her in a while. Part of her thinks they don't care, but another part thinks they miss not having someone to push around. Once she realized that it was getting darker outside, she walked toward the house.

While on her way to the house, she wondered which way she should get in. The window sounded the safest and the obvious. Instead of going to the window, she stood in front of the front door. Katherine didn't know where all of this bravery came from suddenly. Maybe she didn't care anymore, or maybe she knew God was watching over her.

If I get hurt tonight, It's not God's fault. She told herself. *I know that one day, I will be free. I will have peace one of these days. What's happening to me? Am I no longer scared of what happens to me in this house? Who am I kidding? I'm terrified. I have to fight through all of this though. My rain will come.*

Katherine opened the front door and as soon as she walked into the house, her mom talked.

"Well, well, well," Sarah said with a nasty attitude. "Look who it is. We haven't seen you here in a while. I was thinking you ran off to live under a bridge or something."

Her mom looked at Katherine, moving her eyes up and down.

"Look at you. All dressed up. Where were you tonight?"

Katherine looked down and mumbled, "On a date."

Sarah burst out laughing.

"A date? Who would want to go on a date with you? You're not even pretty enough to go out on dates."

"A guy from church says I'm beautiful," Katherine mumbled as she tried to hold the tears back.

"Church!?" Sarah yelled as she chuckled. "You went to church? There's nothing at church but a bunch of stuck up idiots who believe in fairy tales."

"They aren't like that, and God isn't a fairy tale."

"Excuse me?"

Sarah got off the couch slowly and walked over to her daughter. Her mom looked angry.

"You want to say that again?"

Katherine wept and tears rolled down her cheek as she looked away from her mother.

"G-God is real."

Sarah slapped her daughter and snatched the Bible that John gave her out of Katherine's hand.

"No!" Katherine shouted.

"Shut up! You're nothing but a worthless brat. You're nothing but a mistake."

Sarah threw the Bible to the floor.

"Why are you doing this to me?" Katherine asked as she looked up to her mother.

"Because, if you were my kid, you would have gotten me out of this dump by now."

Sarah pushed her out of the house. Katherine then fell onto the ground, getting her new dress dirty.

"Look at you. Do you think you're too good for us now? Make yourself useful for once and clean up this yard."

Katherine got up, still crying. Her dress was filthy. Dirt was all over it. She wiped tears away as she cleaned up the yard. The yard was covered with beer bottles, cans, tops, and a ton of paper. *This will take me all night to clean up.* She thought as she heard her mom slamming the front door.

An hour had passed before she sat down to take a break. *Maybe she fell asleep by now. No. I better not risk it.* She looked up at the night sky. The stars seemed like they were brighter than normal. It was as if they were shining brighter, just for her. The moon was giving her the light to see the yard. She made separate piles for everything. So far, the biggest pile was the beer bottles. *He's next. Dad. I wonder what he will do when he gets here. Hit me, or not even notice I'm here?*

John said God is a loving God. He also said you should fear God. Does He allow bad things to happen, to see if we continue to believe in Him? Katherine looked up at the night sky once again. *I believe in You, God. I may not understand much, but I know that You're real. I will read that Bible every day, and I will read a ton. I need to know what Jesus did. I need to get to know Jesus. Nothing will stop me. Not my mom and not my dad.*

Headlights pulled up in the driveway. It was Kenny. He cut off the truck and stumbled out. He was drunk. He saw Katherine sitting in the yard, staring at him.

"W-What are you looking at girl?" he said with a drunk voice.

"Nothing." She mumbled.

"What?"

"Nothing." She said louder.

"Don't you yell at me! I don't understand why I got stuck with a no-good daughter like you. You do nothing around here. You keep going to that school; for what? You're not going anywhere."

I know that I shouldn't say anything. That will just get me hurt. Just, please, go inside and fall asleep. Please, leave me alone. Kenny walked next to Katherine. His breath smelled strong with alcohol.

"You're nothing by trash." He said as he leaned closer to her. "Just like your mother."

That was it. Katherine stood up and looked straight at him. Her heart was pounding, and she was breathing heavily.

"What?" he said. "This time he stood straight up. "What are you going to do? Hit me?"

"I-I'm not trash," Katherine said.

"You are what I say you are!" Kenny yelled.

"N-No. I'm going to graduate and get away from here."

"Oh yeah? Who's going to help you? God?"

"Y-Yes."

"Oh, so you believe God will help you?"

"I know He will."

Kenny took off his belt and waved it in Katherine's face.

"Well. If God will help you get out of this town, let's see if He can get you out of a whooping."

Kenny then slapped his daughter so hard that she fell to the ground. As she laid on her stomach, he walked over to her side. When she got on all fours, Kenny hit her with the belt. He continued to hit her back with the belt over, and over, and over again. Katherine went to bed bleeding that night.

Picnic

It was Tuesday night and John was making food for the picnic tomorrow. He decided that instead of the coming weekend, he would ask Katherine on a second date tomorrow afternoon. *She has to say yes.* He thought. He cooked everything himself. This would be the first time he would have cooked for someone who wasn't a relative. *I hope she'll like my spaghetti.*

Since their first date, he couldn't stop thinking about her. Her smile, her eyes, and her sweet voice. His chest was feeling warm again, and he forgot that he was cooking for her. *Snap out of it John! You almost set the house on fire. Finish the spaghetti, and then you can continue your daydreaming.*

John finished making the food and put it in the fridge. He thought about making it after school, but he was too excited. If they go on this picnic, he will ask her to the prom. The butterflies came back when he practiced on asking Katherine to the prom. *Calm down. If you can ask her to go on a date, then you can ask her to the prom. Just relax.*

Before going to bed, his mind rewound back to earlier that day. It was after school and he was having a conversation with his parents. Luckily both weren't working today. Michael and Mary were watching T.V. when their son came into the room. He asked his folks if they could talk.

"Sure, son," Michael said. "What's on your mind?"

"It's Katherine," John said.

Mary cut the television off and both of his parents just stared at him.

"I-I'm going to ask her to the prom and-"

"Oh, how wonderful!" Mary shrieked.

Her face glowed with excitement, and she ran up to hug him.

"Mom, I can't breathe."

She released me and sat back down with her husband, who was smiling.

"Good luck," Michael said.

"Actually, I'm wanting to ask you guys something."

"Oh, alright."

"If she says yes, I was wondering if you, mom, could go with Katherine to find a dress or something. I don't think her mom will do that with her."

"How do you know?"

"It's a feeling. I don't think her mom spends any time with her."

"Oh, okay."

"Thanks. Could you make it seem like it's your idea?"

"Sure," she mumbled.

"And dad, could you go with me to find a suit or something?"

"Sure thing," he agreed.

"Thanks. This means a lot."

Man, I have the coolest parents in the world. He thought as he was lying in bed. It was eleven o'clock at night and John was still wide awake thinking about tomorrow. Suddenly, he wondered why Katherine wouldn't let him walk her to the front door on Saturday night. *Is she embarrassed by me? No, that can't be it. Could her parents embarrass her? Now that could be a possibility. Maybe I should ask. No, that would be rude.*

He kept tossing and turning until he finally fell asleep. He did his nightly prayer, and the last thing on his mind was Katherine.

It was another warm, cloudless sky morning, and John was having trouble putting clothes on before school. First, his pants were inside out and then he put his shirt on backward. After getting everything straightened out, he ate breakfast and went to school. Katherine wasn't there during the first class. She eventually showed up in the middle of Biology.

She's been coming late since Monday. I hope that everything is alright. She hasn't been saying much during study hall either. I'll see what's wrong in study hall today. Maybe she's feeling better.

Study hall came, and John sat next to Katherine as he has been the past couple of days.

"Hey," he said

"Hi."

"Is everything ok?"

"Yeah, why do you ask?"

Her voice was low, and a little shaken. It was like she was hiding something. Something she didn't want John to know.

"Well, you've been late to school for a couple of days now. Is everything alright?"

She looked down and mumbled. "Everything is fine. I just keep sleeping in. My alarm clock broke."

"Oh. You also have been looking kind of ill. Are you feeling okay?"

"Yes."

"Good."

She's not fine. Something is wrong, and she won't tell me.

"Katherine, would you like to go on a picnic with me today? Around six?"

She looked up at him and smiled.

"Really?"

"Yeah, I couldn't wait till the weekend to go on that second date."

He blushed and looked away.

"I would love to."

"Great!" he said with excitement.

John said it loud enough that the teacher shushed him.

"One question."

"What?"

"What's a picnic?"

He smiled as he looked into her beautiful ocean blue eyes. "I'll show you."

It's been a couple of days since Katherine's beating from her dad. Since then she has been having trouble getting out of bed. It now takes her longer to put clothes on. She didn't go to the bathroom much because she was in so much pain. However, on Sunday, she took a bath in the pond. Even though she had to stop twice for a break, the bath was worth it. The water felt nice on her back. When she looked in the mirror, she couldn't believe her eyes. The fresh wounds were hideous. The bleeding stopped during the night of the beating, but she slept on a pile of clothes to help the wounds.

Thankfully, her dad hasn't noticed the bible. Mainly because Katherine grabbed it while everyone was asleep Sarah completely forgot about it, so it was never mentioned to Kenny. Because she had nothing to do at the house, she was able to read a good amount of the New Testament. She had read the books of Mathew and Mark. When she read about the death of Jesus, a tear would run down her cheek.

She was late at getting to school on time for Monday and Tuesday. Her back was in so much pain that she missed the bus both days. Still, she was determined to go to school; not just so she could still graduate and get out of Bruce, but so she could also see John. Since she's been hurting so much, she hasn't been saying much to him.

I hope he doesn't think I no longer like him because I still do. The prom is next weekend and I hope that he will ask me to go with him. It's been two days and I'm sure he's suspecting that something is wrong with me. He can't know. If he does, I'll get in trouble and I don't want that. I can't have that, not again. My back feels a bit better, but not enough for me to catch the bus. I'm so tired of walking to school. It hurts too much. I have to make it through today and then I can come home and read.

"Home," she mumbled to herself.

Why did this place have to be my home? Why couldn't I have nicer parents who weren't so mean to me?

Katherine missed the bus again that Wednesday morning. Like usual, she climbed out through her window to avoid her parents. Kenny lost another job because of alcohol. The last thing she wanted was to see him again. Once again, she was late for school and missed the first class. She had to stop a couple of times to rest. Holly asked what was wrong with her while Katherine was working. Katherine was drifting and cried once or twice. She told Holly that nothing was wrong and continued working.

All I want is another date with John. Another nice day of talking, laughing and smiling. Another day of spending time with him that doesn't involve school. I don't want to eat at another restaurant though. No, I want to go eat somewhere quiet. Somewhere beautiful and peaceful.

She got her wish in study hall when John pushed their original weekend date to that night. She was so excited that she even jogged to the house. Her back was aching, but she didn't mind it. Now instead of waiting until Saturday to go on a date, they will be going out tonight. He told her they will go on a picnic, but she didn't know what that was.

I have a feeling that it will be a quiet date I've been wanting. Hopefully, this time, I will be able to go to bed with no marks on my back. That blue dress is covered with dirt and stains, so I can't wear that. Maybe I can find something to wear for tonight.

After jogging most of the way to the house, Katherine had to take a rest. Her back felt like a pile of burning coal beat it. *I'm right there.* She saw the mailbox and driveway to her house a few yards away. *You can make it. I know you're tired but keep going. You have a date tonight and you need to find what you need to wear, what you can wear. Take a deep breath and just go. You're going on a picnic.*

⚭

John was wearing a purple button-down shirt with black jeans. He combed his hair and sprayed cologne.

"Good luck son," his dad said from the living room.

"I will need it," John replied.

The picnic basket was full of food and drinks. He also packed a couple of plates and picked flowers that were growing near the house. He put everything in the truck and grabbed the key from his dad.

"Wait!" Mary yelled as she waved John down to stop.

"What's wrong mom?"

"Here, take this. Your dad gave it to me shortly after we went out."

Mary put a pearl necklace in her son's hand.

"Mom, I can't take this. This is yours. Besides, Katherine and I aren't going out. I haven't asked if she would even want to be my girlfriend."

"Give it to her, anyway. She seems nice and I know how much you like her. Invite her to church this Sunday."

"Alright. Thanks, mom."

"Good luck!"

She hugged him and watched him drive away.

Katherine was wearing a plain pink shirt with blue jeans when he picked her up. *She looks more beautiful every time I see her. She seems so excited about our date tonight, for someone who doesn't know what a picnic is.*

Her smile makes him smile. *When she's happy, I'm happy. If she's upset, I'm upset. Tonight will be fun and hopefully romantic. Sure hope she will have a wonderful time. I don't like it when she's not happy like she has been in school for the past two days.*

"So," Katherine said with a huge grin on her face. "Where are we having this picnic thing at?"

"You'll see," he replied, smiling.

John drove to the pond where he, his dad, and Katherine went fishing. He wanted this date to be where they spent the first time together. Where they had fun.

"Here?" she asked with a puzzled look.

"Yeah, it's where we hung out for the first time."

They got out of the truck and John got everything ready. John prayed for them and they began to eat. Katherine loved his spaghetti. As a matter of fact, she had two plates of it. Then for dessert, they had chocolate cake. For drinks, they had sweet tea. Sweet tea isn't much of a romantic drink, but it was the best that John could do.

Katherine told him she read the first two books of the New Testament, and she cried when Jesus died on the cross.

"I felt so calm when I read the Bible," she said.

"I know what you mean. If I ever get upset or anxious, I can always read what it says in the Bible about that stuff and the feelings will go away. All that weight will lift off my shoulders. Do you want to watch the sunset?"

"I would like that."

John and Katherine watched the sun go down, and some stars came out.

"The night sky is so amazing," Katherine mumbled. "When you can see the stars, anyway."

"Yeah, God's work is amazing. You know, when I look up at the stars, I like to think it's one giant canvas that God painted over. One night the stars will be out, shining. Another night, He could paint the sky cloudy with a hint of moonlight shining through the clouds."

"Wow."

"Yeah."

He turned his head toward Katherine, who also was staring at him. John took out the necklace that his mom gave him.

"Katherine, would you like to go to the prom with me?"

Her jaw dropped, and a tear rolled down her cheek.

"Oh, John. Yes! I would love to!"

They hugged, and he put the necklace around her neck. Both of them felt something between them that night.

Shopping

It was Saturday, and Katherine was working at Holly's flower shop. Since the picnic, Katherine has been acting a little weird. She's been forgetting stuff, losing her school supplies, and she's been having trouble falling asleep. Usually, she could go to sleep, even with her folks making loud noises. Last night, they were throwing bottles and plates at each other. After about an hour, it finally got quiet.

Before she snuck into her room last night, she was at the William's house, having supper. They had pepperoni pizza with extra cheese. It was the best pizza she ever had. After pizza, they watched an action movie. John sat right beside her. She never saw a movie before, except for documentaries at school. Before she left their house, John's mom asked if she could help her shop for a dress for the prom. Katherine gladly said yes.

So, after work today, she and Mary will be dress shopping. For the first time, it'll be like Katherine is bonding with a mother. It wouldn't be her mom, but she is still a mom. *I wish my mom would spend time with me.* She thought. *This is what mothers and daughters are supposed to do together. Fun stuff like shopping and laughing. Not having the mother being cruel to her daughter and knocking her down to the ground.*

"Katherine," Holly said, worried. "Are you alright?"

"Y-Yeah, I'm fine."

"Are you sure? Because you're putting the sunflowers where the roses go."

"Oh, sorry."

"What's on your mind?"

"I-I got asked to the prom and I'm a little nervous."

"Well, that's exciting."

"Yeah."

"I know what you're going through. I was so nervous about my senior prom."

"Really?"

"Oh yeah! I went with my high school crush, so I was extremely nervous. I was a nerd back then, too. I'm still a nerd, but that's not important. Anyway, I used to wear glasses when I was in school and got made fun of because of it. For some reason though, the guy asked me to the prom. I said yes, of course. I wore a green dress and wore my mom's earrings. I'd never felt so happy before. Before the prom, though, I was getting nervous. Actually, I had a panic attack."

"Oh, wow."

"Yep. Anyway, my date saw I was having an attack in his car. You know what he did?"

"No. What?"

"He pulled the car over, put it in park, and held me tight. Then he whispered that everything will be alright and that he was there for me. I calmed down and had an amazing night."

"What happened to him?"

"We went out. However, he passed away from a car accident."

It got quiet for a while and Katherine just stared at her. After a couple of seconds, Katherine gave Holly a hug and thanked her.

"Thank you for being my friend."

"You're welcome. Feel better?"

"Yes, thank you."

Mary picked Katherine up from work, and they went to grab a bite to eat. Mary paid for Katherine's food and then they went to look for a dress for the prom.

"How was work?" Mary asked Katherine.

"It was fine. How was your day?"

"Oh, it was nice. Can I ask you something? It's personal."

"S-Sure."

"Do you like my son?"

Uh oh. She wants to know what I think about her son. Of course, I like him. He's nice, sweet, handsome, and fun to be around. He makes me feel safe and calm. When I look into his eyes, I see the most amazing guy ever. Someone who could never hurt me. How do I tell his mom that though? This is weird.

"Y-Yes ma'am. He's kind and respectful. I don't think I have ever met someone so nice before."

"Yes, he is a kind young man. That's not what I was asking though. What I meant was, do you like him in a way that you might be falling in love with him?"

Love? I never thought about that. I don't think I ever loved someone before. I'm not even sure what love feels like. Hmm. I know that I like him more than a friend, but I'm not sure how to tell him that. He asked me to go to the prom with him. Maybe he likes me, how I like him. Great, now I am paranoid.

"I-I don't know. I do like him though. You're not going to get mad at me, are you?"

"Of course not, dear. I'm just curious is all. You're the first girl he brought over to our house. You're the first girl he went on a date with. I'm just looking out for my son."

"Oh, okay."

"You seem to be a lovely girl. Are you excited about going to the prom?"

"Yes, ma'am. I'm also nervous though. It's in a week. The closer it gets, the more nervous I am."

"Oh, I'm sure everything will be fine. How about this one?"

Mary pulled out an orange dress that was a little short.

"Looks a little short."

"Yes, it looks a little too short. So, John told me you are reading the Bible. How's that going?"

"Great. I enjoy reading it. When I read it, my body feels like … like … I can't explain it. It's a good feeling though."

"Good. You're supposed to feel that way. That is Christ, in your heart and soul. It's an amazing feeling."

"Yes, it is. I'm not used to it though."

"You will be. Trust me. Are you saved?"

"Saved?"

"Yes, dear. When you accept that Christ is your Lord and Savior and that Jesus died on the cross for you, that's when you're saved. You can't just know who God is. You have to KNOW that He is real. You have to KNOW that He sent His Son on the cross to die for your sins."

"I-I don't know."

"Then you're not saved. You'll know when you are though. It's the best feeling ever."

Katherine nodded and pulled out a pink dress. It was longer than the other one, which is what she wanted. It went past her knees, almost touching the ground.

"How about this?" Katherine asked.

"That's cute. Go try it on, and we'll see how it looks on you."

"Okay."

What Katherine didn't know, was that the dressing room had a lock on it. When she went in, she thought the door was closed. Mary noticed it and went to tell Katherine to lock the door. Before she said anything, Mary saw the bruises on Katherine's back.

Katherine walked out of the dressing room and noticed that Mary had a concerned look on her face.

"Are you alright?" Mary asked.

"Y-Yes ma'am," Katherine replied, nervously. "Why do you ask?"

"Are you sure you are alright? You can tell me if something is wrong. I'm here for you."

What is going on? Katherine thought. *Why does she keep asking me if I'm alright? I know what I want to tell her. I want to tell her I'm not alright, but at the same time, I'm great.*

I'm great because I'm shopping for a dress for the prom. In a week I will be on a date with a guy who makes me happy and safe. At the same time, though, I'm not fine. I'm not fine because my back is in so much pain, I want to collapse to the floor and cry. I want to be in a happier and safer home. I can't tell her I'm not fine; because if I do, I might get another beating, and I don't want that.

"I'm fine," Katherine mumbled. "I promise."

Mary sighed and said, "Okay. How about I buy you some heels to go with the dress? This is the dress you want, isn't it?"

"Yes, ma'am. You don't have to buy me heels though."

"Oh, I want to. Prom is a special time in your life."

"Do you think John will like it?"

"He'll love it."

"Um. Can I ask a favor?"

"Sure, sweetie. Anything."

"C-Can I leave the dress and heels at your house and get ready over there? I don't really have any privacy or anything."

"Of course. You can use some of my makeup too."

"R-Really?"

"Yes. What time does it start?"

"Seven o'clock."

"Well, next Saturday you come over around four. Okay? That way you'll have a couple of hours to get ready."

"Thank you."

"Anytime."

It was one week until the big dance, and John was already sweating like a hot pig at a farm. He never thought he would go to the prom, especially with a girl who he has feelings for. Just thinking about going to the prom with Katherine made his heart race like a racehorse. At one point, he thought he would have a panic attack. He was able to calm himself down though.

He's been working at the shop to earn extra money to buy him a nice suit for the prom. He asked his dad to help him pick a suit. Michael suggested that they could spend Saturday together. Just the two of them. No girls allowed.

They watched the morning game and had burgers for lunch. Michael closed the store for the day, so there wouldn't be any interruptions. Mary knew today was a boy's day, so most of the time she'd be keeping to herself. She would read and then do some cleaning. She'd be picking up Katherine at the flower shop later to find a dress for the prom.

After the game and lunch, John and his dad had their own Bible study. They never did one with just the two of them, so it was exciting. After that, they went to the next town, where the store for men was at. Bruce didn't have one for guys and girls. So, the girls will go to the store in Bruce, while the guys will go to one of the stores in the town next over. It wasn't far, though. Just a couple of miles.

The sun was bright as always, and there wasn't much of a breeze outside. On the way to the clothing store, the boys listened to some <u>Casting Crowns</u>. They sang along with the lyrics, trying to out-sing each other. John won.

The store wasn't that busy, so finding a suit shouldn't be too difficult.

"Alright son," Michael said. "Let's go hunt you a sharp-looking suit for your woman."

John chuckled and said, "She's not my woman, dad."

"Why not?"

"I haven't asked her to be my girlfriend yet."

"Well, are you going to ask her?"

"I want to. I'm just nervous. Do you and mom even like her?"

"Son, it doesn't matter if me or your mother like her or not. The important thing is that you do. I mean she seems like a fine a girl. I don't have a problem with her. Your mother has to get to know her more, for her to decide if she likes Katherine or not. Still, whether or not she likes her, doesn't matter. What matters, is you liking her. Do you like her?"

"Yes, sir. A lot. She's beautiful, smart, and kind. When I look at her, it feels as if my heart is trembling. Like it's weak."

"What does it feel like when she's not around?"

"Empty. I mean, it's filled with Christ, of course. No question about that. I know God loves me, He's my Savior. It's just that, when Katherine isn't around, my heart feels like it's missing something."

"Son. You're in love."

"What? I just met her dad. I can't be in love."

"It doesn't matter if you just met her. You're falling in love with her. It seems to me that she's the one you're supposed to be with. I'm not you though. Does she feel like the one?"

"I don't know. I like her a lot, but I don't know if I'm in love with her."

"You'll figure it out. How about this one? It looks nice."

Michael pulled out a blue blazer. John looked at it but didn't like what he saw.

"It doesn't look right."

"What do you mean?"

"It doesn't seem like the right suit. You know what I mean?"

"Yeah, I know what you mean. I had to have the perfect suit when I took your mother to the prom. If the suit didn't look or feel right, then I didn't look right. I wanted to look the best I could for your mother."

"And did you?"

"Of course."

They chuckled and continued to look for the right suit. *Should I ask Katherine to be my girlfriend?* John thought. *I do like her after all. Maybe I should. I love being around her. I'm already nervous about going to the prom with her. Asking her to be my girlfriend will be nerve-racking. Terrific. The butterflies are back.*

"I think I found one," John said as he pulled out a suit at the back of the store.

It was your average looking suit. All black with a white shirt. Normal. Classy. *It's a classic. Just the way I like it.*

"Nice suit." His dad said. "A classic."

"I agree. This could be the one. I'll go try it on."

While John was in the dressing room, his dad randomly asked him a question.

"John, have you figured out your gift yet?"

That was random. Why would he ask me that? Maybe to see if I found my gift. Unfortunately, no. I sure wished I did though. It hurts to not know what God wants me to do with my life. Worship Him, obviously. But what else does He want me to do? I know He doesn't want me to be a manager or have my own business.

"No, sir. Sadly, I haven't."

"Maybe you should have your own business."

"No, that doesn't feel right. I don't think I'm supposed to run my own business."

"Do you have any clue what you ARE supposed to be doing? Any sort of hint?"

"I'm leaning toward something creative. You know? Something I can make."

"Hmm."

"How do I look?" John asked as he stepped out of the dressing room.

"Looking good, my man. It doesn't matter what I think though. The question is, do you think it's the right suit?"

John looked in the mirror and said with confidence, "Yeah. It's the right one."

Calm

I t was eight o'clock and John was in his room, waiting for his mother to come home from shopping with Katherine. He and his dad came home a couple of hours ago. John got himself a suit for the prom from a clothing store at the town next over. His dad cooked supper and then John has been in his room ever since. As soon as he went into his room, he prayed.

"Father, I'm praying to You now to ask for something. I ask that You give me a sign; a sign that lets me know if Katherine is the one. Ever since she came into the church at the beginning of the month, a lot has happened. She became my friend, and I slowly had feelings for her. I ask You, Lord, to please let me know if Katherine is the right path. Is she brought into my life for a reason, other than to show her the way to Christ? Please, I need to know. Amen."

John then went to his desk and took out his journal from the drawer. A couple of years ago, he wrote his thoughts onto paper, a journal. He wouldn't write in it every day. Just the important stuff, like his journey on finding his gift. His mom and dad thought it was a good idea. Only half of the journal has been written.

In it, John would write what he believes are signs from God, hunches, or anything that involves a clue that would get him closer to finding what God wants him to do. Now something tells him he should do something creative and artistic. He grabbed a pen and began writing.

Lately, I have had thoughts about my future; my gift. I believe God is trying to tell me I should do something creative with my life. What could that be though: painting, designing, or drawing? I have a feeling that whatever my gift is, Katherine will lead me to it. Did Jesus bring her into my life to show me what I'm supposed to be doing? I don't know.

I know one thing though. I know that God brought Katherine to me, to help her. I believe He wants me to show her the way. To show her that Christ is real. That she needs Him in her life. That through Christ, anything is possible. She has been reading the Bible that I gave her. It seems like she has plenty of time on her hands. Something tells me, though, that there is darkness in her life. She's hiding something, but what? I have a feeling that I will find out. Very, very soon.

John heard his mother downstairs. He put his journal up and went downstairs to see her. She had a dress in her arms and looked a little shocked. It was like she saw a ghost or something.

"What's wrong?" Michael asked.

"I need to talk to you," Mary mumbled. "Alone."

While his parents talked privately in the kitchen, John went into the living room and sat down in one of the chairs. *I hope mom is alright. She looked worried. Is Katherine alright? Why did she bring the dress here?*

Michael and Mary walked into the living room where John was. They both, now, had a worried look on their faces.

"What's going on?" John asked.

"Son," Michael said in a calm voice. "We need to talk to you about Katherine."

"What's wrong? Is she alright?"

"Mary sat on the couch and looked at her son with watery eyes.

"Have you ever met Katherine's parents?" Mary asked her son.

"No, ma'am. She refuses to let me walk her to her front door. Why?"

"We believe she's being abused by them."

John's jaw dropped, and his eyes filled with fear.

"H-How do you know?"

"I saw her back at the store. It's covered with bruises. Some looked fresh. That we know of, she only goes to school, the flower shop, and her house. You haven't seen any of the girls at school bullying Katherine, have you?"

"N-No, ma'am. She doesn't talk to anyone at school, except for me."

"Your dad says Katherine's dad likes to drink. A lot."

John's eyes watered as he covered up his mouth with one of his hands.

"W-Why?" John said with his mouth still covered. "Why would he do that to her?"

"I don't know, sweetie. Has she seemed different lately?"

"She came to school late a couple of days and she looked weak and upset on those days."

"John." His dad said as he stood beside him, putting his hand on John's shoulder. "As parents ourselves, your mother and I believe we should do something. However, since you are almost a man and you have feelings for this girl, we believe the decision should be yours. What do you want to do, son?"

I don't believe this. Katherine. Why would someone do that to their own daughter? Why is that person allowed to have alcohol in their hands? Why would they allow evil into their heart and soul? Don't they know they are destroying their family? Destroying their own lives? Well, no more. I'm getting Katherine out of that house. No one deserves that kind of treatment.

John looked at his parents and said, "I know what to do."

It was Friday, and Katherine was getting nervous about the prom tomorrow night. It's been almost a week since she and Mary went shopping for a prom dress. Katherine picked out a cute pink dress and a pair of black heels, and Mary bought them. Katherine couldn't help keep wondering about her and Mary's conversation from Friday.

Katherine was ready to go to their house to get ready for the prom. However, she must survive one more night at her house. For the past few nights, all Katherine heard was her mom and dad yelling; telling each other they're lazy and stupid. Every night they would throw something at each other. Then, if that wasn't enough, they would slam each other in the wall and push each other around.

I want one night of peace. One night where I don't have to be afraid. One night without yelling and fighting. One night without crying myself to sleep. For the past week, I had to sleep on my sides. My back was hurting too much to lie on it. It has healed some, but not enough to lie on it.

The only time that Katherine had any peace was at school and the flower shop. The only time she saw John in the past week was at school. When they talked, he would always ask how she was feeling. If she was okay. *Why does he keep asking me that? He asked me every day if I was okay. I want to tell him everything so badly. I don't want to hide anything from him.*

Even with the flower shop, Katherine still has a lot of time in her hands. She's been reading the Bible a lot, even with the loud fighting going on at home. Sometimes she would go to the pond to read. She was on Hebrews now, in the New Testament. The more she reads the Bible, the warmer her heart and soul feel. The more she understands.

Before she falls asleep, she would think about what she has read. Sometimes she would talk to God. It didn't feel weird talking to Him. It didn't feel wrong. It felt right. She knew someone was listening. After she would get done talking to Him, she would fall asleep with a tear in her eye. She wasn't sure if it was a happy tear or a scared one. She just knew someone was listening, and they were watching her.

I feel like I'm in a storm. It's dark, and the rain is just pouring down hard on me. I can barely see and I'm freezing because it's so cold. I can see where the storm ends, but I can't seem to get out of it. I can't get out of the storm. It's like the storm is darkness and at the end is light. The storm is bad, and the light is the answer to being happy and free. The thing is, I don't remember seeing that light before. I don't think it was there before. That light showed up after I ran into that church for the first time. At first, it was small, but then it grew over time. I've been wanting to go to church on Sundays, but I'm afraid. What if everyone looks at me with a nasty look? What if my folks find out? I don't know what to do.

When I see the light, I imagine that rain theory a while back, before I talked to John at the church when we were by ourselves. Could the light be my rain? Not actual rain, but a rain of goodness? A rain of happiness and peace? If I look hard enough, I can see that cross in the light. It's a little faded, but I can still see it. I WANT to be in that light. I WANT to be closer to that cross. It seems as if something is holding me back. But what?

After work, Katherine walked home. Thinking about the light and prom made her forget about home. Instead of walking through the window, she went through the front door. When the door shut, she realized what she had done. *Oh, no. Dad's home. So is mom. I didn't realize that I walked in by the front door! No. No, no, no, no, no. What will happen to me? What are they going to do?*

"Why are you home late?" Sarah asked.

"I-I was ..."

"Never mind. I don't want to know."

Sarah said nothing else. She didn't get up to yell or hit Katherine. She sat on the couch, staring at the TV. *That's odd. That's all she's going to say and do? I better not jinx it.*

Katherine walked toward her room, but before she could open her door, her dad walked in.

"How have you been doing?" He asked in a soft tone.

Katherine turned around and saw her dad standing in the kitchen doorway. Something was different though. For some reason, he didn't have a beer in his hand. He wasn't drunk. He didn't yell at her or beat her with his belt.

"F-Fine," Katherine mumbled, confused.

She didn't know when he would take his belt off and hit her with it. *Why hasn't he hit me yet? Why hasn't he yelled? What's going on? Am I dreaming? Why does everyone seem so calm tonight? Something is wrong. I'm not sure if I like it or if I'm scared.*

"Good. How's school?"

How's school? Did he really ask me that? Is he sober for once? I'm not sure what to think about this.

"F-Fine." She mumbled again.

"Good."

Kenny walked off and Katherine just stood there, shocked. She didn't hear anything else for the rest of the night. No yelling or fighting. Just silence. Calm. If she only knew what would happen tomorrow night after prom. Tomorrow night will be the greatest time of her life and the scariest.

Prom

I t was around nine in the morning when John woke up on the day of the prom. Usually, he would sleep a little later on Saturdays, but he was too excited. He did his morning stretch and went to the window. When he opened the blinds, the sun shined light into his room. It was another warm day, with no signs of a cloud in the sky.

Another beautiful day. He thought to himself. *Hopefully, most of the day will go by fast. I'm ready for prom. I'm ready to dance with Katherine. First, I must do my morning prayer. It's always good to talk to God, first thing in the morning.*

Every morning, John would pray to God. It was a must. If he didn't pray before he started his day, everything would feel wrong. It would be like not talking to a friend for the entire day. Sure, it's only for a day, but knowing that you haven't talked to them makes you feel uncomfortable and alone. It makes you feel like you are missing a piece of your life. John got on his knees in front of the window and prayed.

Father, I thank you for letting me wake up to another gorgeous day. I thank you for bringing Katherine into my life. I thank you for giving me amazing parents. I pray that today will go great and that you will watch over all of us. I pray that you will protect Katherine and me tonight as we will be going to prom together. Some seniors like to sneak alcohol and drink on nights like these. Please watch over us. Amen.

John got up and smelled breakfast from downstairs. He could smell the bacon, eggs, and waffles. It all smelled delicious. *I wish Katherine could join us for breakfast. I miss her. Sure, I see her at school every day, but that's not enough. I wonder what she's eating for breakfast this morning.*

He remembered what his parents told him about Katherine last week. Remembering that made him a little upset. *Her back was covered in bruises, mom said. What did she do to deserve that? To have been beaten like a weak animal. Nothing, that's what. She doesn't deserve that. No one does. She's been in that darkness for I don't know how long. How come her parents haven't been reported to the police? Is she scared to tell someone? Maybe she thinks no one will believe her, or that if she told someone she will get another beating. How is she able to sleep at night? Mom said once that Katherine smelled. Could she be scared to take a shower at her own home? Does she think her parents would burst in to hurt her? Man, I don't think I could even imagine being afraid to be in my own home. I mean, this is home. Home is meant to be happy and safe. Parents are supposed to discipline you, sure, but not beat you. My gut tells me she never has done anything wrong. They just beat her for the fun. Well, God will help her. He made it so that my mom saw Katherine's back. He made it that mom told me. He wanted my mom to see her back, so I would know about it.*

A couple of tears ran down John's cheek. He wiped them away and headed downstairs. The closer he got to the kitchen, the more his stomach growled. *I need to get my mind off that dark subject and eat some food. Everything will be alright. I know it.*

Michael and Mary were already at the table, eating breakfast. They figured that John would have slept in like every Saturday.

"Well, good morning." His dad said, a little surprised.

"Good morning," John replied.

"You're up early. Excited about tonight?"

"Yes, sir!" John said in an excited voice.

"Mom, I've been wondering about something."

"What is it, dear?" Mary asked.

"Why is Katherine's dress here? I've been meaning to ask you, but the question kept slipping away from me."

"She's going to get ready over here. She asked me, and I told her yes. Your dad is fine with it."

"Oh, okay."

"Is that alright with you? It doesn't make you uncomfortable, does it?"

"No, ma'am. I don't want her in that house anymore. I prefer that she would get ready over here. What time is she coming?"

"Around four I believe."

"Alright. Mom, did you see the suit I bought?"

"Yes, I did. It looks very nice. You did an excellent job picking it out."

"Thanks."

"I have a question." His dad said after he swallowed a mouthful of eggs. Are you going to ask Katherine to be your girlfriend tonight?"

65

"W-What?" John said nervously.

"Well, with big nights like this, you have to do something. It's prom. Either you ask her to be your girlfriend, or you tell her you love her."

"I like her a lot, but I'm not sure if I love her."

"Well, then you have to ask her to be your girlfriend."

"W-Why? Why tonight?"

"Because it's prom. Something major always happens on prom night. You don't want her to be your girlfriend? Is that why you don't want to ask her?"

"Yes, I do. I just didn't know when I would ask her. Are you sure it's best to ask at prom?"

"Definitely."

Katherine showed up a little before four o'clock. John couldn't believe how beautiful she looked. She wasn't even in her dress or had any makeup on. She was gorgeous, just the way she was. *I can't believe that I will be dancing with her tonight. The most beautiful woman I have ever seen. My heart is pounding as if it wants to jump out and land right into her hands. Calm down, John. You're not at the prom yet. Keep it together.*

"Hey, John." She greeted with a smile. "How are you?"

"G-Great. What about you?"

"Same."

They just stood there, smiling at each other. Not saying a word. Smiling was enough for them. Just being close to each other made John happy. *That's it! I can't take it anymore. Tonight, I will ask her to be my girlfriend. I'll ask her when we are dancing. It'll be romantic. I want to ask her now, but it's not the right time. The timing has to be perfect.*

John wasn't prepared with what happened next though, it just happened. He didn't even think Katherine knew what she did. Or did she know? What Katherine did made John form the biggest grin on his face that anyone has ever seen. She kissed him on the cheek.

———

Another day, another morning where Katherine woke up in a hot room. Her back was sweating as if she's been in the sun for too long. That wasn't the only thing that was considered normal though. Her folks went back to their old ways. She knew that they would. Her dad threw, what sounded like, a beer bottle. Katherine heard it smash against a wall. After a bottle was another plate. *How many plates are left?* Katherine asked herself. She rubbed her eyes and sat up. *I'm surprised that we haven't run out already.*

She turned around, ignoring the fighting. The sun was shining as always, with no clouds anywhere to cover it up. Katherine sighed as she stood up. She pulled her shirt up at the mirror, so she could see her back. There was never a day where there wasn't a bruise on it. Just once she would love to have a bruise-free back.

She grabbed the least dirty clothes she had and went to the pond. When people look at her, they give that look when they know that she smells bad. Every now and then, someone from school would ask why she smells. Her answer is always that the pipes in her house are broken. The truth is, though, she's scared. She's scared to take a shower in the house because her dad walked in a couple of years ago and hit her with his belt. She did nothing wrong. He was just drunk and had no one at the time to beat. Her mother was in town, buying drugs.

Now, she bathes in the pond. The water was a little dirty, but it was either that or get hit again. She can't smell too bad now, though. She has deodorant. She also bought herself a bar soap with the money she earned from the flower shop.

Every time she would take a bath in the pond, she would cry. She didn't want to clean herself in dirty pond water. She wanted to use the shower in her own home, but no. She wasn't allowed too. If she did, she would get hurt again. Katherine didn't want that. She didn't want to get hurt anymore.

In a way, she was happy. She has John. A friend. A friend that she likes a lot and wants to be with all the time. She wants to be his girlfriend. Katherine, as depressed as she used to be, ever since she met John, has grown happier every day. And since she's been reading the Bible, her soul seemed happier as well. She couldn't really explain it, but she was experiencing peace at a spiritual level.

She also has Holly and John's parents. All of them have treated her with nothing but kindness. That's all she wanted from her parents. Kindness. She witnessed that some last night. From her dad at least. Her mom just didn't yell at her.

When she finished and put her clothes on, she sat on the grass to rest. Her back was aching, and all she wanted to do was lay down and cry. She didn't though. Something was different. Something inside of her told her that everything would be alright. In one month she will graduate, and she will leave this place. Did she really wanted to leave though?

If I leave this town, I'll be leaving John. I'll be leaving Holly. The only friends I have. Do I really want to leave, or should I stay? Wow, I never thought I would ever ask myself that. I never thought I would stay here. If I stay, I won't be living with my parents. I can't stay over there. Maybe I could ask for full time at the flower shop, and then I'll be able to afford my own place. It'll be small, but it'll be where I can use my own shower and not have to worry about getting hurt. I don't know.

Why does it feel like I'm forgetting something? I know that I'm supposed to do something today, but I don't remember what it is. Katherine sat there, trying to remember what was so important about today. She listened to the ducks that swam around. They quacked as if they were talking to each other. The birds were chirping in the trees. Suddenly she remembered.

Prom! I can't believe that I forgot about prom! I'll be dancing with John tonight! I'll be having the most handsome guy in school beside me. My dress and heels are at his parents' house. Let's see. The sun isn't all the way up in the sky yet, so I have a couple of hours left before I must walk over there. What do I do in the meantime? I guess I'll just lay here and relax.

Katherine laid down and closed her eyes. She listened to the wilderness as she relaxed. Her back was in pain from taking a bath in the pond. Of course, it always ached. She thought about the Bible and God. *He created the sounds that I'm hearing. The animals. He created the stars I see in the sky when it's dark out. He created John, the boy I have feelings for. He sent His Son down to die on the cross for me. For everyone. Every time I think about this, my whole body feels different. In a good way. I feel more at peace. The question is, do I know and accept that Jesus is my Lord and Savior? I don't know. I don't know what is stopping me from accepting it.*

After a while, Katherine got up and walked toward the Williams' house. It was a decent walk, and it made her back hurt, but she made it in time. John was the one who opened the door after she knocked. Not his mom or dad. John. As soon as she saw his face, she just smiled. They asked each other how they were and just kept smiling.

What she did next was shocking, even for her. She didn't know why, but she kissed him on the cheek. She couldn't stop it. *What did I just do!? Did I really kiss him on the cheek! Why did I do that? Something inside of me made me do it. Oh no. No, no, no. What is he going to do? Is he going to get mad at me? Does he no longer want me to go to the prom with him? Why is he smiling!? He liked it!*

They blushed and heard John's parents walking toward them. *Thankfully, they didn't see the kiss.*

"Hey, Katherine," Mary said with a smile.

"H-Hey," Katherine replied nervously.

"Are you ready?"

"Yes, ma'am."

"You can use the bathroom upstairs. It's the second door to the right. If you need anything, call me."

"Thank you."

After a couple of minutes, Katherine called Mary to help her with the makeup. She used the usual stuff: eyeliner, lipstick, etc. As Mary was helping Katherine put makeup on, they started a conversation.

"Are you excited?" Mary asked.

"Very. I can't wait to dance with John."

"Do you know how to dance?"

"Kind of. I would watch people dance at the pond. When they would dance, I would copy what they would do. It's silly, I know, but I enjoyed it."

"Well, I'll show you some moves after we get done here. How does that sound?"

"Fantastic!" Katherine shouted happily.

Mary showed her some slow dancing moves and then they both headed downstairs where John was dressed up in his suit. *Oh, wow! He looks so handsome! His hair is slicked back and everything!*

"Y-You look amazing," John told her.

He made another huge grin as he watched her walk down the stairs. Katherine took a couple of deep breaths.

"You look handsome." She replied.

She could feel tears wanting to come out of her eyes. *Don't cry. I know you're happy right now. Happier than you have ever been in your life. However, you can't be crying in front of everyone. At least, not in front of his parents.*

Mary took a picture with her phone and said, "Have fun, you guys. Be safe."

"We will," John replied.

They got into the truck and drove to the school. They may not have any sports teams, but the school had a gym. That's where the prom will be. They didn't say anything to each other on the way there. They both had the butterflies and felt like if they said one word to each other, they would puke. The sun was getting closer to hiding behind the other side of the world.

"N-Nice sunset," Katherine said.

"B-Beautiful," John replied. "N-Not as beautiful as you though."

Katherine blushed as John parked at the school gym. Then they went inside.

⬯

Music was already playing when they went inside the gym, the lights were down, and the room was filled with the smell of cologne and perfume. They both coughed from the strong smell, trying to catch their breath. *Wow, it smells strong in here!* John thought.

Some people were on the dance floor, while others were sitting in chairs, chatting. *I don't know any of these songs. Maybe Katherine does.*

"Do you know any of these songs?" He asked Katherine.

"Not really." She responded. "I have heard little music before. Is this what some people would call Rock?"

"No, I think this is Blues or something. Rock is faster paced."

"Well, what do you want to do? Do you want to dance?"

"How about we get something to drink first? There's punch on the other side of the room."

"What's punch?"

"Oh, it's awesome. Come on."

They walked around the dance floor and grabbed themselves some cups. The music was loud, and the talking was even louder. *How can people be louder than music? I need to focus less on that and be more focused on dancing with Katherine. I hope I remember the moves. Dad taught me once or twice.*

I'll never forget what he told me while Katherine was getting ready ... ...

"This dance could be the dance that would begin your life with that girl." His dad said while watching John put his tie on.

"What do you mean?" John asked.

"I mean, this dance could lead to even more dances. Date dances, engaged dances, maybe even married dances. You need to choose if you want to have those dances with Katherine."

"Dad, she's not even my girlfriend yet. I'm not sure if she will even say yes when I ask her."

"She will."

"How do you know?"

"I can see it in her eyes. She's falling for you, son. You're falling for her too. I can tell."

"Really?"

"Yes. This dance is important to you and to her. Do you remember the moves I taught you?"

"Yes, sir."

"Show me."

John showed what he remembered from his dancing lessons. He did pretty well, and it impressed Michael.

"Good. Good."

"I'm nervous, dad."

"I know you are, son. Everything will be okay though. This is a big night. Tonight will change your life. It'll change her life."

"Dad. Thanks for never, you know, hitting me or anything."

"I'm a dad. A real dad doesn't beat his children. A real dad is there for his kids. A real dad never abandons his son or daughter. One day, I hope, you'll say that to your children."

"You got it."

John looked at himself in the mirror. He was wearing the suit he bought at the clothing store. He didn't look too bad.

"You look sharp," Michael said.

"I do, don't I?" John agreed.

Michael took a deep breath and looked away.

"Dad, are you crying?"

"No. I just can't believe how much you've grown. You're becoming a man more and more each day. Next month you will be a man."

"Well, I had some help from the greatest man I know," John said as he turned around, looking at his dad.

They hugged and walked downstairs to wait for Katherine. When John saw Katherine in her dress, he wanted to cry. She was so gorgeous. He never saw someone so beautiful in his life. He fought back the tears and just stared at her. She was like an angel.

Now, he's standing next to her, drinking punch and watching the other students dance on the floor.

"This punch stuff is fantastic," Katherine said.

"I know right?!" He replied.

"So, what kind of music do you listen to?"

"Gospel. That's pretty much it. Every now and then I would browse around the internet to see if I could find any Christian rock or something. Nothing would catch my eye."

"Maybe you could let me listen to some Gospel sometime. I mean, if you want to."

"I would love to. Can I ask you something? It's kind of personal."

"What is it?"

"Do you like living at home? Home with your parents?"

Katherine looked down, away from John. He could tell that she wanted to tell him the truth. That she was afraid to live in that house. He could tell by the look on her face. At first, he thought she would cry. John didn't want her to cry. Not now, not ever. Just thinking about her crying makes him feel depressed. Seeing her hurt would make him hurt.

"I'm fine," She mumbled.

That's it? Just fine? Please, tell me. I want to help you. I care about you. An instrumental love song came on, and everyone began to slow dance. Neither one of them knew what the song was, they just knew that it was romantic. John took a long deep breath and took Katherine's hand.

"W-Would you like to dance?" he asked in a nervous voice.

"I-I would love to."

They sat their cups down and went to the middle of the dance floor. John put his hands on her waist so gently, as if she would break if he put any pressure on her. She wrapped her arms around his neck, looking straight into his eyes. They danced.

"You're good at this," He breathed.

"Your mom taught me after helping me with my makeup."

He chuckled and said, "Well, she did a good job at teaching you."

"You're good at this too."

"My dad taught me a move or two."

A tear ran down Katherine's cheek. She shifted her eyes away from him, so he wouldn't be able to look at her.

"Why are you crying?" he asked, concerned.

"B-Because I'm so happy. I've never been this happy before. I have been battling the darkness that has been surrounding me my whole life. Since you came into my life, I now have something to look forward to, when I wake up every morning. You make me smile and you gave me that Bible. The more I read and understand it, the closer I am to finding peace and complete happiness. It's like I can see the cross, but I can't reach it."

"Katherine, I have never felt this way about anyone, like the way I feel about you. When I'm not around you, it's like a piece of my heart is missing. I want you to be in my life. You make me happy and I always can't wait to go to school, just so I can see your face. You're kind, sweet, beautiful, and amazing. I've never met a girl like you. I want you to know that I care about you. A lot. I NEVER want to see you hurt. Never."

"R-Really?"

"Katherine."

"Y-Yes?"

There was a small pause for a moment. They looked into each other's eyes as if they would never see each other again. They no longer were listening to the music. They didn't care about anyone was around them. Their eyes and ears were only focused on each other.

"Would you like to be my girlfriend?" he asked softly.

Another tear ran down Katherine's cheek, as he said, "Yes."

They smiled at the same time and held each other tight, finishing their dance.

Prom night was amazing. Katherine danced with the most awesome guy ever, and he asked her to be his girlfriend. She couldn't believe her own ears. She said yes, of course, and was so happy that she cried. It was the most romantic night of her life.

I can't believe it! She thought to herself. *He wants me to be his girlfriend! This night couldn't get any better. I had punch for the first time, heard different types of music, danced with John, and now I'm his girlfriend. I wish tonight didn't have to end. I wish I didn't have to go back home. No, I don't want to think about home right now. I just want to enjoy the rest of this incredible night. I'm in his arms and dancing with him.*

God, if you're there. Who am I kidding? Of course, You are. I just want to say, thank You. Thank You for leading me to that church. Thank You for bringing John into my life. Thank You for everything. I admit that I'm not sure about accepting Jesus into my life just yet. Something is holding me back and I need to find out what it is, so I can push it away. I want my heart, mind, and soul to submit to You and all Your glory. Please, help me. Help me find this invisible wall that is between You and me. I can see the Cross. I can see the light. I just can't reach it; I want to though. One more thing. I have a feeling that tonight might end horribly. I can't explain it, but I just have a feeling. Please, protect me.

They finished their dance and walked to the truck. They didn't talk to anyone while they were there, nor did they dance to the fast music. John drove her home, and they both were smiling as if some hooks caught them.

"Well, how was your night?" John asked her.

"It was unbelievable," She said back.

"I really like you, Katherine."

"I really like you too."

"Would you like to come to church tomorrow morning with me and my folks?"

"Um. Maybe. I'm not sure how the other people will react."

"What do you mean?"

"Well, the last time I was there, they stared at me. It made me uncomfortable."

"That's because you walked in during the middle of the sermon. This time, you'll be with me and you'll be joining us before it even starts."

"I guess that helps me feel better."

"Good."

He pulled up into Katherine's driveway and opened the truck door for her. She hugged him tight and didn't want to let go.

"Do I have to let go?" she asked.

"Unfortunately." He said. "I don't want to go but I have to. Good night, gorgeous."

"Good night."

She watched him drive away and then looked up at the sky. The sun was down, and the stars were shining brighter than ever. Katherine sighed and walked toward the house. She didn't care if her parents were yelling at each other. She had the best night of her life and nothing was going to ruin it.

When she walked in, she saw her parents yelling, but not at each other. Her mother wouldn't stop laughing. She saw her daughter walk in and yelled at her, but not angrily.

"Well, look who it is, Kenny!" Sarah yelled. "It's our daughter!"

"Our daughter!?" Kenny yelled back.

"Yeah! You know, the girl that lives with us."

"Oh, that lazy thing!"

Her parents laughed, but that didn't get to Katherine. She would not let them destroy her happiness. She saw that there was some kind of white powder on the coffee table in front of her mother. Katherine would see it there every now and then. Sometimes it would be needles. Her dad, of course, had a beer bottle in his hand. This time, though, they were wilder than ever.

Kenny stumbled into his room and Katherine walked toward hers. Before she could turn the knob, Kenny came back out with a gun. She saw it in his hand and began to breathe heavily. She never saw a gun in his hand before. Her heart was pounding with fear, and she walked away from him.

"Woo!" Kenny shouted.

He pointed the pistol to the ceiling and fired it. The gunshot was loud and when Katherine heard it, she ducked down to the floor. She crawled behind the old TV. Tears were rolling down her cheeks again, but this time it was from being terrified.

Why does he have that thing? Why is he shooting it in here? Does he know that he could really hurt someone? How much did he have to drink tonight? I need to get out of here. I need to get away. What if he sees me though? What if he sees me trying to get away? God, please help me! I need You!

Kenny fired again at the same spot on the ceiling.

"Woo!" he shouted again.

After the second gunshot, the front door was knocked down and a couple of police officers came running in. Two tackled Kenny, trying to disarm him. Katherine crawled and hid at the side of the couch. Then another two police officers took down Sarah. They put handcuffs on them and took them out of the house. She witnessed her parents being shoved into the police cars.

After a couple of seconds, the sheriff walked in.

"Come on out, sweetie." The sheriff said in a calming voice. "Everything is alright now. You can come out. I won't hurt you. I promise. I'm a police officer."

Katherine slowly stood up with tears pouring out of her eyes. Her body was shaking uncontrollably. The sheriff ambled toward her and wrapped his arms around her.

He patted her on the back and said, "Everything is alright. You're safe now. Do you have anywhere you can go? Somewhere safe? Someone that'll take care of you?"

"Y-Yes, sir …"

"Come with me, and I'll take you there."

"C-C-Can I get my Bible?"

"Of course."

Katherine went into her room and grabbed her Bible that was lying on the floor. When she walked out, she looked where her dad was shooting. Some pieces of the ceiling fell onto the floor, forming a cross. That night, she knew that God was watching over her.

A New Home

I t was around eight-thirty and John just pulled up into the driveway. He cut the ignition off and sat there, staring up at the night sky. He didn't want to go home just yet. Sure, he was already parked at the house, but he didn't want to go inside yet. He wanted to sit there in the silence, in the dark. He knew his parents probably heard the truck pull up.

I had a great night tonight. He thought. *I went to prom, and I went there with the most amazing girl I have ever met. I asked her to be my girlfriend, and she said yes. I have a girlfriend now. I never had one before, so I'm not completely sure what I should do first. Maybe she and I can watch a movie over here. We still have bags of popcorn left. I don't know. Doesn't sound good enough for a first date as boyfriend and girlfriend.*

The moon was shining on him like it was trying to tell him something. He couldn't put his finger on it, but he knew that tonight wasn't over. Yeah, the prom is over, and he dropped Katherine off. However, something inside of him is telling him that tonight isn't over. There is more to come.

What could it be? Something good? Something bad? What is it? Am I going to walk into the house and have my parents tell me something bad or good? If so, please let it be good. The bad thing that happened today was dropping Katherine off at her house with those bad people. I need to get inside before my folks suspect something.

John walked into the house and went straight to his room to change. He changed into his plain white pajamas. Boring look for some people, but he liked them. That's all that mattered. While he was up there, something was telling him to make a phone call. An important one. He dialed on his cell phone and made that phone call. Did he do the right thing? He won't know until later.

He then walked downstairs and greeted his parents in the living room. They were watching a movie. His dad paused it and his mom turned to face John.

"Well, hey," Mary said. "How was prom?"

"It went amazing," John replied. "I asked Katherine to be my girlfriend."

"Really!?" Mary shrieked with excitement. "What did she say?"

"She said yes."

"Oh, congratulations!"

"Congratulations, son," Michael said.

"Thanks," John said.

He shifted his eyes and his voice sounded upset. His parents knew that something was wrong. They've had years of practice of telling when something is wrong with their son.

"What's wrong, John?" his dad asked.

"Something is wrong. I just know it."

"With Katherine?"

"Yes, sir."

"Are you going to do something about it?"

"I already did. I just hope it was the right thing to do."

"Good. I'm sure it was."

A few minutes later, there was a knock on their door. John went to the front door and opened it. A police officer was there with Katherine. *Oh, no. What happened?*

"Are your parents home?" the officer said."

"Y-Yes, sir," John replied.

He went to his parents, telling them that an officer was at the door with Katherine. They got up and went to the front door and talked to him.

"What's going on, officer?" Michael asked, concerned.

"This young lady's parents were just arrested. When I asked if she knew a safe place to go to, she said this address. Is it alright if she stays here?"

"Of course," Mary said.

"Now from what I could get out of her, she'll be graduating this year. So, there's no sense of finding a legal guardian or sending her to an adoption agency. Graduation is next month and by the time the papers would come, she'll be free to live wherever."

"She can stay here."

"Good. Now that's out of the way. How are you doing Michael?"

While the officer was chatting with his parents, John let Katherine come inside. They went into the living room and sat down. Her makeup was ruined by crying. Her body was shaking uncontrollably, and she looked terrified.

"Hey," John mumbled as he held her close. "Everything's alright. I'm here."

"I-It was horrible," She whimpered. "My dad was so drunk that he was shooting his gun. T-Then the p-police came and tackled him down and arrested him and my mom"

John rubbed her back, trying to calm her down.

"It's okay. I'm here for you. I'm not going anywhere. Are you alright?"

"M-My head is killing me."

—

Katherine told the police officer she might can go to the William's house. They were kind people, and their son just became her boyfriend. The officer put her in the back of the car and drove her to their house. While on the way there, he asked her some questions.

"What grade are you in, hon?" he asked.

"Twelfth," She mumbled while she cried. "I-I graduate next month."

"Well, that's neat. Do you make good grades?"

Katherine nodded and faced the window. She didn't want him to see her cry. Her headache came back, and it was hurting more than ever. Part of her tears was from the pain and the rest were coming from what she went through. Her dad shot a gun and her mom was on a huge amount of drugs. The police came and tackled her dad and arrested both.

My head is in so much pain. She thought to herself. *I just want to twist it off and never worry about headaches again. What just happened? I mean, I saw them get arrested, but I don't understand how it suddenly happened. Did someone call on them? Who? Either way, I knew that God was watching me. Thank You, God. Thank You so much for watching over me.*

"Do you have any relatives that live close by?" the officer asked.

"N-No, sir. I don't have any other family."

"Okay. How are you doing back there?"

"F-Fine, I guess."

He pulled up to the William's house and opened the door for her. He knocked on the door and the first person Katherine saw was John. She couldn't feel more happy and safe. Seeing him made her relaxed and comfortable. He left the door and brought back his parents. They said she could live at their house and then John brought her inside.

"M-My head is killing me." She said while John was holding her tight.

"I'll get you some headache relief," John said. "I'm sure we have some left."

He got up and walked away. *Headache relief? What's that? Some kind of medicine to make my headache go away? I sure could use some right now. My head hurts so much! I want it to go away. I want all of this to go away. This situation, this fear, everything. I want all of it to just disappear.*

I can't believe that his parents will let me stay here. They are so kind! I don't want to be a burden though. I don't want to give them any trouble. John lives here though. He's my boyfriend. Does that mean he's going to take care of me? Where will I be sleeping? What will happen to my parents? A lot of questions, but no answers. I can't stand that.

John came back with a glass of cold water and two pills.

"Here," He said. "These will help your headache."

She took them and drank all the water.

"T-Thank you."

"Your welcome. Are you alright?"

"I'm a little better. It was so scary."

"I bet it was."

They heard the front door shut and John's parents walked in.

"Are you alright, Katherine?" they asked.

"I'll be okay."

"Do you want anything to eat?" Mary asked.

"I'm not hungry. You don't have to let me stay here if you don't want to. I don't want to cause any trouble."

"Oh, no trouble at all! Come on, we'll show you where you can sleep."

They walked upstairs and into an empty room. It was a little bigger than her old room. This one, though, had a dresser with a full mirror, instead of a broken one.

"For now, you can use an air up mattress," Michael said. "Monday, we'll go and buy a real bed."

"Y-You don't have to."

"I want to."

"Monday while the guys are getting the bed, we can go clothes shopping," Mary said to her with a smile. "How does that sound?"

"S-Sounds like fun."

"Great!"

"T-Thank you. You're too kind."

"Don't mention it," Michael replied. "I think we have some spare quilts in one of the closets. I'll go look."

"Are you going to be okay?" John asked her.

"Y-Yes. Thank you for being here for me."

"Of course. I will always be here for you. No matter what."

Michael came back with two quilts and a pillow. He set them down on the mattress for her, and everyone told her goodnight. Katherine unfolded the quilts and got herself comfy. The mattress was more comfortable than what she used to lie on. A lot more.

She looked at her hands and realized that they were still shaking from earlier. She tried to calm herself down. First, she took long deep breaths; that helped some, but not enough. Katherine got up and opened the window curtains, allowing the moonlight to shine into the room. She grabbed her Bible and read some of it by the window. The moonlight helped her see the words. The closer she gets to the end, the more she understands it. The more it makes sense.

After reading for about an hour or two, she looked up at the moon. It was beautiful. *It's like John said. It's like a giant canvas that God paints over. A masterpiece, every single time. It never gets old.*

She then went back to lie of the mattress and stared at the ceiling. She still wasn't tired enough to sleep. Tossing and turning didn't help. For once, she could lie on her back, and she couldn't fall asleep on it; but the mattress didn't hurt it at all. Finally, she figured out what was wrong. Something was telling her to pray.

"God," She said out loud. "Thank You for all that You have done for me. Thank You for keeping me safe tonight and for bringing this family into my life. They are so kind and understanding. I believe that I'm getting closer to You. To Jesus. I'm closer to being out of the storm and into the light. I can feel it. I can see it when I close my eyes. I'm getting closer to that cross. Thank You. Thank You for a new home."

Katherine closed her eyes, and as soon as she did, she fell asleep. It was the first time in a long time that she slept well.

That next morning, she was woken up by someone knocking on the door.

"Wake up, sleepyhead!" John yelled from the other side of the door.

"Come in," Katherine mumbled.

"It's Sunday. Do you want to come to church with us?"

"Not today. I'm not sure if I'm ready. Maybe next Sunday."

"Oh, okay. I'll remember that next Sunday, then. What are you going to do while we're gone?"

"Read some."

"Well, you know what? If you're not worshipping the Lord at church, at least you're worshipping Him somewhere."

"Yeah. Have a good time."

"You too. You look beautiful by the way."

Katherine smiled and rubbed her eyes. She was sleeping so well. She didn't want to get up. After she sat up, there was another knock on the door.

"Come in," she said

Mary walked in and handed her some clothes.

"I figured you could wear my clothes until we go shopping tomorrow," Mary said. "We look about the same size. I hope they fit."

"O-Oh thank you. Um. C-Can I use your shower?"

"Of course, you can! You don't have to ask. You live here now. You can use my shampoo and stuff for now."

"T-Thank you."

"You're welcome. John told me you might come to church with us next Sunday. I hope so because the church would love to have you there."

"O-Okay."

As soon as the Williams left for church, Katherine immediately went into the bathroom and took a shower. No more taking a bath in dirty pond water. No more having fish biting her toes. No more smelling gross. She cried while she was in the shower, but it was a happy cry.

After that, she put on the clothes that Mary gave her. Blue jeans and a plain yellow shirt. It wasn't much, but it was a lot better than the clothes she used to wear. She knew that she couldn't wear her prom dress forever.

The pants are a little big, but that's alright. I think they're big only because I never ate much while I lived at my parent's house. Maybe after living here for a month, I'll gain weight. I need too. I think the reason I get so many headaches is that I barely eat anything. The only time I eat is at school and I've eaten once or twice over here. I need to do something nice for them. Maybe I could clean. Yeah, I could clean something. Kitchen, maybe?

It took a few minutes, but Katherine found the broom and mop. She swept the kitchen and the hallway. After that, she mopped. Then she grabbed the vacuum that was beside them and vacuumed the living room. She didn't vacuum their rooms because she didn't want to invade their privacy. That would be rude.

When she got done, she went upstairs and grabbed her Bible. She then went downstairs and sat on the couch. Now, she can read on a comfortable seat instead of the hard floor. She read until the Williams got back.

"Hey, Katherine!" John yelled for her.

"In here," She said from the living room.

John walked into the living room and sat down beside her.

"What's up?"

"We need to think about graduation."

Different

"Graduation?" Katherine asked.

"Yeah. It's only a month away." John said, "We need to get measured up, so we can order our gowns tomorrow at school."

"Oh. I don't know my size."

"That's okay. My mom will get you measured tomorrow when you go shopping. You can order yours Tuesday."

"Alright."

"We also need to plan a party afterward. Like a cookout or something."

"A cookout?"

"Yep."

"Is it really a month away? I can't believe last month went by so fast."

"I know right?! I'm so excited."

I am excited. John thought. *I'll be a man and it's only a matter of time before dad will give me the talk. The talk about being a man. He will probably talk to me about college too. The thing is, I don't know what I want to go to college for. I still haven't found my gift. Maybe I should stay around here, just until I find it.*

"Hey, John," Katherine said.

"Yeah?"

"What's a cookout?"

"You never had a cookout before?"

"No ..."

"Well, you grill food outside like hamburgers, ribs, and those kinds of stuff, then you invite friends and family to come and join you if you want. You eat and chat with them and have a good time."

"Grill food?" Katherine said, looking puzzled.

"You never had grilled food before? Oh, we are going to change that."

John went to his dad and asked him if they can have some grilled burgers. His dad agreed and went to get everything ready. John brought Katherine outside to the backyard and sat in the lawn chairs. They watched Michael put the charcoal in the grill and fired it up. It amazed her when she saw the fire. After Michael got it under control, he put the meat patties on the grill to cook them.

"Wow, that smells great!" Katherine said with excitement.

She never had grilled food before and was ready to try it. Smelling it made her stomach growl and her mouth water. John saw her and chuckled.

"What's funny?" she asked.

"Nothing. I just love seeing you try new things. So how was your alone time?"

"It was great. I cleaned some of the house."

"Yeah, my mom noticed. She's impressed."

"I read some of the Bible too. Getting close to the end."

"Oh yeah? What are you going to do when you finish it?"

"Probably start over, but this time I'll begin with the Old Testament."

"Good."

"The closer I get to the end, the closer I feel that I am getting out of the storm. I can see myself at the edge, reaching for the cross. But, as soon as my hand touches the light, I wake up. I open my eyes and I can't picture it again for a while."

"Sounds to me you are getting closer to being saved. It's only a matter of time."

"Yeah."

"So how are you doing with living here now?"

"It's different."

"What do you mean?"

"I don't have to get into my room by climbing through the window now."

"Well, your room is up the stairs." John chuckled.

"No, I mean, I'm not scared to walk into the house by going through the front door. I know that when I walk into this house, I won't get hurt. I'm actually welcomed."

"Of course, you're welcomed. I never want you to feel unwelcome. I don't want you to feel scared or unwanted. Do you understand?"

Katherine smiled at him and said, "Yeah. Are the burgers almost done? I'm starving."

"Almost, I think. What else is different?"

"The people that live at the house. When I come here, I know that they won't be mean and treat me rudely. They'll treat me with kindness and love. I'm not used to that."

"I know. You'll get used to it though. I promise."

"I know."

John felt the sun beaming down on him. It was warm and comfortable. *I wonder what will happen to her after graduation. I want to ask, but I don't think it's the right time. I know mom will ask her tomorrow, though. I want Katherine to feel loved and welcomed. I don't want her to be afraid of anything anymore. I don't want to see her hurt. I don't want to see her sad. I want her to be happy and enjoy herself.*

John turned to her and kissed her on the cheek. She looked surprised and blushed.

"I-I ..." Katherine mumbled.

She couldn't get anything to come out of her mouth. She didn't know what to say. She sat there, smiling and blushing.

"Is the food done yet?" She asked again. "It smells delicious!"

"I'll go check."

John got up and walked over to his dad to see if the food was almost ready. The burgers smelled great. His stomach growled when he got next to his dad.

"I saw that," Michael said.

"Saw what?"

"That peck on the cheek. Kissing now, are we?"

They both grinned and John said, "Just on the cheek. Are they almost done?"

"Yep. Go get the buns and stuff. We can eat out here and enjoy the rays."

"Sounds like a plan."

Everyone fixed themselves a burger and sat down to eat under the sun. Midway through lunch, the backyard became darker. They looked up and saw a couple of clouds above.

"Clouds?" Mary said, surprised.

"We might get rain soon," Michael replied to her. "It's been a while since we saw a cloud around here. We sure could use some rain."

"It would be nice to have something different," John said as he looked at Katherine. "Sometimes, different is good."

It was around eleven am Monday morning, and Katherine and Mary were in the clothing store where Katherine got her prom dress from. Mary wouldn't allow Katherine to go another day of school wearing old, torn, small clothes. Today they will get Katherine some clothes for her size. Then they will be having lunch. John went to school, and Michael will buy a bed for her after he gets off work. She won't know what it looks like until she goes back home.

Home. She thought to herself. *It's strange to call their house my home now. It's different. Everything is different. My new home, the adults I now see when I come home. No yelling, no fighting, no fear. It's relaxing and I do enjoy it, but it all just feels weird. Like John said, I'll get used to it. I hope Mary won't buy all of these clothes for me. I don't want to be a burden. I'm sure I can pay for some of these clothes myself.*

"How about these?" Mary asked.

She showed Katherine some jeans she found.

"They look nice."

"Go try them on and see if they'll fit."

"Okay."

They all fit and Mary put them in the basket she was carrying. Mary was looking for jeans and socks while Katherine was looking for shirts and other clothing. She needs new shoes, too. Katherine found a couple of cute short sleeves and one or two dresses for church. *Church.* She decided that she'll be going to church this coming Sunday. The Williams was happy to hear about that. Katherine, on the other hand, was nervous. This time, she won't be running into church randomly. She'll be going with John and his parents. Katherine took a deep breath and continued looking for new clothes.

She remembered what John said yesterday about graduation. *I need to think about what I want to do with my life. I want to go to college, but something tells me I need to stay here. I don't know. Maybe I should stay here. To be honest, I'm more worried about the cloudy weather that suddenly appeared. It's strange that the clouds just popped up out of nowhere. Is it really going to rain? So far, it's just been partly cloudy. It's a nice change though. Maybe John is right. Different can be good.*

"So, Katherine," Mary said randomly. "What are your plans after you graduate? Going to college?"

"I want to, but I think I'm going to just stay here."

"Why would you want to stay here? It's a small town. Not much you can do around here."

"I know, but I think I should."

"Okay. Well, what are you going to do?"

"I'm going to see if I can get a full-time job at the flower shop. Save up for my own place. I-Is it okay if I stay with you and your husband until then?"

"Of course. You take your time."

"If you did go to college, what would you go for?"

"I think I would go to be a therapist or something like that."

"Oh, really?"

"Yeah, I want to help people."

"Then why stay here? Go to college so you can become a therapist and help people."

"Something is telling me I should stay here though."

"It could be God."

"Maybe. You know, you guys don't have to do this for me. You don't have to buy me a bed or anything."

"We know, but we want to."

"Why?"

"Because it's the right thing to do. Besides, John likes you, and to be honest, I do too. You're a nice girl and you make John happy."

"R-Really? I make him happy?"

"Oh, yeah!" Mary picked up a pair of shoes and said, "How about these?"

"I'll try them on."

The shoes fit, and she got those and a pair of heels for church. She got the rest of the clothes that she needed and went to lunch with Mary. They went to that country restaurant she and John went to on their date. Katherine had catfish this time, and Mary had a big salad.

Next, they went to get Katherine some cleaning supplies: shampoo, toothbrush, and her own towels. Mary bought them for Katherine, and they headed home. When they got there, they went straight up to Katherine's room.

The bed was set up in front of the window, and it was nice. The headboard had a gold look to it and at the foot of the bed was a chest. Michael bought some new quilts, pillows, and sheets to go along with it. The quilts were blue, and the sheets were the same color.

"Wow!" Katherine said happily. "That's pretty."

"Thank you," Michael said, sneaking up on them.

The girls jumped and giggled. Mary helped Katherine put her new clothes in the dresser.

"Did you ladies have an enjoyable time?" Michael asked.

"Yes, sir," Katherine replied. "Um. What's the chest for?"

"Anything you want to put in it."

"Cool. Thank you again."

"You're welcome."

There was a knock on the door and Michael went downstairs to answer it.

"I'm glad you enjoyed yourself," Mary said.

"Me too."

Michael called Katherine to come downstairs. When she went, she saw the same policeman at the door that brought her here just a few days earlier.

"Hello, young lady." The officer said. "Do you remember me?"

"Y-Yes, sir."

"Well, I have some news for you. Your mother has checked herself into a rehab facility."

"W-What's that?"

"That's a place where people go to get clean. To help them get off of drugs and to, hopefully, stay off of them for good. She'll be in there for a while. I wrote the address for you, in case you wanted to go see her."

"T-Thank you." She said as she took the paper from him.

"Also, your dad's trial will be this Saturday, and you will need to testify against him."

"T-Testify?"

"Yes. You will need to tell the judge and jury, what you saw him do that night. Your mother also said your dad beat you with a belt. You will have to show them your back and tell them he did that to you. Do you still have bruises on your back?"

"Y-Yes, sir. A good bit is still there."

"Alright. Mary and Michael will take you to the courthouse this Saturday at four pm. You all have a good night."

"I-I can't believe that I have to go to court and tell everyone what my dad did to me. I-I'm scared."

Court

It was Monday, almost midnight and John has been tossing and turning, ever since he lay in bed that night. He couldn't sleep. His mind wouldn't allow him to go to sleep. Katherine had shown him the bruises on her back last night, and he was shocked. He told her he promised that she will never get hurt again. Then they hugged each other good night and went to bed.

Everybody else was asleep. At least, his parents were. He could hear them snoring from his room. Their snoring never bothered him though.

John had enough and got out of bed. He was wearing his plain black pajamas tonight. He walked to the window and pulled the curtains, allowing a partial moonlight shine into his room. Ever since Sunday, it's been cloudy nonstop. Even at night, the sky would be partly covered up by clouds, but you could still see some stars here and there. *A new painting.* John thought to himself. *Tonight, God was painting a cloudy night. I can see that He's going with very little moonlight tonight. A star over there, and a couple over there. What is He trying to say? It can't be just that we might get rain soon. No. It must be something bigger than that. What could it be though? Maybe I'll find out soon.*

John snuck out of his room and tiptoed downstairs and into the kitchen. He didn't turn the light on, worried that he would wake up his parents. He grabbed a glass cup and put a handful of ice in it. Then he filled the cup with water from the faucet. Some people liked bottles of water, but John thought good ole fashion ice water from a faucet was the best water that anyone could get. That was his opinion, though.

He sat down and rubbed his head a few times. *Why can't I sleep?* He kept asking himself that question over and over. Suddenly, someone turned the kitchen light on. John turned his head and saw it was his dad. Michael rubbed his eyes and walked over, sitting next to John.

"What's wrong, son?" Michael asked.

"I can't sleep," John replied. "How did you know I was up?"

"I didn't. I was thirsty."

"Oh."

"Why can't you sleep? Worried about Katherine going to court?"

"I guess that's it."

"Talk to me about it. My eyes and ears are open."

"Her dad abused her."

"Yes."

"A lot. With a belt."

"Yep."

"Have you ever thought about hitting me with a belt? Hitting me at all?"

"No, son. I haven't. I try to never allow evil to get anywhere near me. I believe in discipline, but not beating a child."

"How bad do you think she's hurting?"

"I don't know, son. I'm sure she's hurting a good bit."

"Do you think she will ever get better? Mentally, I mean."

"I'm sure she will. I can tell that she's letting Jesus more and more into her heart, every day."

"Me too. She showed me her back. It was bad. She said it's been healing some. Slowly though."

"Well, healing takes time."

A tear ran down John's cheek as he said, "I-I don't know how to help her. It hurts my soul that all I can do is watch. She's hurting and there's nothing I can do about it."

Michael put his hand on John's shoulder and looked straight into his eyes.

"Look at me," Michael said in a strong tone. "John, look at me."

John did, and he saw that his dad was serious.

"John, you can do something. You can be there for her. You can pray for her. When you're a man, you know that you must take responsibility. Whether it's yourself, other people, or your woman. There will be times where you can't help physically, but you can still help. You can be there for her. You pray for your woman. Do you understand? You pray to God that He will help her. That He will heal her."

John nodded and wiped his tear away. Before he went to bed, John prayed for Katherine. Shortly after, he fell asleep. For the rest of the week, he helped Katherine. Mary gave her chores she could do around the house.

Washing the dishes every night was one. They had a dishwasher, but it was broken. John would do them for her while she dusted around the house.

By the time it was Friday, Katherine sat John down in the living room. His dad was in his room, reading. The sun was setting, and Mary should be home from work any minute.

"John, I know what you're doing," She said.

"What?"

"You think since I'm in pain, that I shouldn't be doing many chores."

"I care about you. I don't want to see you in pain."

"I know that, but you can't prevent it. The bruises will be there for a little while longer. Alright? Then they'll be gone for good." She held his hand and kept talking. "I want to do the dishes. Okay? I want to feel that I'm useful. I love feeling useful. It makes me feel good. You have your chores and I have mine. You have mowing the yard and vacuuming. I have washing the dishes and dusting the house. Please, let me do my part of the chores."

"Okay." He mumbled. "You know, tomorrow is the day. You'll be telling the judge everything. About your dad beating you with a belt."

"Yeah, I know. Um. There's something else that I need to tell you."

"What is it?"

"When I used to live over there, I would take baths in the pond."

"Wait, what? Why?"

"Because I was afraid to take a shower in the house. Once my dad barged into the bathroom and hit me. I never took a bath in that house since then."

"I'm sorry."

That was a theory I had. I could never imagine what it would be like to be in her shoes. To be honest, I'm afraid to find out. If I could, I would have taken her place. I would have taken the beatings for her if I knew that she would be okay.

John grinned and said, "You are so gorgeous."

Katherine blushed and said, "Thank you. You've been telling me that every day."

"Because it's true. Are you ready for tomorrow?"

"No, but I know that you will be there by my side."

⌒

It was Tuesday after school, and Katherine was at the flower shop. The flower shop was a little busy today. There was always a customer. She and Holly would take turns helping a customer out. It slowed down near closing time. Now that the store has calmed down, Katherine could work with the flowers. She did her usual work. Snipping, watering, and basically making sure that all the plants were healthy.

After she was done, Holly came in.

"Katherine," Holly mumbled. "I-I've been wanting to talk to you."

"Is everything okay?"

"I-I heard what happened to you and your parents."

"Oh."

Katherine looked down. She was so embarrassed that she turned away from Holly. *How did she find out?* She asked herself. *How did she hear about that? Oh man, this is so embarrassing! I can't even look at her right now.*

"This is a small town," Holly said. "Word travels fast. I'm so sorry."

"W-Why?"

"Because you went through a terrible thing. If you need anything, let me know. Alright?"

"Y-Yes ma'am."

"Are you okay?"

"I-I have to go to court this Saturday and tell the judge what my dad did to me."

"It'll be alright. I promise."

"C-Can I ask you something?"

"Of course."

"After I graduate, is it alright if I work here full time?"

"You don't want to go to college?"

"Not yet. I think I should stay here for a while. Save up money for my own place."

"Of course, you can work here full time. It'll be like we're partners."

"Yeah."

Holly counted the money and closed the store. John's dad had the truck, so Holly took Katherine home.

"So, you're living at the William's house now?" Holly asked. "How is it over there?"

"It's nice. They are really caring."

"That's good."

It was good. Katherine had her own bed now and some new clothes. She was free. Well, she was free from her parents. She didn't feel completely free though. It was strange. Something told her she will be free, soon.

For the rest of the week, Katherine did the chores that Mary gave her. John kept helping her, so she had to ask him to stop. She knew that he cared and was trying to help, but she loved the feeling of being useful. She enjoyed helping around the house.

Even though she has her own bed now, she would be up on some nights, worrying about court. *What am I going to say? What am I going to do? Anything I say will be important. Extremely important. What if my dad runs over and hurts me? No. Don't think like that. He won't hurt me. There will be a bunch of people around. He wouldn't do it. At least, I hope not.*

Saturday came, and everyone was getting ready. John and his parents were coming with Katherine for support. They told her they will be there with her, so she shouldn't feel afraid. Katherine wore a t-shirt with a panda on it and black jeans. She wanted to wear a dress, but she knew that the judge would have to see her back.

While waiting at the courthouse, John held her hand.

"Everything will be fine," John said. "I'm here for you. I've been praying."

"T-Thank you." She replied. "I'm scared."

"I know. Just remember that God is here and watching over you."

"Okay."

"Do you want to pray before you go in there?"

"S-Sure."

John, Mary, Michael, and even Katherine, all prayed that everything will go well. That Katherine will keep calm and be safe. Katherine was called for her dad's case. The William's sat in the seats behind the gate, while Katherine sat in a big seat, next to the judge.

"Hello, young lady," The judge said. "Do you know why you are here?"

"Y-Yes, sir," Katherine said.

"You will be asked a couple of questions about your dad. Are you ready?"

"Y-Yes, sir."

A man-made her swear on the Bible to tell the truth. When he walked away, the questions began.

"First," the judge said. "How would you describe your dad?"

At first, Katherine didn't say anything. She was so nervous that all she could do was sit quietly and stare in the distance. After a few seconds, she took a deep breath and answered the question.

"M-M-Mean." She answered, frightened.

"What mean things did he do?"

"Y-Yell and …"

She cut off and stared at her dad. He stared back with a cold face. She could tell that he wanted to hit her right then and there. *God, please help me. I-I can't do this without You. I'm scared.*

"And what?" the judge asked.

"And beat me with a belt."

"Can you stand up and show me?"

Katherine stood up and raised the back of her shirt slowly, revealing the bruises. They healed a good bit, but you could still see them. Instead of dark colors, the bruises turned into a dark yellow color. When she showed him, everyone gasped. Some people whispered to others while the rest covered their mouths in shock. The judge made an angry face and told Katherine that she could put her shirt down.

"How long has your dad been doing this?" he asked.

"A-A long time. Years."

"Are you afraid of that man?"

Katherine cried as she said, "Y-Yes sir. He came into the bathroom once and hit me while I took a shower."

"Why?"

"I-I don't know. I had to take baths in the pond after that."

"You were so scared, that you had to take baths in a pond?"

She nodded and wiped some of the tears away.

"Does your dad drink?"

"Y-Yes, sir."

"How much?"

"He always had a beer in his hand."

"Can you tell me about the time when the police came and arrested him?"

"H-He had a gun, a-and shot it at the ceiling."

"How many times?"

"T-Two."

"Why did he do that?"

"H-He was drunk."

"Have you ever seen that gun before?"

"N-No, sir."

"I understand that you are graduating this month. Are you living with someone to take care of you?"

"Y-Yes, sir. The William's"

Katherine pointed them out, and the judge told her she can go sit with them. The jury didn't take long for them to decide. They were only in the other room for about two minutes. When they came out, they said they have found Kenny Lee, guilty.

Rain

John and Katherine watched Kenny being taken away. After they walked out of the courtroom, Katherine wrapped her arms around John. He held her tight, allowing her to cry on him.

"Shhh," John said quietly. "Everything is going to be alright. I'm here for you. Cry as much as you need to."

Katherine wiped the rest of her tears away and thanked John for being there for her.

"Anything for you," John said.

"I just know that he hates me even more now," Katherine whimpered. "I can feel it."

"I'm sure he doesn't hate you. Besides, this will help him with his drinking problem. Maybe after a while, he'll find Christ and become a better person. A kind person."

"Yeah, I guess you're right. Can we go home now?"

"Of course."

When everyone walked out of the courtroom, they noticed that the sun wasn't shining on the town. Everything looked darker. They looked up and saw that the sky was completely covered with dark clouds. It made the weather a little cooler as well. There was not one piece of blue sky that you could see.

"Oh, wow," Michael said. "It's sure getting dark. We might be getting rain soon."

"Maybe," John replied.

"I heard," Katherine mumbled to John. "That when it rains, that means that someone has found peace. Sometimes it could mean that it's a sign. Like something is going to happen."

"Really? Well, that's interesting."

I sure could use a sign. John said to himself. *I need to know if I'm heading in the right direction. I wonder if Katherine found peace, now that she no longer has to worry about her parents. No. She can't find peace until she finds Christ. Hopefully, that will be soon.*

"I think so. John, didn't you say once that you are trying to find your gift? Maybe after this rain, you'll find it."

"That would be nice. Maybe you will find peace."

"Maybe. I know that I don't have to worry about my parents and their abuse anymore, but I don't feel at peace just yet."

"You'll find it. Trust me. So, what do you guys want to do tonight?"

"How about some family time? I know that I'm not a part of it, but all of you make me feel like I am a part of the family."

"Awe!" Mary said with excitement. "Of course, you are part of this family, dear. We care about you!"

"I'm almost finished reading the New Testament. I got Revelations left. I will read some tonight before I go to bed."

"Well, that's good," They said to her.

For the rest of the day, Katherine and the Williams spent it together. They watched a movie and ate supper. They had corn, green beans, and pork chops. It was so good that John had to have a second plate. Then they played a couple of card games. Katherine won most of the games. Mary won one or two. After that, they did their own family Bible study. They even let Katherine join them. She enjoyed it.

After all the fun and games, everyone went to their rooms and went to bed. Except for John. No matter how much he tossed and turned, he just couldn't go to sleep. He did his prayer.

"Lord," he prayed. "Thank You for watching over Katherine and my family. Thank You for giving Katherine the strength to go up to that stand and stand up to her dad. I pray that You will give her the peace she needs. I know that the only way for her to find peace is through You. I pray that You will give us this rain that we desperately need. Farmers need it for crops, and we need it to cool down this weather a bit. Father, I ask that You help me find my gift. It seems like the closer I get to graduation, the more I feel worried and scared. I don't think I will discover my gift in time to use it after graduation. I want to be able to find it and put it in use as soon as I graduate. Of course, I know You will show me my gift when the time is right. It's just hard sometimes to not know what I'm supposed to do. Anyway, I pray that You will watch over us, as we will be going to church tomorrow morning to worship You. In Jesus's name, I pray, amen."

Not being able to sleep, John got up and walked over to the window. He didn't close the curtains since the dark clouds covered the moon. It almost looked pitch-black outside. No stars, no moonlight, nothing. The only thing he could see was the streetlights from the side of the road.

A new painting. Everything seems so calm. I don't hear a sound. The crickets aren't even chirping. So calm. So peaceful. What if Katherine is right? What if something IS going to happen? Will it be bad? Will it be good? Or will the crops just get watered and that's it? Only time will tell. What will happen, Lord?

John stood there at the window, staring out. Every now and then he thought he could see a piece of a cloud, moving across the sky. He kept wondering what's going to happen. It could be anything. Eventually, he changed the subject. Now he was wondering if Katherine would come to church tomorrow. He thought about his gift and all the possibilities on what it could be. After a few minutes, he went to his desk and turned on his lamp.

He pulled out his journal and a pen. He figured that since he was still wide awake, he would write his thoughts.

What is my gift? That's a good question. I don't even know what it is yet. I'm still patiently waiting to find it. I need to know what it is, so when graduating comes, I'll know what to do with my life.

Anyway, I'm looking forward to the day when Katherine gets saved. It's going to be a day she will never forget. Who knows, maybe she'll get saved tomorrow at church. I love it when she smiles, when she laughs, I even love it when she's just sitting on the couch doing nothing. I love spending time with her. She makes me feel like she could be the one. To be honest, I think she could be. I'm falling in love with her.

It was Saturday night, and the clouds were covering the stars that usually show up when it's dark outside. Katherine couldn't even see the moon, shining in the night sky. That's okay though. It was nice to see something different.

She had fun today, besides going to court to tell the judge what her dad would do to her. That was terrifying. She could tell that he wanted to hurt her. Even though he didn't look at her when he was taken away, she could feel the hate. She could feel that he was angry at her and wanted to beat her with his belt. She doesn't have to worry about him and his belt anymore though. That's all over. She's free from him. Free from the abuse.

Katherine opened her window and let the cool air flow into her room. After being in the hot sun every day, it's nice to feel some cool air. Might as well enjoy it while it lasts.

She turned her bedroom light on and grabbed her Bible. Revelation was the last book she had to read in the New Testament. Even though it was the last book to read, she didn't want to put it up after she finished it. She wants to start over from the very beginning. She wants to read the Old Testament and then read the New Testament over again. As a matter of fact, she wants to read the Bible every day. It doesn't matter how many times she would read it over and over again. Just as long as she could read some of it every day. A chapter would be fine. Now it's like she couldn't go to bed without reading one verse in it.

She read half of Revelation and went to close the window, but before she did, she felt a small breeze. *Oh my.* She thought to herself. *That breeze feels good! It seems like it's picking up. I should close the window.* She locked the window, so the wind wouldn't open it up later that night.

Katherine then tucked herself in her bed. *No longer do I have to worry about my dad hitting me with his belt. No longer do I have to deal with the bruises on my back. Once they're gone, they're gone. No more beatings. No more struggling with putting on clothes. I'm safe. You know what? I'm going to go to church tomorrow. I'm going to get up extra early, so I can finish Revelation, and then I will attend church with everyone.*

Katherine woke up early that Sunday morning. She put on a yellow dress that went down to her ankles. After that, she brushed her teeth and finished off reading Revelation. The closer she got to the end, the more she felt warm inside. It was like something, or someone was calling her name. Telling her to come and enjoy the grace. To enjoy the love and peace.

She snapped out of it when John knocked on her door.

"Come in," she said.

"He"-he stopped before finishing his sentence.

"What's wrong?"

"Y-You look gorgeous," He blushed. "Um. Are you coming to church?"

"Yes, I am."

She smiled and put her heels on. When they got to the church, everyone greeted her. She never had so many people being nice to her at the same time. They all smiled and shook her hand. *It's a lot better when I'm not running in during the middle of church and having a ton of people staring at me like I'm weird.*

"It looks like it's going to rain any minute now!" one man said to Michael.

He looked about seventy years old. No hair was on his head, and he had a walking cane with him. It shook when his hand shook. It was like the cane was the only thing that was holding him up. He dressed up nicely, though. A white button-down shirt and blue jeans. The shirt was tucked in, and she could smell the cologne attached to him. It was a little strong, so she had to back away a little bit.

"Yes, sir," Michael replied. "I enjoy the sunshine every now and then, but sometimes I would like some rain."

"I agree. Crops aren't going to last much longer if it doesn't."

Everyone sat down and listened to the pastor. Today he was talking about being saved.

"Let me ask you something" the Pastor shouted. "Are you saved?"

"No," Katherine mumbled under her breath.

"Do you know what it's like to be saved?"

"No," Katherine mumbled again, as a tear ran down her cheek.

"Do you know Jesus Christ? I'm not talking about knowing who He is and what He's done. I'm talking about knowing Him in your heart, mind, and soul. Do you know Him?"

"No."

"Jesus Christ died on the cross for YOU! He died for your sins! That's what love is, people. Can you feel Christ in your soul? Can you hear Him talking to you?"

Another tear ran down her cheek. "Yes."

"Do you want to be saved?"

"Yes."

"For those of you, who want to be saved and want to know Jesus Christ better, please come forward. Let God into your soul. Let Him be your King. Let Jesus into your heart."

Katherine slowly stood up and walked toward the pastor. When she got to the front, she looked at the cross and knelt down. She closed her eyes and cried, allowing tears to pour out of her eyes. Then she felt a hand touch her shoulder.

"Young lady," a voice said. "Do you accept that Jesus Christ died on the cross for your sins?"

"Yes."

"Do you believe- no- do you KNOW that He is your Lord and Savior?"

"Yes."

"Then let Him in your heart, mind, and soul. Let Him into your life and follow His word and guidance. Let the one and only Lord set you free."

God. Father. I know that You sent Your one and only Son to die on the cross for my sins. I know that Jesus Christ is my Lord and Savior. My life is in Your hands, Lord God. I worship You and ONLY You. Please, forgive me for my sins.

Katherine felt a strong warm feeling inside of her, and when she did, she could see the cross with her eyes closed. She was out of the dark, raging storm and inside of the light. The feeling was unexplainable. Suddenly, there was loud thunder. Everyone in the church heard it. The pastor closed the sermon, and everyone walked out of the church.

When Katherine got up and walked out, she looked up at the dark clouds. Then she felt a raindrop hitting her nose. Then another, and another, and another. It poured. Katherine finally found her rain.

Tired

Katherine was saved recently. Spiritually, she never felt better. No longer felt afraid. Sure, her parents were away and could no longer hurt her, but after they left, Katherine still felt afraid. She didn't know why. She just knew that she was scared. Something inside of her still felt uneasy. Sad. Like there was something missing in her life. That all changed after being saved on a Sunday morning at church. Now she's not afraid. She's not afraid to die or anything. She's happy. Now, she's at peace. Now, she feels complete. That hole in her soul and heart has been filled, thanks to Christ.

It rained Sunday and Monday, just about non-stop. Every now and then the rain would calm down long enough for a cloud to spread open, allowing the sun to shine in town for a couple of minutes. Then it'll go back to being cloudy. Darkening the entire town. That was okay though. The plants and wild animals needed the rain.

It was Wednesday afternoon, and Katherine was at the flower shop once again, working after school. John's parents ordered her cap and gown for graduation. They didn't have to, but they insisted. It's only a matter of time until she will get her diploma and starting her life as an adult.

Katherine was doing her usual work at the flower shop. Snipping and watering the plants. She thought about buying flowers to bring to the house, just to brighten up the place some more. It's been about two hours since she worked for the day, and she was already feeling tired. She sat down for a bit to rest.

Why am I tired already? She asked herself. *I've only been here for two hours and have done little. Could it be my back? No, it can't be. It's been healing a good bit, and it doesn't really hurt that much anymore. Usually, I would be tired because of the pain. This is strange though. I'm not hurting at all. So why am I tired?*

"Katherine?" Holly asked as she walked where Katherine was at.

Katherine was sitting next to an aisle of roses. They smelt nice and never looked so beautiful.

"Yes, ma'am?" she replied.

"Is everything alright?"

"Yeah, I just feel tired for some reason. I'm not sleepy and the work isn't that tiring. I enjoy working here. It's fun and relaxing."

"Do you feel dizzy?"

"Dizzy? No."

"Have you eaten much today?"

"Now that I think of it, no. I ate a tiny bit at school, but that's about it. I wasn't that hungry."

"So, you didn't have breakfast?"

"No, ma'am. Again, I wasn't hungry. Even for me, that's a little odd. The eggs and bacon looked delicious, but for some reason, I couldn't get myself to eat it."

"Take a break and eat something. You can have some of my lunch. A girl needs her strength to work."

"Oh, no. I can't take your food."

"That's alright. I can buy myself some lunch. Now eat."

"Yes, ma'am."

Katherine went to the back room and had some of Holly's lunch. After that small lunch break, Katherine was back on her feet. She felt a little better. Holly let Katherine run the cash register for the rest of the day while she worked with the flowers.

The shop wasn't that busy, so Holly decided to close up early. They haven't had a customer in two hours. Later that night, Katherine did her usual reading. She was starting in the Old Testament now. Now that she has a busier life, she didn't have time to read half a book in one night. She made time though.

Something was weird about John tonight. He seemed out of place. Like he was annoyed or something. I wonder what it could be. Maybe it's the whole graduating thing. He hasn't found his gift yet. He'll find it. I just know it. He has to have faith and keep praying.

Speaking of gifts. I wonder what mine is. I never really thought about it. Hmm. I don't think I have one. I mean, I know that God has plans for me, but I don't think I have any gifts. Maybe I'm supposed to be there for John, or maybe I'm supposed to help him find his gift. Now, that's something to think about. I need to read. I'm almost done with Genesis.

Katherine finished her nightly reading and stood up to go to the bathroom. When she did, she felt tired and a little weak. She sat back down on her bed and took a couple of deep breaths.

What's going on? Why am I feeling tired again? I feel like I just did eight hours full of hard work. I ate supper and I don't feel that sleepy. Maybe I'm getting sick. Two students weren't at school today because of a cold. Could that be it? I don't know. Right now, though, I'm not going to let anything come between me and that bathroom.

Mary walked out of her and Michael's room and saw that Katherine looked exhausted.

"Oh, my!" Mary said. She sounded concerned and felt Katherine's forehead. "Are you alright? You look sick."

"I feel tired, but that's about it," Katherine replied.

"You don't have a fever. Maybe you just need sleep."

"Maybe. Goodnight."

"Goodnight, dear."

Mary went downstairs, and Katherine used the bathroom and went straight to bed. She slept well that night. However, the next morning, she felt awful.

John was happy that Katherine got saved Sunday morning. When they got home from church, he gave her a huge hug. Since that day, she has been smiling a lot more and being more open. She would be a part of the discussion about Christ and no longer sound so quiet and afraid. That was good though because he didn't want her to fear anything. He wanted her happy and smiling.

Now we can move further into our relationship. John thought. *Spiritually. We can grow together with God as a couple. I know we're not married, but I feel like I want to spend the rest of my life with her. Maybe I am falling in love with her. Is it too soon for that, though? I don't know. Maybe, maybe not.*

The next day, most of the seniors got measured for their cap and gown. He was excited, but at the same time, nervous. Graduation is next Friday, and he has yet to find his gift. What is he going to do after he graduates?

I guess I could go to college, but what would the point be, if I don't even know what to go there for? I need to figure this out. I have little time left. I don't want to go to college without knowing what I want to do with my life. What God wants me to do. I guess, until I find my gift, I could work full time at dad's shop. I'll be able to buy Katherine some nice stuff like flowers and necklaces.

Monday and Tuesday, John was too distracted at school by being worried about what he should do after graduation. He kept tapping his pencil against the desk. Katherine would sit beside him and stare at him with a worried look. At study hall, she would keep asking him if he was alright.

"I'm fine," He would always tell her.

"Are you sure? You look worried about something."

"Nah, I'm good."

She would hug him before she would go to work at the flower shop and kiss him on the cheek. He would kiss her cheek right back. Even though he was worried about finding what God would want him to do, Katherine would always put a smile on his face. She would smile back at him. He loved seeing her smile. It was the highlight of his day, knowing she was happy and enjoying life.

For supper Wednesday night, he cooked everyone spaghetti. At the dinner table, he would keep lightly tapping the table. He was still worried about his gift. About what he was supposed to do with his life. Deep down, he knew that he's supposed to do something amazing. Something creative and talented. But what?

John kept bouncing his leg under the table while they would eat. He did a great job with supper. After supper, they watched a movie as an entire family. For the past two days, it was just he and Katherine watching a movie each night. They would eat some snacks while watching the movie together. John figured that peanut butter and jelly sandwiches were her favorite snack since she had them on each night.

"It's the best sandwich ever!" she would always say.

John would chuckle and say, "If you say so."

His mother wanted to watch a Christian movie tonight. After the movie, they did a small Bible Study. Katherine participated and closed it out with a prayer. It surprised everyone, but at the same time, proud of her. She has come so far.

Everyone told each other goodnight and went into their own rooms. John didn't go straight to bed though. He stared out the window once again, looking at the night sky. There were a couple of small clouds floating around the moon. It's like God didn't want them to cover the moon up. He wanted the moonlight to shine into John's room. To shine at the town.

A new night, a new painting. I never get tired of staring at the sky. It doesn't matter if it's cloudy or if you could see the stars. It's beautiful to look at the Lord's work. It's also good to look at it while thinking. Put the mind at ease.

Katherine looked a little tired when she went to her room. At first, I thought she was going to fall down. Thankfully, she made it to her room. Maybe she's getting sick or something. Hopefully, she'll get better soon.

John took a deep breath and closed his eyes. He stood there, letting his mind race. From Katherine to his destiny. He kept asking himself what he should do with his life.

If I keep this up, I'm going to drive myself crazy. I need to calm down and let it come to me. Hmm. What about being an architect? That's creative. You get to design the buildings and such. It's worth a shot.

John walked over to his desk and took out a pencil and some paper. With each piece of paper, he would try to design his own building, or a backyard, or something. He even tried to design a playground for a park. Nothing worked. Either he couldn't picture the design right, or nothing came to mind at all.

No. This doesn't feel right. I don't feel like an architect. If I'm not supposed to be an architect, then what am I supposed to be?

John tapped his finger on the desk. He kept tapping it until it got on his own nerves. Then he would tap all his fingers on one hand on the desk. He sat there and tapped the desk for a good hour, trying to think of what he was supposed to be. What his destiny was.

Father, what am I supposed to do? What do You want me to do? I sit here and keep trying to think. I think, and think, and think, but nothing comes to mind. I can feel that You are leading me toward something, but I don't know what. I don't know how long it will be until I find out what it is. I need more patience. I know I must wait to find out, but I can't help myself. I feel like I'm losing control of myself and, soon, I'm going to panic. Again, I ask You. What am I supposed to do?

John got up and went downstairs to get a glass of water. While he was in the kitchen, he opened the window and listened to the crickets. He couldn't explain it, but the chirping sounded so peaceful. He looked at the time on the microwave. It was almost eleven-thirty.

Close to midnight. He heard a cat meowing in the distance. He knew it was outside but didn't know where it was. It was faint though. It meowed a second time. Now it was getting closer. *It must be hunting, or maybe it already has what it caught. It must be nice to be a cat. No worries whatsoever.*

Who am I kidding? I love being a servant of the Lord. I love worshipping Him. I wonder if animals do that. Do they worship God? Or do they just know that they are alive and have to eat other animals to survive? I wonder. Either way, I need to go to bed.

John finished his water and went back to his bedroom. He prayed and tucked himself in. At first, he couldn't go to sleep. He laid there, wondering about that cat. *What was the cat's destiny? Maybe just to survive and be loved by humans.* Finally, after a few minutes, John fell asleep.

Worried

I t was now Friday, one week away from graduation. John has been having trouble sleeping for the past few nights, due to being worried about what his gift could be. Last night was no different. He would wake up, lay there in bed for a couple of minutes, and then fall back to sleep. He continued to ask himself what his gift is, trying to think of ways to find out. He even made himself a list of possibilities on what he could do with his life. So far, nothing.

John woke up on the warm Friday morning by his alarm clock. It was sunny once again. When he got up, he walked to his window and moved the curtains. Not a cloud in the sky. It was back to pure sunshine with no chance of being cloudy. He opened the window and noticed that there wasn't even a breeze.

Not even a breeze? He asked himself. *It's going to be a hot day. Who knows when we will get more rain? Oh, man. My neck hurts. I must have slept on it wrong last night. It wouldn't be the first time though. It seems like, lately, that I've been having trouble with sleeping.*

John moved his neck around, trying to make it feel less stiff. He then did his normal morning ritual: brushing his teeth, combing his hair, etc. After he put his school clothes on, he realized that he was shaking. You couldn't really tell unless you saw his hands. He looked at them.

My whole body is shaking, but mainly my hands. Am I that paranoid about graduation? About this whole gift thing? I need to calm down before my parents and Katherine see me like this. They'll be worried. Just take a few deep breaths, John. Stay calm.

He grabbed his backpack and headed downstairs and into the kitchen. His mom made eggs, pancakes, bacon, ham, and some toast. It smelt delicious. He got himself some milk and made himself a plate. After filling his stomach, his dad came in sounding excited.

"Next week you'll be graduating!" Michael said with a smile.

"Yep," John replied, with a less exciting tone.

"You don't seem so happy about that. Everything alright?"

"It's just that, I haven't found what God wants me to do yet. I haven't found my gift or anything."

"He'll show you when it's the right time."

"I know, but what if I don't know what it is after I graduate? I don't want to go to college without knowing what I'm supposed to do in life."

"I don't know, son. I'm sure you'll figure it out. If that happens, then maybe you can work at the shop, full time."

"Maybe."

I could do that, I guess. Work at the hardware store until I know what I'm supposed to do. It'll help me to buy Katherine some stuff for the holidays and on dates. Speaking of which, where is Katherine?

Mary sat down with her breakfast and a cup of coffee. So did Michael. There were three people at the table. Not four.

"Where's Katherine?" John asked his parents. "She needs to eat before we go to school."

"Oh," Mary mumbled. "She's not feeling too well."

"What's wrong?" John asked, concerned.

"She's sick. She was vomiting earlier this morning and said she felt tired and weak. I told her to stay in bed and rest for the day. It might just be a bug that's going around."

"Oh, man. That stinks. I hope she'll feel better soon."

John finished his milk and hugged his parents.

"I'm going to tell Katherine goodbye and then go to school," John said.

"Oh, sweetie, she's sleeping. You don't want to wake her up. Let her rest."

"Oh, alright. When she wakes up, can you tell her I said to get better?"

Mary smiled and said, "Of course. Have a good day at school."

John walked out of the house and went to school. On the way there, he noticed that his hands were still shaking. *How did they not noticed that my hands were shaking? Were they even shaking when I was in the kitchen? I don't know. Right now, I just hope that Katherine will feel better soon. We have graduation next week, and I want us to walk together on the same day.*

The air was warm, and John thought it was a good idea to get exercise and walked to school. For the rest of the day, John kept thinking about

Katherine and his gift. Every now and then he would catch his hands shaking. No one seemed to ask if he was okay, or how he was doing. *Father, please help me.*

━━

Katherine woke up a few times, feeling uneasy. Once she looked at her phone and saw it was four in the morning. She didn't know what was wrong with her. She just knew that she didn't feel good. Now Friday, she was only one week away from graduation. She hoped that she would get better before getting her diploma next week.

An hour later, she felt like she was going to vomit. When she got out of bed, she felt tired and weak. She knew she was tired from lack of sleep, but this felt a different kind of tired. A weak tired. Like she was lifting weights all day without rest. She took a deep breathed and forced herself to walk to the bathroom.

After vomiting, there was a knock at the bathroom door. *Who would be up at this time?* She thought. *Are they sick too? We can be sick buddies and I won't have to go through this alone.*

"Who is it?" Katherine asked.

"It's Mary," Mary announced herself. "Are you alright? Can I come in?"

Before Katherine could answer, Mary let herself in. She looked tired herself, but not in the way Katherine was feeling. *She looks more like she just woke up and wanted to go back to sleep kind of tired. Better than what I'm feeling, I bet.*

"I don't feel so good," Katherine mumbled to her.

"I can see that. It might just be a bug or something. Stay home today and see what happens."

"Maybe I can get better sleep," Katherine said as she flushed the toilet.

Mary grabbed a small rag and soaked it with cold water. Then she rubbed it on Katherine's forehead. The rag felt nice and a little relaxing, but Katherine knew that she couldn't go back to sleep on the bathroom floor. She stood back up, just to fall back down again. Mary helped her up and walked her to the bedroom.

"That's one nasty bug you got there," Mary said.

"Definitely."

Katherine was able to get herself into bed and immediately fell back to sleep. She didn't wake up again until around lunch.

When Katherine woke up, she felt a little better. No longer did she feel sick. However, she still felt tired. She stretched and got up to pull open the curtains. The sun shining on her felt nice. *I should probably go in the backyard and enjoy the rays.*

I can't believe that I'm graduating next week! My parents may not be there, but at least Mary and Michael will. I like to think of them as my parents. Mary was acting like a mom earlier when she put that cold wet rag on my forehead. For the first time, it felt like I had a real mom. One who actually wanted to take care of me.

Katherine read some of her Bible and heard a knock at her bedroom door.

"I'm awake," She said loudly.

"Hey, there sleepyhead," Mary said as she walked in with a bowl of soup. "How are you feeling?"

"Better."

"Well, that's good. Here, I brought you some chicken noodle soup."

"Thank you."

"John said to get better."

That made Katherine smile. *Awe! He's worried about me. So sweet. It's Friday, so he's at school. I do wish that he could have stayed at home though. We would have spent the entire day together then. Oh, well. School is important.*

"I thought you and I could do something together," Mary said. "We can plant sunflowers in the yard if you're feeling better."

"That sounds like fun," Katherine replied. "It looks nice outside too."

"Good. Finish your soup and then come downstairs. We can have a girls' day."

"Sounds like a plan to me."

Katherine finished her soup and put on some clothes that she figured she could wear to get dirt on. After that, she headed downstairs and walked to the backyard with Mary. They planted the flowers on each side of the doorway. The sun felt warmer while working on the flowers. It felt nice, but at the same time, it made her want something to drink.

"How about we make ourselves some lemonade?" Mary asked.

"Sounds good, but I never made lemonade before."

"Oh, it's easy. I'll show you."

They went inside and made lemonade. Then they finished up with the sunflowers and put on some clean clothes. Mary insisted that they go get their nails done and then come back home and watch a movie. Katherine gladly agreed.

While they were at the beauty salon, Mary asked Katherine a serious and personal question. "You and John seem to be doing great. Do you see yourself with him in the future?"

That's a good question. I want to say yes, but I'm worried about what she would say. Does she even want me to be the girl that takes her son away? Oh, man. I'm getting nervous.

"I-I don't know," Katherine replied nervously. "I like him a lot and I want to be around him all the time. I miss him right now, as a matter of fact. I want to say yes, but I don't know how he feels."

"Do you feel strange and warm when you're near him? In a good way, I mean."

"Yes, ma'am."

"Do you feel safe around him and know that he will always be there for you?"

"Yes."

"There you go."

"R-Really?"

"Yep. At first, I didn't want you to be around my son. Now, though, I would be happy if you two end up getting married."

That made Katherine's day.

John had a decent day at school even though his hands shook non-stop. *Hopefully, Katherine is feeling better.* He said to himself. His future has been on his mind all day. When is he going to find out his gift? How will he find out? Will he be able to go to college shortly after graduating, or is he going to have to wait?

He will be a man soon and has no idea what he will do with his future. However, he does see Katherine in his future. No matter where he pictures himself, he sees her. Always side by side and holding each other's hand.

Lord. I want to thank You for bringing Katherine into my life. Even though I am worried about my future and when I will find out about my gift, thinking of her makes me smile. She added a new piece of a puzzle into my heart. One that I can't lose. I may not know what I'm supposed to be doing in the future, but I do know that I want her there by my side.

While on his way home, he kept holding his hands together. They were shaking all day. No matter how hard he tried, he couldn't stop thinking about what he should be doing for the rest of his life. He was starting to panic. Out of nowhere, he breathed heavily. Before he walked into his house, he took a few long deep breaths, trying to keep himself under control.

Calm down, John. Everything will be okay. God has this. Let Him take away all your anxiety.

John then walked inside and went straight upstairs and knocked on Katherine's door.

"Come in," She said.

"Hello, gorgeous," He said as he walked in. "How are you feeling?"

"Better. Your mom thinks it was just a small bug."

"She's usually right about those kinds of things. I see that you've got your nails painted."

"You noticed, did you?" she said happily.

"Yep. They look pretty."

"Thank you. Your mom and I had a girls' day. We planted sunflowers and went to get out nails done. Then we watched a movie."

"Sounds like you had a lot of fun."

"I did. Wish you could have joined us though."

"I think my nails look fantastic just the way they are."

Katherine giggled and gave him a tight hug. He hugged her back and kissed her head. *I know that it was for only a day, but I missed her so much.*

"I missed you," She said.

"I missed you too. So, have you thought about what you want to do after graduation?"

"I think I'm just going to stay here and work at the flower shop full time."

"Really? No big plans on going to college or searching for your destiny?"

"No. I think God wants me to stay here. What about you? Have you figured out your gift yet?"

"Not yet, unfortunately. I don't want to go to college empty-handed, so I'll stay here for a while."

I don't want to stay here though. I want to use my gift and go to college. Maybe find my own place. If Katherine is going to stay here though, then so will I. Maybe she'll come with me when I find out what I'm supposed to do with my life.

"Where will you be working at?" she asked.

"My dad's hardware store."

"Sounds good."

They talked until they went to bed. While he was with her, he noticed that he wasn't shaking at all. As soon as he closed her door and went to his room, his hands went back to what they were doing earlier. John was panicking.

Panic

It was now Thursday, one day from graduation. Katherine and the Williams slept in today. Katherine woke up around eleven o'clock. Lunchtime. When she woke up, her stomach was already growling. She got up and went to her window as usual. She pulled back the curtains to look outside. It was mostly sunny with a couple of small clouds in the sky, scattered around.

She opened her window and inhaled the fresh warm air. It was as if she felt brand new. A new nose, new legs, new eyes. She didn't feel weak or tired. Not right now, anyway. Staring out the window for a couple of more minutes, she suddenly remembered that she will be graduating tomorrow. A smile formed on her face with excitement.

I can't believe that tomorrow is the day! She told herself. *Tomorrow, I will no longer be a student at Bruce Alabama High School. I will be an adult. A woman. Then I will be working full time at the flower shop and saving up for my own place. Hopefully, John will stay in town for a while.*

She didn't hesitate. She walked out of her bedroom, still wearing her white flower pajamas. Katherine wasn't the only one who just woke up. Mary was in the bathroom, brushing her teeth, and Michael was walking down the stairs, probably to make coffee. Katherine walked over to John's bedroom door and knocked loudly.

"Wake up, sleepyhead!" she said. "Lunchtime!"

She walked downstairs to join Michael and made herself a cup of coffee. When Mary came down to the kitchen, she took out some lunch meat and cheese, along with ketchup and other sauces.

"Sandwiches for lunch," She mumbled, trying to get herself to wake up. "We can have lasagna tonight."

"Sounds good, dear," Michael responded.

Everyone made themselves a sandwich and took out a bag of chips from one of the cabinets. It was odd to have coffee with sandwiches, but they didn't care. All of it was good.

"So, Katherine," Michael said. "Are you ready for graduation tomorrow?"

"Yes, sir," She replied.

"Are you going to continue to work at the flower shop after tomorrow?"

"Yes, sir. I'm going to work over there full time and save up money for my own place. Hopefully, I won't be a burden for you guys for too much longer."

"Oh. You're not a burden! We enjoy having you here. We just want to make sure you know what you will be doing with your life."

"I would say go to college, but I don't think that's what I'm supposed to do with my life. I think, for now, I should just stay in town and wait for God to show me the way."

"Sounds like a plan."

It sounded like a plan to her. For now, she knows what she wants to do with her life. Work at the flower shop and have her own place. She never would have thought about staying in this town before. She figured that she would leave shortly after she graduated and never look back. Who knew that she would end up staying in this small town?

I wonder what's taking John so long. He should be out of bed by now and in here talking with us. Is he not excited about tomorrow? He must be upset that his gift hasn't shown up yet.

"John should be down here by now," Mary said.

"I'll go check on him," Katherine answered.

Katherine walked upstairs and knocked on his door again. *It's not like him to act like this. To not get out of bed and come downstairs to spend time with his family and his girlfriend.*

She knocked on his door again. "John, are you alright?"

She opened his door without waiting for an answer. She knew that it seemed rude, but she was worried that something was wrong with him. When she opened the door, she saw that his room was empty. John wasn't in his room. John wasn't anywhere at all.

Before going back downstairs, she wanted to make sure he wasn't just in a different room. She looked in all the rooms, the bathroom, his parent's room, the living room; she even looked in the backyard. Nothing. She finally went back to the kitchen to tell his parents she couldn't find their son.

"That's not like John at all!" Mary said, sounding worried. "W-Where could he have gone? He would have told us if he were to leave the house. Oh, no. What if he's hurt and can't get help!?"

"Mary," Michael said to her. "Calm down, sweetie. He's a grown man. He can handle himself now. I'm sure he walked out to clear his head. He doesn't know what God wants him to do yet, and it's really getting to him. I'm sure he went out for a walk or something. He'll call us from his cell phone if something happens."

"Um," Katherine mumbled. "He left his phone on his nightstand that's beside his bed."

"What?" Michael asked, now worried. "He left his cell phone? That's definitely not like him."

"What are we going to do?" Mary asked.

"Going to look for him. We can go to the pond and then the restaurant. Let's go."

They first headed to the pond. Katherine looked around to see if he left anything behind. Nothing. She looked out and watched the water form bubbles from the fish. *Come on, John. Where are you? What's going on?*

They then went to the restaurant to see if John would have gone there to eat lunch. Michael even went into the men's room to see if his son was there. He wasn't.

Why would he leave the house like this? He would have at least told me or one of his parents. Does he not think we wouldn't have noticed? He could be hurt, and we don't know where he could be.

They then went to the flower shop. They were sure he didn't go there but just wanted to see in case he did. He wasn't there either.

"Where could he have gone, Michael!?" Mary shrieked.

"I don't know." He said back to her.

"He's not a man yet. He has today and most of tomorrow before he can pull this kind of stuff. Even then, I want him to tell me if he's safe."

"Wait!" Katherine blurted. "Of course. Why didn't we think of this first?"

"What?" they asked.

"I have a hunch where he could be at."

⸺

It's been a stressful week for John. Actually, he's been stressed out for a while. He's just now feeling the effects of it. It was Thursday morning and John woke up early. He looked at his phone and saw it was eight in the morning. This wasn't the first time he woke up randomly. He's been waking up a few times every night for the past two weeks.

Since last week, his hands have been shaking just about nonstop. No one seemed to notice it or even asked if he was alright. He couldn't get mad though. He usually is fine and calm. So, people would never notice his hands shaking. Hiding his hands under the table and in his pockets would also be why no one asked if he was alright.

John got up and went to the window. Every day he would look out the window to see what kind of day it was. Today could be pure sunshine, or mostly cloudy, or even thunder and lighting. When he opened the curtains, the sun was beaming down on him. It was a little warm, but that was alright.

He looked at his hands and they were still shaking. Not that much at the moment. Tomorrow will be graduation, and he still doesn't know what his gift is. How much longer would he have to wait? Another day, another week or month? He never planned to stay in this town for the rest of his life. He knows that he's supposed to do something great, but he doesn't know what that could be.

He examined the sky. There were a couple of small clouds moving along the sky. Not enough to cover the sun, though. It seems like the clouds didn't want to cover the sun. It was like they were trying to avoid it.

I don't know why, but I have a craving to go for a walk. He thought. *Maybe even a jog. Yeah, I like that idea. I can jog this stress away. That might help.*

John put on some shorts and a sleeveless shirt. Then he put on a pair of his shoes and walked outside. No one else was up, so he thought he could make it back before they would notice that he was gone.

He jogged all the way to the pond. The sun continued to beam down on him as he jogged his way there. When he got to the pond, the trees were giving him shade. He sat down in the grass and rested. While he relaxed, he listened to the wildlife that was surrounding him.

Birds were chirping in the trees that were a few yards away from him. He always loved the sound of birds chirping. It was a relaxing sound and soothed him. A breeze snuck up on him and gave him a chill down his spine. It felt good, but he wasn't expecting it to be windy.

He continued to sit there for another hour. He crawled over to the pond and splashed some water in his face. After that, he stared at his reflection in the water. He breathed heavily and smashed his fist into the water.

Why am I so impatient about this whole gift thing? What is wrong with me? I keep worrying about this whole future thing and I can't seem to keep myself calm. I feel like I'm going to lose it. I keep waking up at night. I keep tossing and turning. I just want to pull my hair out and scream. This is so unlike me. I know that God has plans for me, great plans. I can feel it. But why am I so impatient about it? Why do I keep trying to rush it?

John began to have trouble with his breathing. *What's going on? Why am I having trouble breathing? It's like I'm running out of oxygen or something. A-Am I having a panic attack? I-I need to get out of here. Father, I need You. What do I do?*

John didn't know what to do, so he just ran. He ran away from the pond. He didn't go back home though. He didn't even think about home. He forgot all about going back home. He even forgot that he had a home. All he knew right now, was that he had to get away and get to a safe place. A place where he can breathe. A place where he can calm down and be safe. He knew exactly where to go to.

The church. I need to get to the church. I'll be better there. I'll be able to breathe. Lord, please help me to get to the church. Let me make it. I can't do this without You.

John made it into town and could see the church. He was almost there. He wanted to stop and take a break, but he knew that if he did, he would collapse. Who knows what would happen to him then? He could pass out and hurt himself.

As he got closer to the church, he had more difficulty breathing. He knew that if he didn't get inside that church, he wouldn't be able to breathe anymore. He builds up the strength and ran faster. He was in the open, but it felt as if something was closing him in. He was feeling claustrophobic.

Almost there! Just a few more yards. I can see the entrance now. Come on, John. I know you can make it. You have to make it. Don't give up now. Don't quit! Fight through this.

John finally made it inside the church. When he ran in, he stopped in the front where the cross was at and fell onto his knees. He looked up at it and took long, deep breaths. He was breathing easily again. No longer did he feel claustrophobic. The air felt cool, and he wiped the sweat off his forehead.

"Thank you," He said as he looked up. "I can always count on You."

He stood up and walked over to one of the benches. He sat down and thought about everything. About his panic attack and his gift. He sat there, staring at the cross until he heard the front doors open. He looked behind him and saw that it was Katherine.

"How did you know I was here?" he asked her as he watched her walk down the aisle.

"I just had a feeling," She said. She sat down next to him and gave him a hug. "We've been looking all over for you."

"We?"

"Your parents and I. We didn't know where you were. You left your cell phone and didn't tell anyone where you were going. We looked at the pond, the restaurant, and even the flower shop."

"I'm sorry that I caused such a panic."

"It's okay, as long as you're safe. How long have you been out?"

"Since around eight or nine, I think."

"You've been here this whole time?"

"No. I was at the pond first. Then I felt weird and ran here. I was scared. I think I had a panic attack, Katherine."

"Oh, my!"

She wrapped her arms around him and squeezed tight. He wrapped his arm around her and leaned his head on top of hers.

"Why did you have a panic attack?"

"Because I've been so stressed out about finding my gift and what I would do if I can't find it in time."

"God will lead you the way. He'll let you know when the time is right. You just have to have faith, John. He knows what He's doing."

"Yeah, I know."

"Do you feel better?"

"Yeah. A lot better."

"Good. Now let's go, so your parents can chew you out. Then we can get ready for graduation tomorrow."

They both chuckled and walked out of the church.

Graduation

J ohn woke up the next day. It was Friday morning. Later, today he will
be graduating, and he couldn't be any more excited. He had a good
night's sleep and felt rested. It has been a while since he had a good
night's rest.

He stretched and got out of bed. Rubbing his eyes, he walked over to
his window and opened the curtains. It was cloudy outside and was raining.
It wasn't raining hard though, just sprinkling. Still, he was hoping for the
sun to be shining. *Maybe the sun will be out later today.* He thought.

For some people, the rain was calming and relaxing. Some people
even enjoy a good rain. John knew that the town needed rain, but he
always preferred sunshine. Rain is good, it helps the crops grow, but it's
still gloomy weather. At least, for him anyway. He always thought the rain
had a depressing feel to it. He didn't know why he always felt sad when it
poured. However, he would not let this rain stop him from feeling excited.
Today is graduation day. Nothing would make him feel blue.

John sat at his desk and took out his journal. Ever since Katherine has
come into his life, he's been writing more than usual. That was okay with
him though. Writing makes him calm, and he enjoys it.

*For the past couple of weeks, I've been feeling different. My hands were
shaking and sometimes my entire body. I thought I would explode at any minute.
I did yesterday. I went out on a jog and ended up breathing heavy. I didn't know
what was going on, but I knew that I had to run before I got worse. The church
was the first place I thought of. It was the only place I knew that could help me
feel better. My chest was tightening as if it was closing inside. As I ran closer to
the church, it was getting more difficult for me to breathe. I made it though.*

*Once I was inside, I felt better. My chest was more relaxed, and I could
breathe again. When I was in front of the cross, I could feel the freedom. I could
feel the chains of my anxiety and stress break away from me. I was free. If it*

122

wasn't for Christ, I don't know what would have happened. I could have passed out and no one would have found me. Or I could have ended up in the hospital. I scared my family and Katherine. I was even scared. I had my first panic attack. Thankfully, the Lord was watching over me.

Anyway, I came to realize that I'm in love with Katherine. Today I will talk to my dad about that and on how and when I should tell Katherine. My only worry is, what if she's not in love with me?

After John finished writing, he prayed and went downstairs for breakfast. His mom did a wonderful job as usual. This time there were grits, biscuits with gravy, pancakes, scrambled eggs, bacon, toast, and even a steak for breakfast. Everything smelt delicious, and everyone enjoyed their food.

"Graduation Day!" Mary said happily. "Are you excited?"

She took a picture of John and Katherine eating. Mary told them she would take pictures all day as memories for this special day. His parents didn't want to forget it.

"Yes, mom," John chuckled. "Very excited. Your baby boy is a man now. What do you think of that?"

Mary put her phone down and said, "You're not a man until you hold that diploma! Even after today, I'll wipe that gravy off your face any time if I want to"

Everyone laughed and continued eating. Later on that day, Michael was in John's room, talking. It was a couple of hours away from the ceremony, and the sun decided to come out from hiding.

"Well, today is the day," Michael said. "It seems like only yesterday I was cleaning you up from playing in the mud. I remember you smearing that mud all over your mother's face. I laughed so hard!"

John smiled and sat down next to his dad on the bed.

"It'll be okay, dad," John replied.

"You're gonna become a man soon. I did all that I could to raise you right. Now, the choices you make are your own. Good or bad. Wrong or right. The jobs you'll get or the college you go to. It's all on you. I'm proud of you, son."

"Thanks, dad. That doesn't mean that you will get away with giving me advice. I need to talk to you about something."

"What's that?"

"I think I'm in love with Katherine."

"You think?"

"I know I am. Am I too young to be in love?"

"I don't think so. I can tell by the way you look at her that you truly love her. It's the same way I look at your mother."

"Really?"

"Oh, yea. I still look at her like that. She makes me happy. She makes me smile, laugh, and I don't know what I would do without her. Yes, she gets on my nerves sometimes, but that's fine with me. I get on her nerves too. Even if she's mad at me, I'm just glad she's with me. Because something could happen, and I might not see her tomorrow. So, whether or not she's mad at me, I'm still thankful and happy that she's with me."

"It's the same with you, son. I try to spend as much time as I can with you because I know that once you're in college, I won't be seeing you as much. You're going to start your own family and be with them. I thank the Lord that I'm able to have the time with you and your mom. You two are blessings to me."

"Wow, dad. I don't know what to say."

"You don't have to say anything. So, when are you going to tell Katherine that she's the woman of your dreams?"

"I'm not sure. What if she doesn't love me how I love her?"

"She will."

"How do you know?"

"I just do. You just make sure you tell her. Because if you don't, then you might lose her forever."

"I don't want that."

"Then I suggest that you tell her. She was brought into your life for a reason. Maybe it's because you two belong together, or maybe it's something else. Either way, tell her how you feel."

"Thanks, dad."

"Don't mention it."

"Now I have to think on when to tell her."

Katherine woke up on Friday morning. She had the best sleep in her life. She got out of bed and went straight to the window. It was sprinkling. That didn't bother her though. She enjoys the rain, and not only because she can splash in the puddles. For her, rain is peaceful. It's relaxing. She could sit outside all day and just watch it rain.

Even though she enjoys it, she hopes that the sun would shine later. She doesn't want to be soaked when she gets her diploma. They are having their graduation outside. The principal thought it was a clever idea. *Rain some other day.* She thought to herself. *I got a graduation to go to later today.*

Graduation. She still couldn't believe that today is the big day. Today, she will become a woman. After today, she'll be working full time at the flower shop and saving up money for her own place. Scary, but still very exciting. As long as she has God with her, she's not afraid of anything.

Katherine let out a huge yawn and leaned against the window, still watching it rain. Mary and Michael will be in the crowd, watching her walk. Not her parents. Even though they were mean to her, she still wanted them to watch her graduate today. They're her parents for crying out loud. They should be there on her big day.

Maybe I could visit them one day and show them my diploma. Maybe they'll be proud of me. Of course, they could also tell me to leave them alone and never come back. It's worth a try though. I have to try. I wonder how they're doing, anyway. Dad's in jail and mom is in some kind of rehab place. I hope that they're doing okay.

Katherine went downstairs and had a big breakfast with the Williams. Mary was taking pictures of her and John. She wanted them as memories for her photo album.

"I know that you're not our relative, Katherine," Mary said as she kept taking pictures. "But you're a part of this family. That means you will be in our album as well as John."

"I'm glad I could be a part of this family," Katherine told everyone. "All of you have treated me with such love and kindness. If it wasn't for all of you, I would probably be sleeping in a ditch or under a bridge. Thank you for everything."

"You are most welcome, dear," Mary answered.

"You can stay here until you save enough money for a house or an apartment," Michael told her. "We won't charge you for your room or anything."

Katherine smiled and said, "Thank you."

More importantly, I want to thank You, God. If You hadn't been watching over me, who knows where I would be at right now. You were there for me, even when I didn't know who You were. I know that You will continue to watch over me and everyone else. Whatever happens to me, I know that everything will be okay.

"Are you wanting Holly to come to the cookout after graduation, Katherine?" Mary asked her.

"Yes, please."

Unfortunately, that's her only friend she had, who wasn't a part of the family. She wished that she had more friends, but that's alright. She'll make more friends down the road in her life. As long as John is by her side, she doesn't care if she makes any more friends.

She didn't want John to leave her. If he ever moves out of town, then she would have to go with him. That is if he lets her. He makes her so happy. He's always there for her and making her laugh. She cares about him so much. Maybe even more than usual.

Yes, she likes him as a boyfriend, but deep inside she feels something stronger. Could it be love? She didn't know. She would have to talk to Mary about that.

Later that day, her and Mary were in her bedroom. Mary was helping her decide on what to wear for the big day. Sure, she would wear a cap and a gown, but after the pictures, she will be wearing normal clothes.

Katherine opened the window, letting the sunshine into her room. It stopped raining, and the sun came out an hour ago. She could feel the sun beaming down on her. It felt nice. Relaxing.

"Can I talk to you about something?" Katherine asked Mary.

"Of course," Mary responded. "Anything."

"Um. I had a dream last night, about John."

"Oh? What about him?"

"We were in church, holding hands."

"Really now?" Mary sounding excited. "Were you wearing a white dress?"

"I'm not sure. I don't remember what I was wearing. Anyway, after we left the church, we would be at a house or a grocery store together. We would still be holding hands."

"Well, that sounds sweet."

"I was wondering if you knew what that could mean."

"My best guess is that you're in love."

"In love?"

"Yep. It's okay, I won't get mad at you for being in love with my son. To be honest, I don't think any other girl would be better for him."

"I enjoy being around him, and I never want to leave him. I don't want him to leave me either. When I'm around him, my heart feels so warm and weird. It's like, if he's out of my life, I'll hurt inside. I want him to be with me for the rest of my life. He makes me so happy and I care about him so much."

"So, you can see a future with him?"

Katherine thought about it for a while. "Yes. I do, actually. I can't picture myself without him in my life. I think I am in love with him."

"You think, or you know?"

"I know I am. It's an unconditional kind of love."

"Tell him. He needs to know how you feel."

"What if he doesn't feel the same way about me?"

"You have to try. He can't read your mind."

"Okay."

"Now, he will get on your nerves sometimes. That's okay though because he'll be worth it."

"Does your husband get on your nerves sometimes?"

"Oh yeah! A lot. However, I'm still in love with him. I never want to leave him or him to leave me. Never, have I ever thought about leaving him. I can't picture the rest of my life without that man. Just thinking about it makes me want to cry."

"Oh, please don't cry."

"Tell John that you are in love with him. If you don't, you will regret it for the rest of your life."

Katherine had a small headache for a few minutes, trying to think of what she should do. *When she should tell him she's in love with him?* She had to rest for a little while before leaving the house. Once again, she was feeling tired and weak.

Now is not the time to feel this way. I need to get my energy back. I have a graduation to attend.

It got warmer when they reached the graduation spot. No clouds were in the sky for miles, from what John could tell. The sun was beaming down on him, making him sweat a little. That's the south for you. It'll be spring, but it will feel like one hundred degrees outside as if it was already mid-summer. Everyone was carrying a bottle of water. Some people had two, just in case they drank their first one before the ceremony started.

The rain from earlier made the ground soft. Not enough for it to make the dirt turn into mud though. Some people wore boots, just in case there was mud.

He looked toward Katherine and noticed that she was looking a little tired. *I thought she got over the flu.* He thought. *She's been looking worse for the past week. I hope she's alright. I'll go ask her if she's feeling okay.*

John walked over to Katherine and took her hand. When he looked into her eyes, he could tell that something was wrong. She was breathing heavily and looked a little pale.

"Katherine," he mumbled. "Are you alright? You look terrible."

"Well, thanks," She mumbled with a grin.

"You're beautiful obviously. I was talking about health-wise. You look sick. Are you feeling alright? Do you need to go home?"

"No. I'm fine. I just feel tired is all."

"Did you get enough sleep last night?"

"Yeah. I don't know why I feel like this. I feel weak too. I think I will take a short nap after the cookout."

"Maybe you should go to the doctor and get a shot. That will help you get better pretty quick."

"Maybe. I'll take a nap first."

Man, she looks bad. I hope that all she needs is a nap. She looks like she'll collapse any minute.

"Are you sure you're alright?"

"Yes. Go socialize. I'll be fine."

John gave her a kiss on the cheek and walked toward the crowd of students. He talked to some of his friends. Well, he wouldn't call them friends. He never hung out with them after school or talked to them when school was out.

One guy that he talked to, Mark Hathaway, talked to him about going to college to be a graphic designer.

"I'll make myself some good money," Mark said. "I'll be making album covers, billboard signs, book covers, and many things."

"That's cool," John replied.

It must be nice to know what you want to do for a living. I sure don't. You have your gift already. Drawing and painting. You can already picture yourself making good money from making designs for other people. I must sound mean. I know that God will show me my gift one day. I'm not going to rush it. I will be patient and wait.

Next was Michael. John never knew what his last name was. For a small school, you think he would know it. Michael wanted to be a police officer in one of the big cities like Chicago or New York City. He figured that he could make a difference.

"I want to help people," Michael said. "I could help put more criminals behind bars and hopefully they will learn to not do any more crimes. Maybe I could even convince them to turn their lives around."

"That sounds exciting," John told him. "Just try not to get shot. I would like to see you at our ten-year reunion."

Now John was talking to the teachers. They were going around asking the students what they would do for the rest of their lives. Some told them college for a career; others told them they would join the army and one or two said they just wanted an ordinary job and have a family.

Everyone knows what they want in life. I'm not sure what I even want. I do know that whatever God has in store for me, it will be amazing. I also know that wherever I go, I want Katherine to be there by my side. Katherine is the most incredible woman ever. The way I feel about her there is too much to explain. I'm in love with her.

"So, John," His English teacher said. "What will you be doing?"

"I'm not sure. I'm still waiting for God to give me a sign and to show me the way."

His English teacher looked away when John mentioned God. Most of his teachers didn't believe in God and thought Christianity was a big joke. That never bothered John, though. He tried to get them to believe or at least get them to try to understand about Jesus, but they kept denying it. John tried, that's all he could do.

"Well, you are a dazzling young man. Maybe you should think about psychology or something around that field. You like to help others."

"I'm not sure. Doesn't feel like that would be something I should do."

John talked to a couple of other teachers and walked back to his parents and Katherine. Mary and Michael talked to the principal while Katherine talked to Holly about working full time. *I guess I could do what Katherine is doing. I could work full time at dad's shop and save up for a house or an apartment. At least until I know what to do with my life.*

Michael came over and tugged his son away from his mother and Katherine.

"What's going on dad?" John asked, confused.

"Have you decided what you were going to do about Katherine?"

"You mean about telling her I'm in love with her?"

"Yep."

"Well, I was thinking about telling her after we toss our hats in the air."

"Hmm. That could work. Are you prepared?"

"Not really, but I don't think I will ever be."

"You should tell her when you think it's the right time. Tell her when your heart knows when it's the right moment."

"Yeah. You're right."

"I know I am."

What does my heart say? It says I should tell her after we toss our hats in the air. I can't believe that I'm going to tell her I'm in love with her. What if she doesn't say it back?

Katherine was sitting down while John went to talk to some students and teachers. He checked up on her to see if she was feeling alright. She told him she was fine and just a little tired. She didn't know why she was feeling this way. She felt worse than what she felt earlier that day at the house. Now she feels like she is going to pass out any minute.

She tried to stand up but got dizzy instantly. The weather wasn't helping. The heat made her feel worse somehow. Luckily there was a tree, and she sat under it. Her breathing got heavier when she got there. It was as if someone was squeezing her lungs. She wanted to fall asleep. *Why do I feel so tired?* She asked herself. *I could barely make myself stand up. When I walk, I feel like I'm going to collapse at any minute. Maybe John is right. Maybe I should go to the doctor and get a shot. I might feel better afterward.* After sitting under the shade of the tree she felt a little better; still, everything was spinning some.

Looking around, she could tell that everyone was cheerful. All the parents were proud of their child or children. Mary and Michael weren't her real parents, but they told Katherine that they were proud of her. That made her day. She wished that her real folks would tell her that.

Katherine took a long deep breath and almost fell asleep until Holly came over.

"Hey there," Holly said in a soft voice. "Is everything alright?"

"Yeah," Katherine mumbled. "I just feel tired."

"Maybe you should go see a doctor."

"I might just do that."

"Well, I wanted to thank you for inviting me to come to see you graduate and to the cookout afterward."

"You're welcome." Katherine made a small smile and kept talking. "You're not just my boss, you're also my friend. We are friends, aren't we?"

"Of course, we are."

"I can't wait to be at the flower shop a lot more. I like working there."

"And I like having you there."

"Really?"

"Yep. It's like we're partners. So, are you ready to get your diploma?"

"Yes, ma'am. I've worked really hard for it."

"I bet you have. Well, I'm going to go and talk to some people before the ceremony begins. See you later."

"Bye."

Katherine was glad that Holly left. After watching Holly walk away, she ran behind the tree and vomited. She thought she got over the flu, or whatever it was. After she wiped her mouth, she looked to see if anyone noticed her. Thankfully, no one did. That would have been embarrassing. She felt a little better though.

Not wanting to alarm anyone, she went back to John's parents and waited with them. After a while, John came back and asked her if she was okay.

"I feel a bit better," She told him.

"That's good," He said.

A few minutes later, everyone took their seats, while the students were at the stage, waiting in line. The principal talked about the students and the school. He also talked about how proud he was of the students. In the end, the parents clapped and then the students were called out, one at a time.

After each student received their diploma, everyone would clap their hands. The students were being called by their last names. So, John would be one of the last ones to walk. Eventually, the principal got to the L's.

When he called Lee, Katherine walked up and shook the principal's hand. She looked out and saw John's parents clapping for her. *Even though my parents were mean to me, I still wish they were here to see me graduate. I wonder if they would have even clapped. I want to say no, but you never know. I might go and visit them. Tell them that their daughter graduated. They might not applause for what I've accomplished, but at least someone is. Mary and Michael treated me as if I was their own child. They're proud of me.*

131

Katherine took her diploma and walked off the stage. Then she watched as the rest of the students walked. After John walked off the stage, he and Katherine hugged and waited for the principal to close the ceremony out.

Then, they waited while the photographer was getting ready to take the graduate's picture. *I can't believe it! I graduated! I'm a woman now. Starting on Monday, I'll have a full-time job. I'm actually looking forward to it. Instead of working for a couple of hours, I would be working a full eight hours.*

Once the photographer got everything ready, all the students got in position to have their picture taken. There were three and a half rows of students. Each row had about ten students each. The very back row had four or five people.

Katherine was feeling worse. Not only was she feeling more tired and weak, but a headache was coming along. The sun beaming down on her wasn't helping her feel any better. *I wish we were in some shade. I feel like I'm going to pass out. Right now, I just want to lie in bed where the air is a lot cooler.*

The students had their picture taken and then toss their hats in the air as high as they could. John then turned Katherine around and faced her. He wrapped his arms around her with a smile.

"I'm in love with you," He told her.

"W-What?" she asked.

"I'm in love with you," He said again.

"Y-You're in love with me?"

Katherine's head pounded, and everything was spinning around. Her body dropped, but John caught her and held her up.

"Are you okay?" he asked, sounding worried.

She didn't respond. She couldn't respond. Katherine made herself stand up. She looked up at John and stared into his eyes. Now she was dizzy, and her vision was getting blurry. Everything around her was getting dark.

A tear ran down her cheek and Katherine collapse to the ground. Even though she was staring up at the sky, she knew that people were surrounding her.

"Katherine?" John panicked. "Katherine!?"

She still couldn't speak. A tear rolled down her cheek. She wasn't terrified, but she was wondering what was going on. Now her vision became completely dark. She wasn't sure if she had her eyes closed or not. The last thing she heard was John screaming.

"Call an ambulance!"

Hospital

John didn't know how to react. He was afraid, sad, and angry. He was angry because there wasn't anything he could do to help Katherine. She laid there on the ground, not talking. Her eyes were closed, but she was still breathing. All the graduates and the adults surrounded her. John yelled for someone to call an ambulance.

"Katherine," John said to her. "Can you hear me?"

She didn't respond. He listened as he heard someone talking to the operator on the phone. They told the person what they knew and saw.

"An ambulance is on its way." A random person said.

Come on, Katherine. He said to himself. *Fight, whatever is wrong with you. You can't leave me yet. I love you. I'm in love with you, Katherine.*

John put his left hand under her head, holding it up. He then wrapped his right arm around her. He held her tight, not letting anyone else touch her. He kept telling them to 'give her some breathing room'.

It felt like hours until the ambulance came. The sun continued to beam down on him and Katherine. It felt like it was getting hotter, and John began to cry. His first love was lying unconscious in his arms, and there was nothing he could do to help her. He stared at her and allowed his tears to fall on her face. He didn't wipe them off.

Father, please help her. Please don't let her go just yet. I want to be with her, just a little while longer. Please save her, Lord. She needs You now, more than ever.

"Where's the ambulance?" John cried out.

"They're on their way," Michael told him. "She's going to be alright. God is watching over her."

John could tell that his dad was choking up. He knew, without looking, that his dad was also crying. John looked up and saw that his mother was shedding tears as well. They cared about Katherine as if she was their own daughter. No one else was crying though. No one else didn't really know Katherine. They never talked to her or even tried to be her friend. The only person that knew her, besides John's parents, was Holly. Holly was covering her mouth with her hands. She was speechless and scared.

Everyone behind him mumbled to each other. He couldn't understand what they were saying. He didn't care though. All he cared about was Katherine. He just wanted her to get taken care of. He just wanted her to get better. He just wanted her to wake up and look at him in the eyes and smile.

He knew that something was wrong with her. He could tell by the way she looked. She looked sick and tired. She had told him how she felt weak, and once she told him she got bad headaches every now and then. She mainly got them when she was living with her parents. They've died down some ever since she lived with the Williams.

I should have taken her to a doctor. I should have made her go to see what was wrong. Why didn't I? Where is that ambulance? Where is the medic? Why aren't they here yet to take her to the hospital?

What felt like hours was only about two or three minutes. John finally heard sirens. *Thank You, Father.* He kept crying as the ambulance parked on the side of the road. A couple of medics came out and tried to talk to Katherine, but she wouldn't respond. They then put her on a stretcher and put her in the ambulance.

John didn't hesitate. He got in with her. He would not leave her, not for one second. John held her hand and gave it a light squeeze. Even though she was unconscious, he hoped that she knew that he was with her. Everything seemed to slow down. The medics were moving slower, and the drive to the hospital seems to take forever.

John kissed Katherine's forehead and wiped his tears away from both of their faces. She still wouldn't wake up. Thankfully, she was still breathing, though. *At least move, so I know that you're alright. Your head. A toe. Something.* Nothing happened. Katherine didn't move any body part. John was still thankful that she was still breathing.

"What's wrong with her?" he asked a medic.

"I'm not sure," They said.

He still wouldn't take his eyes off of Katherine. If she were to move, he wanted to be there. If she opened her eyes, he wanted to be the first person she would see. *Please don't go. I need you to stay with me. I don't know what I would do if I lost you. You mean so much to me.*

John prayed as the ambulance pulled up to the ER section of the hospital. The medics took Katherine out and rolled her into the building. John jumped out and walked fast behind them. One or two nurses surrounded Katherine, blocking John's view of her.

"You can help her, right?" he asked them. "Will she be okay?"

"We're going to do everything we can." One nurse said.

They rolled Katherine into a room and shut the door behind them. John stopped in front of the door and stared at it.

"Sir," a nurse said to him. "I need you to go into the lobby and wait, okay?"

"I'm not leaving her," He said as a tear rolled down his cheek.

"She'll be right in that room. We will come and get you once we know something."

John still didn't move. The nurse grabbed his arm and slowly walked him into the lobby. He sat down in one of the chairs and looked at the floor. He didn't know what else to ask them. He felt helpless.

"Everything will be okay," the nurse told him.

He forgot that she was still there. He looked up at her with red tearful eyes.

"I love her," he told the nurse. "I want to help."

"Pray for her. That's all I can say."

"Can you stay here until my parents get here?"

"Of course." The nurse sat down next to John. "Do you believe in God?"

"Yes." He mumbled. "Of course, I do."

"He's wonderful, isn't He?"

"Yes."

"I like to think He sends guardian angels to watch over people. Everyone. Not just to the ones that are hurt, but to the ones that care about the ones who are hurt. God loves His children."

"Yeah, I know." John sobbed. "He sent His son to die on the cross for us."

"Yes, He did. So, believe that God has this. He'll take care of her. He can do, what no one on this planet can."

"Yeah, you're right."

John took a deep breath and bowed his head.

Lord God, I pray that Katherine will be alright. I know that You will help her. I know that she's in Your hands. I don't know what is wrong with her, but I know that You do. Whatever it is, help her. At least take some of the pain away.

I believe in You. I know that whatever happens, there is a reason. I know that
if You take her, it'll be okay; because she will be with You.

When John looked up, the nurse was gone. He didn't hear her walk
away. It was as if she just vanished into thin air. The only people he saw
were the woman at the desk and a few people sitting down, waiting to
hear the news about their loved ones. He didn't know how long he'd been
in the ambulance or in the lobby, but eventually, his parents came in and
sat beside him.

"How is she?" Mary asked him.

"I don't know. They took her and shut the door. They won't let me in."

"She'll be okay, son," Michael said.

"I was just talking to a nurse about God. She pretty much said I should
let Him handle it. I'm not sure where she went through."

"Katherine just collapsed," Mary said. "Did she eat today? I'm pretty
sure that she did."

"Not now, Mary," Michael replied to her. "You're going to scare our
son more."

Mary kept talking like she didn't hear him. "Maybe she fainted from
the heat. She didn't wake up though. Someone should have splashed water
on her."

"I'm going to splash some water on you. Your son is upset about all of
this."

"Oh, I'm sorry, honey!"

Mary gave John a tight hug and held him. They heard Michael's
stomach growl and made a small grin.

"Um … I'm going to the vending machine. John, how about you come
with me?"

"O-Okay," John answered.

They both got up and walked over to the snack machine. When they
got there, Michael counted his change and tried to decide what he wanted
to eat. Everything was quiet. Too quiet. No one else was being rushed in
for help. No one in the lobby was talking. There was just dead silence.

Michael sighed and faced John.

"You know," Michael began. "I forgot that the closest hospital was
about ten minutes away."

"What?" John said. It puzzled him.

"When I was driving, it felt like I got here in under a minute. I think
I was speeding."

"That would be a first."

"I kept asking myself if she was alright. I prayed to God, and I kept trying to calm myself down. She's like a daughter to me. Such a nice kid. First, her parents abused her and now this."

"Yeah, now this." John cried again. "I feel so helpless, dad. When I looked at her, she seemed so lifeless. Sure, she was breathing, but still. I love her so much."

"I know, son."

Michael pulled his son into his arms and held him. John could feel a tear from Michael, running down the back of his head. *Dad's scared, too. It's rare to see him cry. I think the only time I saw him cry was when his mother passed away a couple of years ago. I remember him telling me it's okay for a man to cry. Some might say that it's not okay, but that's only because they are trying to act tough. Deep down, they want to cry. They're just afraid of people looking at them.*

"You should drink something," Michael mumbled. "It's hot outside and I'm sure you're thirsty."

Michael handed his son some change for the soda machine. John walked to it and grabbed himself a Dr. Pepper. He didn't want to wait anymore. He's tired of not knowing what is going on with Katherine. Could she be getting tested? Is she even awake? He didn't know. He hates not knowing.

After they wiped away their tears, they went back to Mary.

"Is everything alright?" she asked.

"Yeah," Michael responded.

"I wish I knew what was going on in there," John mumbled.

His parents watched him pace back and forth in front of them. It seemed like time has slowed down and they would never find out what was wrong with Katherine. Seconds felt like minutes. Minutes felt like hours.

John kept thinking back at the times he had with Katherine. The first time they talked and hung out with each other was on a Sunday morning. Katherine ran into the church during a sermon. When it was over, Katherine, John, and Michael went fishing. The next thing he knew, they were dating. Then Katherine got saved. Earlier today, he told her he loved her. When he told her that, she collapsed.

"Everything will be fine, John," Mary said. "Come and sit down."

"I don't want to," John told her. "I can't."

The hair on his arms was still standing straight up. He never had goosebumps like this before. The last time he had goosebumps, he was watching a scary movie last year. He didn't remember what it was. It was cold in the ER as well. John was shaking; now he'd been in there a long while. He was shaking earlier from being afraid of what was happening with Katherine, but now he's shaking because of the goosebumps and from being cold.

The room has emptied some. A couple of people that were in the lobby before he went to the back to be with their loved ones. He wished that he could go back there to be with Katherine. He would do anything just to see if she was okay. Waiting made him anxious. His breathing became heavier. He wasn't sure if he would have another panic attack or not. He closed his eyes and took a few deep breaths.

Calm down. God has this. He has a reason for what is going on. He'll take care of her. I know that she'll be alright. I wish I could stop shaking though. I'll probably stop once I know that she's okay. Where's the doctor? Why hasn't he come to tell them what was wrong? Is he still with her? What's going on?

"The doctor will have the answers," His dad said.

"I know," John replied. "What's taking him so long though? Does he not know what is wrong with her? Is he doing tests on her? I just want some answers."

"I know you do, son. You must be patient."

Finally, a man wearing a white lab coat walked through the doors from where Katherine went through. He didn't walk toward the couple that was sitting across from the Williams; he didn't walk toward the elderly woman sitting at the other side of the lobby, and he didn't walk to the desk. The doctor walked straight toward John.

"Are you the one who was with her in the ambulance?" the doctor asked.

"Yes, sir," John said in a worried voice. "Is she alright?"

"She's awake, but that's all I can say for right now."

"Can I go see her?"

"Unfortunately, no. We will do some tests to see if there's anything we can find."

"What can I do?"

"Wait."

Wait

Katherine had headaches as far as she could remember. She would usually get them whenever her parents would fight. Other times would be when her dad would beat her, or her mother would push her around and yell at her. She just figured that her parents caused the headaches. Not once has she ever thought she would ever be put into an ambulance over one. Of course, this time it wasn't just a headache. She was dizzy and was feeling tired and weak. For the past few weeks, she's been feeling like that. All this time she figured she had the flu or something.

Before being taken to the hospital and living with the Williams, Katherine thought about going to college a few times. She wanted to help kids that are troubled. Ones who have been abused or bullied. She wanted them to know that there are others like them and that they could talk to her.

A child therapist sounded good to her. Maybe she could help the adults as well, sometimes. Adults need someone to talk to as well. Not everyone will listen to children or adults. Most people don't. Katherine would listen though. She would love to help.

Recently, though, she figured that she should just stay in Bruce for a while. She couldn't explain it, but something told her to stay put after she graduated. So, she stayed. Before graduation, she figured that she could work at the flower shop for a while and save up some money for her own place. John would stay in town also, for a little while. They will still be able to date and not have to worry about being apart from each other.

All of that changed, though. After everyone threw their hats up in the air, John told her that he's in love with her. She wanted to tell him she loves him too, but she couldn't. Not that she was scared to say it, it was that she was losing consciousness. Her headache was worse than ever, and she collapsed to the ground and passed out.

She didn't know how long she was unconscious. Minutes? Hours? Could it have been days? She had a dream while she was out though. She was holding John's hand. She wasn't sure if she was lying down or standing up. Even though she was calm and at peace, John had the look on his face like he was going to cry. Now she's asking herself what was going on in that dream.

She wondered about a lot of other things. Like, where was everybody? What's going on? Why is she in the hospital? What's wrong with her? When can she see John? When can she get out of here? All of these questions and no one was around to answer them.

She woke up a few minutes after arriving in the ER. When she looked around, there was no one there. She was getting scared and was worried that the staff had forgotten about her.

I hope they didn't forget about me. She thought. *They couldn't have. I am a patient after all. Why isn't John in here with me? I miss him. Is he not allowed to come in yet? Are they going to do tests on me? I'm getting scared now. I shouldn't be scared though. God is watching over me and I know that no matter what happens, everything will be just fine.*

Eventually, a man in a white lab coat came in, along with a nurse. He was about six-foot-tall and had short brown hair. His eyes were sky blue, and he wore glasses.

"Hello," The doctor said. His voice was deep and made Katherine nervous. "My name is Doctor Steven. I will be your doctor, and this is Nurse Pam. Could you tell me what happened to you?"

"I passed out at my graduation," Katherine told him.

"What were you feeling before you became unconscious?"

"Um. I had a big headache, and I was feeling tired and weak."

"Have you had headaches like that one before?"

"No sir, but I do get them a good bit. I mainly had them when I used to live with my parents. Now I live with a nice family. I don't get them as much, but when I do it usually is a big one."

"How long have you been having these headaches?"

"Years. As long as I can remember. I think since I was a little kid."

"Okay. Now, what can you tell me about being tired and weak?"

"Um. I didn't really felt tired and weak until a few weeks ago. At first, I thought I had the flu, but I don't think that's it. I vomited once though."

"Okay. Do you get tired and weak easily, or is it after you move around a lot?"

"Easily. I mean, sometimes I can work, but I usually have to stop and rest after a few minutes."

"Alright."

The doctor wrote everything she said down. After about a minute or two, the nurse handed Katherine a gown.

"What's this?" Katherine asked with a confused look.

"A gown," the nurse said in a high pitch voice. "You will need to replace it with your normal clothes."

"Am I going to stay overnight?"

"I'm not sure yet," Dr. Steven said. "First, we will have to do a test or two to see what's wrong."

"Can I see John first? He's my boyfriend and needs to know what's going on."

"That'll have to wait. Right now, I need you to change into the gown. I'll be outside waiting. Let me know when you're done. Then we can find out what's wrong with you."

Katherine made a frown face and mumbled, "Yes sir."

While the doctor waited outside, Katherine changed and laid her clothes onto the chair that was sitting in the corner. Her hands shook. She wanted to cry. The nurse noticed that Katherine seemed upset and tried to help her feel better.

"Everything will be okay," Nurse Pam said. "You can see your boyfriend after we're done."

The doctor and nurse made sure that Katherine wasn't wearing anything metal and rolled her into a room with a machine. The table they put her on was freezing cold and gave her the chills. After shivering a few times, the table wasn't as cold. Her body was warming it up.

Then, a man put some kind of soft cushion around her head. He told her it's to keep her head still. He also talked calmly to her. It looked like he had something green in his teeth, like a piece of lettuce.

"Excuse me, sir," Katherine told him. "You have something in your teeth."

"Oh, thank you," he said.

The table began to move into the MRI machine, scaring Katherine.

"It's alright," the tech said. "It won't hurt you. Just stay still."

The closer she got into the machine, the louder it was. She wanted to cover her ears, but she was told to lay still. She didn't want to make them mad. Her breathing was getting heavy, and she wanted to cry. However, she was able to hold the tears back. The machine was flashing lights, so Katherine closed her eyes. They were too bright for her.

After what seemed like half an hour, Katherine was able to get out and off the table. She did what they told her to do. *That was scary! Why did that thing have to be so loud? Will that machine print out a picture or something? Will I be able to see it? I wish John was here with me. Maybe he's in the lobby, waiting.*

I don't think I have ever been in a hospital before. It smells weird in here. Like some kind of cleaning product. They must keep it clean, so patients won't get each other's germs.

"Your name is Katherine, huh?" the tech said. "That's a pretty name."

"Thank you," she replied.

Her voice was a little shaky, but that was okay if she didn't have to go back into that machine again.

"Does that thing see inside my head?" Katherine asked.

"Yep. We will be able to see what is causing you so much trouble, and hopefully, the doctor can help."

They took Katherine back into the room she was in before. She noticed that some patients had a needle in their arm that was connected to a tube. *Am I going to get one of those in my arm? It looks like that would hurt. I don't want a needle in my arm! This stink. I want a hug.*

For a while, no one came in. Katherine laid there all alone. She kept wondering what John and the others were doing. *Are his parents with him or did they go home? What about Holly? Is she going to let me keep working at the shop? I sure hope so. I enjoy working there. I hope she won't fire me.*

Her stomach growled, and her mouth was getting dry. She wondered if they would bring her any food or some water. A burger sounded good to her. Ten minutes passed by and a nurse walked in, shutting the door behind her.

It wasn't Nurse Pam though. It was a different nurse. She was the same height, but her eyes were a clearer blue than sky blue. Her hair was white, but she wasn't old at all. She must have been in her early thirties.

"How are you doing Katherine?" the woman asked. Her voice was average. Not too high, but not deep either. "Are you doing okay?"

"Nervous, but I'm alright, I guess," Katherine answered. "I like your hair."

"Thank you! It's natural."

"Really? That's cool."

The nurse grabbed a chair and sat down next to her. She had a small smile and never frowned. Her voice was calm and soothing. *Is that what an angel would sound like? Her voice is so pretty. She's beautiful too.*

"There's no need to be nervous." The mysterious nurse said. "God has everything under control."

"I know."

"So, you believe in God also?"

"Yes, ma'am. I got saved recently."

"Well, that's great to hear! He is such an amazing Father."

"Yes, He is."

"No matter what happens, He will always be there for you. You can trust Him. He'll listen to whatever you have to say."

"I know. Ever since I got saved, I have never felt so peaceful in my life."

"So, you're not afraid to leave this world?"

"No, ma'am. I know that even if I pass away, I will be going to a better place. I'll be with Jesus."

"You accept that Jesus is your Lord and Savior?"

"Yes ma'am, I do."

"Well, that's good."

"Do You?"

"I most certainly do. Now, just close your eyes and relax. The doctor will be here any minute now."

Katherine did what she was told and closed her eyes. She took a deep breath, not paying any attention to what else was going on. Letting all the worries go, she felt calm and weightless. Now she was picturing John by her side. Picturing his smile made her smile. She was happy and no longer nervous.

When she opened her eyes, the nurse was gone. She did not hear the door shut or any footsteps. *Where did she go? I didn't hear her leave at all. I wonder where she went. She couldn't have just vanished. I never got her name.*

A few more minutes passed, and Nurse Pam walked in. She had that metal rod with the tube and a needle in her hand.

"What happened to that other nurse?" Katherine asked.

"What other nurse?"

"The nurse with the white hair."

"I'm sorry, we don't have any nurses with white hair."

Well, that's odd. Did she just pretend to be a nurse? How did she get in here if she wasn't a real nurse? How come no one caught her? Katherine had more questions, but still no answers.

"Can I see John now?" she asked Nurse Pam.

"Not yet. Almost, though. Now I will have to stick this IV in your arm. Are you afraid of needles?"

"Not that I know of. Will it hurt?"

"It might sting a little."

It stung a lot. Katherine made a face and bit her lower lip. She kept wondering how long she would have to stay in the hospital. She's pretty sure she had never passed out like this before. At least, that's what she remembers.

She can remember when her parents left her at the house when she was a little kid. They were gone for about two days. Katherine didn't have any food or water. They haven't paid the water bill in a while. So, instead of being able to drink water from the faucet, Katherine had to drink the water from the pond. She remembered how nasty it tasted. She even drank some of the sand that was in it.

She didn't know how to skin or cook a fish, so she went without food. There weren't any berries around either for her to eat. Her stomach growled throughout the nights. When her parents finally came back home, they were somehow able to pay the water bill. She didn't know how they got the money and didn't ask. They were able to buy food as well. However, she had to sneak the food at night from the fridge, since her parents didn't give her any food.

Kathrine didn't have to worry about her parents anymore though. She has food and water now. The Williams are a kind and caring family. John is amazing too. He is sweet, caring, and handsome.

A few more minutes had passed until the doctor came into the room. He pulled the nurse away and whispered in her ear. When he got done, the nurse covered her mouth in shock. She gave Katherine a quick look. The look on the nurse's face looked worrisome.

"Well, I saw the results of your MRI test." The doctor said. You-"

"Wait." Katherine interrupted him. "I want John and his parents here when you tell me what's wrong. John's my boyfriend and his parents took care of me as if I was their own. I want them to be here. Please."

"Alright. I'll go get them. They should be in the lobby."

I don't want to hear the news alone. I want my family to be here. They may not be my biological family, but they put up with me and take care of me. Finally, I'll have some answers.

Answers

John held his breath as he saw a doctor walking through the doors that led from the ER section. He was around John's height with blonde hair. *Could this be the man who will tell me what is wrong with Katherine?* He asked himself. Again, everything felt like it was moving in slow motion. John couldn't breathe. It was as if someone was squeezing his lungs tight. He calmed himself down and took a deep breath. He inhaled through his nose and exhaled out through his mouth. He repeated that two more times.

Instead of walking to John and giving him the news, the man walked right past him and stopped in front of a couple that was on the other side of the lobby. *Not him. He's not the man who will tell me about Katherine.*

He looked behind him as the blonde doctor told the couple some good news. John knew that it was good by seeing the couple's reaction. The woman smiled, and the man exhaled a large amount of breath. The man wiped the woman's tears away, and they got up and went through the ER doors. They could see their loved ones again. They could hug them and kiss their forehead.

What about Katherine, though? When will I know if she's alright? When will I know if I will be able to kiss her forehead and see her smile again? I need to calm down. I need to be patient. God will let me know when the time is right.

John thought back to two Thanksgivings ago when his uncle had a heart attack.

It was the south, so instead of having nice fall weather, they got warm, summer-like weather. It was in the eighties and not a single cloud in the sky. They even had to cut the air conditioner on. Everyone was wearing short sleeve shirts and shorts. One of John's aunts was even wearing flip-flops.

It was the William's turn to host that Thanksgiving. Most of the relatives came. There were a couple of cousins and even an uncle who couldn't come due to being snowed in up north.

Everyone was smiling and telling stories about what had happened throughout the year. His Aunt Betty was now a real estate agent making good money and could finally pay off the house she had been renting to own. Everyone kept congratulating her and saying they were proud.

While most of the guys, and a handful of the girls, watched football in the living room, John was helping in the kitchen. He didn't care that much about football. He was more of a baseball fan. Every now and then, John would hear his family chant for their favorite team. When their team would score a touchdown, they would cheer louder.

Uncle Jim, however, wasn't cheering. John knew that his uncle loved football, so something was definitely off. He knew that Uncle Jim was obsessed with the sport and when John asked him if he was alright, he just told John that he wasn't feeling too well.

When the food was done, everyone gathered around at the kitchen table. John's parents had an extra table they hid away in the garage, for when it was their turn to host on the holidays. They pushed the two tables together, so everyone would sit together as one big family.

The food was delicious. The turkey was nice and juicy, and the mashed potatoes were the best his Mom had ever made. Everyone loves Mary's cooking. Everyone ended up getting seconds, except for Uncle Jim. This time, John wasn't the only one who noticed that Uncle Jim was acting weird. He was sweating and looked like he was burning up.

"Jim?" Michael said. "Are you alright?"

"I'm not sure," Jim responded. "I might need to go to a hospital."

Jim then grabbed his chest where his heart was and fell out of the chair. Mary put a pillow under his head while Betty called for an ambulance. Just about everyone surrounded him and they all were scared. Michael, however, got on his knees and prayed for his brother. When John watched his dad pray, he saw a tear rolling down his cheek and knew that his dad was scared.

Uncle Jim survived the heart attack, and all the family kept surrounding him at the hospital. They kept asking him if he was alright. The doctor told him he should go on a diet if he wanted to live longer. Thankfully Uncle Jim did what the doctor said, and he lost forty pounds and he looks and feels a lot better.

John was scared that day. He didn't know if he would lose his uncle or not. God was watching over Uncle Jim though, and John knew it.

There was another time when something bad happened to one of his relatives. It was last Christmas and John and his parents were heading over to Mary's cousin's house. They lived in Mississippi, so John and his parents didn't have to drive too far. It was warm weather for being in December.

John didn't really mind having warm weather during the holidays like Christmas. Every now and then, though, he would enjoy seeing a snowflake or two.

When they got there, almost everyone was there except for Michael's second cousin. She was running late and said that she should be there in about an hour.

John loved his mother's cousin's home. It always smelt like vanilla when he was over there. She had a chihuahua that loved to lick everyone. He would bark at them sometimes, talking to them when he wasn't noticed. Sometimes he played with people's toes, just so they would give him attention. John never saw a dog that wanted so much attention in his life.

Even though Michael's cousin was running late, the food was already out and steaming hot. All of it smelt amazing. There was ham, green beans, corn, beets, stuffing, and more food that John can't even remember. Instead of alcohol, there was juice or sweet tea.

Thirty minutes passed, and everyone's stomach was growling. You could hear their stomachs from another room. Whoever heard the other person's stomach would tell them to calm down. Some thought that was funny, while others were getting grumpy from not being able to eat anything.

"Rachel should be here any minute now," Michael told everyone.

An hour and a half had passed by since Rachel called. Michael was getting worried and was thinking about calling her to see where she was at. After another thirty minutes went by, Michael couldn't handle it anymore.

"I'm sure she's okay," Mary said.

Before Michael could press Rachel's cell phone number, he got a call. It was a medic. Rachel was in a car accident and was in rough shape. She broke her left arm, and she wasn't responding.

Michael, Mary, and John rushed to the truck and drove to the hospital where Rachel was taken. She was taken by an ambulance to a hospital in Memphis, Tennessee. When they got there, Rachel was all cleaned up and had a cast on. But unfortunately, she was in a coma. Even though they took two hours to get there, it felt as if they were only on the road for forty-five minutes.

The car hit her hard, and both cars were pretty much destroyed. The driver that hit her left the hospital with only a couple of scratches and a big bruise. Rachel had no one else, so Michael stayed there with her until she woke up. While he was there, Mary worked at the hardware store part-time with John.

Two months later, Rachel woke up. She didn't remember what happened and was confused with being in a hospital bed. The doctor told her all that happened. While she was in the coma, Michael would take her hand every day and pray that she would be alright.

Now they're back at the hospital, but this time it isn't a relative, it is Katherine. John looked at his parents and they both had a concerned look on their faces.

"Please sit down, son," Mary said.

"I can't. I have to know what is wrong with Katherine."

Another doctor walked through the doors, and this time he went straight to John.

"Are you John?" Dr. Steven asked.

"Yes, sir," John replied. "Is Katherine alright?"

He ignored the question and told him who he was. "Katherine wanted all of you to be there when I tell her what the results were."

"Results?"

"Yes. Please, follow me."

They followed him through the door. *What results? Did they give her a cat scan or something? I hope she's alright. Please, let her be alright.*

John could see in some of the rooms when they would pass by them. One guy had a neck brace on, and his face was covered in bruises. Another guy had both legs in casts. John was now wondering how bad Katherine is. *Will she have to stay overnight? That scares me.*

As they got closer to Katherine's room, John's heart pounded harder and faster. He tried to calm himself down by taking a couple of deep breaths, but that didn't work this time. They finally reached the room where Katherine was in. *Please be okay.*

The first person who Katherine saw walking through the door was John. A huge smile formed when he walked over to her and kissed her forehead. *Has he been crying?* She asked herself. His eyes were red, and she could tell that he was shaking.

"Why are you shaking?" she asked him.

"I'm worried about you," He answered. "Are you alright? Are you hurt? How are you feeling?"

"I feel fine. They put me in a loud machine. They said they could tell what was wrong with me with the machine."

John put one hand on her head and held one of her hands with the other. He looked into her eyes and didn't blink once. His eyes watered, but Katherine wiped them away with her right hand.

"Did you see a nurse with white hair by any chance?" she asked him in a quiet tone.

"Yeah. She talked to me while I was in the lobby. She disappeared, though. I didn't even hear her leave."

"Really? Me too! It was like she vanished. How weird is that?"

"Very weird."

It was weird. Her and John saw the same woman who disappeared on both of them. *I wonder who she is. An angel? I'm not sure about that, but you never know. Right now, I'm just glad that John is here, holding my hand.*

John's parents asked Katherine if she was alright, and she told them she felt fine. The doctor was behind them, waiting for them to finish up their conversations. After they've settled down, they faced Dr. Steven.

"Is she alright?" John asked him.

"I'm sorry to say this, but Katherine has a tumor in her brain."

The whole room went silent. Mary and Michael covered their mouths in shock. John's jaw dropped and couldn't move.

"A-A tumor?" John choked.

"Yes."

"Can you get it out?" Katherine asked, with a tear rolling down her cheek.

"Unfortunately, no," Dr. Steven said. "It's too deep inside the brain. If we try to get it out, you will die."

"H-How long does she have?" John asked.

"I can't say. My guess is, she could have a few months to a year left. The cancer spread quickly."

The Williams burst into tears, and John held onto Katherine tight. Katherine took a deep breath and hugged John back. *I have cancer. I might not live any longer than a year. I don't believe it. All those headaches were mainly because of the tumor.*

"We can try chemotherapy," Said Dr. Steven. "It will only slow down the cancer, though. With it, she can probably live longer, but I am not sure how much."

John looked at Katherine, waiting for her to say yes. *Do I want to do that? To be honest, I don't think I do. I'll probably feel worse with it.*

"No," Katherine told him.

"W-What?" John asked in shock. "Why?"

"I've been afraid my whole life. I was afraid of my parents, of other students, of my future. I wasn't at peace. Ever since I found Jesus, I have never been so peaceful. I'm not afraid anymore, John. I'm okay with going without the chemotherapy. I'm not afraid to die. I know where I'll be going when I leave this earth. I know where my soul will be going, and that place will be glorious. I'm not afraid, I have Jesus." She turned to the doctor and said, "No chemotherapy."

"If that's your choice," Dr. Steven said.

"It is."

"Alright, well, we will be keeping you overnight. Just in case. We will move you into a normal patient room in a different part of the building."

"Alright. Thank you."

A nurse came in with a wheelchair. Katherine sat in it and was rolled into another part of the building. She had fun riding in the elevator.

"Wee!" she said with a smile. "I have never been in an elevator before. That was fun."

Everyone chuckled and walked onto the third floor. She caught John wiping his tears away in a reflection. She knew that this would be difficult. Not just for her, but for everyone else. She looked up and closed her eyes.

God, even though I had it rough for most of my life, this life was a blessing. John is a blessing. Thank You for bringing him into my life. No matter what happens next, I know that You will be there, by my side, watching over me. I'm not afraid to leave this body. I know that You have and always will be there for me. I know You have a reason for this. I trust You, Father, and I am looking forward to being in Heaven with You, for eternity.

The nurse pushed her into a room, and Katherine got onto the bed. Her stomach growled, and everyone heard it.

"When's supper?" she asked the nurse.

The nurse smiled and said, "We'll bring you some food shortly."

"Thank you."

John sat in the chair beside her and held her hand. Mary told her she doesn't have to do any more chores and she can just relax when they get home. Katherine declined, of course. She didn't want to lie around and do nothing. She wants to help as much as she could.

"I hope Holly will let me keep working at the shop," Katherine said.

"I'm sure she will," Mary replied.

John looked at Katherine and said, "I'm staying here tonight with you. I'm not leaving you. Not for a second."

"You don't have too."

"I want to. I want to spend as much time as I can with you. You mean so much to me. I want to cherish every moment with you."

"Okay. Thank you for staying and not leaving."

"I will never leave you."

Overnight

Katherine was in her new room at the hospital with an IV in her arm. She didn't really like it. She thought it was annoying. The room was quiet, and John was sitting in the chair beside her. He told her that the chair turns into a bed, so he will be able to stay the night with her.

"Hey, John," She said to him. They haven't talked to each other much, and it's been driving her crazy. "Can you cut the air up? It's a little chilly in here."

"Sure," He answered.

She watched him get up and mess with the thermostat. After a few minutes, it finally got warmer in the room. Now Katherine wasn't freezing. She wasn't too comfortable wearing the hospital gown either. She felt naked, and that made her uncomfortable. Thankfully, the nurses gave her some blankets to cover herself up.

Her room smelled like Lysol and Bleach. The smell was strong, but she was able to handle it.

"Thank you," She told him.

A nurse asked her what she wanted for supper. Katherine told her that a salad would be just fine. She wasn't really that hungry. She hasn't eaten anything since that morning before graduation. *Why wasn't she hungry? Was it the cancer?* She didn't know.

The salad was alright. The nurse gave her water and left. A few minutes later, she came back and took Katherine's tray. She didn't want to eat, but she forced herself to, anyway. She didn't want John to be any more worried than he already was.

All this time and I haven't told him I loved him. She thought to herself. *He might think I don't love him back. How could I have forgotten to tell him? What's wrong with me? Look at him. He's worried about me and has been looking out for me. I can tell in his eyes that he's still scared.*

"I love you too, by the way," she told him.

He turned his head from the window and looked at her. His mouth was open, and he looked surprised.

"W-What?" he replied. His voice was a little shaky.

"I'm in love with you too."

"R-Really?"

"Yes. Sorry that I waited so long to tell you. I've been kind of busy for most of the day. I had a couple of meetings."

John chuckled. "It's alright. I understand."

He got up and walked over to her. He then wrapped his arms around her and gave her a huge hug. She missed his hugs, and she missed him holding her and holding his hands. She hugged him back, and they stayed like that for a good half an hour. Not saying a word. Just holding each other.

John sat back down but scooted the chair closer to her. She reached out and held his hand.

"Want to see what's on TV?" she asked him.

"Sure."

She flipped through the channels to find something for both of them to watch. A couple of sports was on. There were also some criminal shows, some sitcoms, and some cooking channels. The cooking shows made her feel sick to her stomach. They decided to watch one or two crime shows, and then they changed the channel to a sitcom. They would laugh every now and then.

Watching John laugh made her smile. She wanted him to laugh. She wanted him to smile. Seeing John upset made her upset.

After a couple of hours, she turned the TV off. They weren't paying attention to it anymore, so there was no use in having it on. John went back to looking out the window, and Katherine was listening to the silence. She didn't know how it got quiet again. They had a conversation during one of the TV shows, but then they got quiet after that.

She didn't like the silence. It made her feel uneasy. Every now and then she could hear a patient in the next room, cough. Sometimes she could hear what they were watching, and now they were watching music videos on TV. A nurse would come in sometimes to tell them to cut the volume down. The patient would cut the volume back up a couple of minutes after the nurse would leave. Once, Katherine heard someone pushing a wheelchair. She heard the wheels squeak. Whoever was in the wheelchair was talking about sports. Nothing that Katherine was interested in.

I wonder what happened to that nurse with the white hair. She seemed nice. I haven't seen her since I first arrived here. Maybe her shift was over or

153

something. Maybe she had other patients to help. Could she only work in the ER? That would make sense of why I haven't seen her here.

It was now around nine pm, and Katherine heard the rain hitting against the window. It didn't rain hard. Still, she enjoyed it. However, she knew that the rain made John upset. He told her before that he didn't like the rain, even though he knew that the plants and crops needed it. The rain made him sad. He didn't know why.

"John," she caught his attention away from the window. "I don't want you to be sad. I know you're worried about me, but I don't want this to take away your happiness. I want you happy. I want you smiling. I want you to laugh when something is funny, like earlier on TV. Please."

John took her hand and held it. Usually, his hands felt strong and secure. This time though, his hands felt soft and gentle.

"Okay," He agreed. "If that's your wish."

He leaned over her and kissed her forehead. She didn't want him to let go of her hand. She asked if she could fall asleep while they were holding each other's hands.

"Of course," He said.

"Do you want to pray for us, before we go to bed?"

"Sure."

John prayed for them and cut the lights out. Before Katherine could fall asleep, a nurse came in to check her blood pressure. Every now and then a nurse would come in to check up on Katherine. She didn't mind it. She knew it was their job to see if she's alright. The nurse told her she might come in again while Katherine is asleep to see if everything is okay.

"That's okay," Katherine told the nurse.

After the nurse left, Katherine looked up and talked to God.

"Thank You. Thank You for everything that You have given me. I am truly blessed and thankful. I know that the rest of this road will be rough. I know that I'm going to feel worse, but this life is only temporary. Take me when You are ready, Lord. I know that everything will be alright. You gave me life and I thank You for that. I thank You for everything. I just ask that You watch over everyone after I leave this place. John and his parents. Even my parents."

With that said, Katherine finally fell asleep. She only woke up once, and that was when the nurse came in to check up on her.

John didn't like seeing Katherine in the hospital bed with an IV in her arm. He didn't like her in the hospital period. It made him cry. He would look out the window with tears running down his cheeks. He didn't want Katherine to see him like that.

Katherine only wanted a salad for supper. *How come she didn't want something more? He asked himself. Is the tumor making her less hungry? Is she losing her appetite? She was cold earlier. Was that the tumor as well? Is she going to eat less throughout the rest of the time she has left? Is she going to get colder? Is she going to get pale? She already gets tired easily. What's going to happen through the next year or less? I'm going to have to watch her slowly fade away. I'm going to have to watch her suffer. She's going to hurt more and more, and there's nothing that I can do to help her feel better.*

He realized that he was shaking. He wanted to stop thinking about what will happen to Katherine so he'll stop shaking. Eventually, he was able to stop. Katherine told him she loved him. *She loves me back. I can't believe it. I should be happy. I am happy. The girl that I'm in love with loves me back.*

John looked at her from the reflection in the window. He smiled a little. He is happy. He's also scared at the same time.

The room was a little warm for him, but he was okay with that. Katherine wanted it warm, that's all that matters. He wants her to be happy and comfortable. *I wonder what all she wanted to do in life. Maybe I should ask. Would that be rude? I don't know.*

They watched some TV together. Through one sitcom they were watching, they talked.

"I wonder if Holly will let me keep working at the shop," Katherine said out loud.

"I don't know. You shouldn't be working though. You should relax and enjoy yourself."

"Oh, no. I'm not going to be lazy and do nothing. I want to do stuff. I want to work at the flower shop. I love working there. It's fun!"

"Are you sure? You don't have to."

"I'm positive. John, I don't want to lie around and do nothing. I want to do stuff that I enjoy. Please, don't try to stop me from doing that."

"Alright. If that's what you want. I want you to be happy."

"Thank you. I want you happy too."

I don't know why she wants to work instead of having fun and relaxation. I will not argue with her though. I don't want to make her upset. I just want her happy. If working at that flower shop makes her happy, then I won't try to stop her.

"Is there anything you have been wanting to do?" he asked her. "Something that you've been wanting to try."

"Hmm. Camping."

"Camping? Why camping?"

"I heard people at school talk about it. It sounds like fun! You get to sleep in the woods at night. Can we do that? We could lie under the stars. It'll be romantic!"

Katherine's voice was getting higher as she got more excited about the idea of camping. John couldn't help but smile. He even chuckled a little. *She's so adorable.*

"We can do that. My dad has a couple of tents. I'm sure he'll let us use them if we ask. I'll find a day we can go and we can go fishing too if you want."

"That sounds terrific! We can have a picnic too. Oh, and we can roast marshmallows! I heard people talking about that too, and it sounds amazing."

"Alright." John grinned. "We can do all of that."

"Yay!"

"Is there anything else that you would like to do?"

"Not that I know of."

"Alright. I'll see what I can do."

They watched TV for a little while longer and then went to bed. John prayed for them.

An hour passed, and John couldn't sleep. He was wide awake. He heard a nurse keep telling a patient to cut the volume down on their TV. John thought it was funny, but the nurse didn't. He could tell by her voice that she was getting annoyed.

He wished it wasn't raining. Rain made him a little depressed. The rain was gloomy, and John didn't like gloomy. He preferred sunshine and birds chirping. He loved happy, warm weather.

A couple of more hours passed, and John still could not sleep. He looked on his phone, and it was one in the morning. He knew why he couldn't sleep; he worried about Katherine. He couldn't get her sickness out of his mind. *Why didn't she want the chemotherapy? She'll live longer. Maybe she thinks she would just hurt more if she went through the therapy.*

John got up and went to the vending machine. He wasn't really hungry, but he wanted to eat something. He didn't want to keep laying there, worrying about Katherine. It just made him upset, and he didn't want to wake Katherine up.

The vending machine wasn't far. It was in its own small room, along with a soda machine. He looked around for a good two minutes, trying to decide on what he wanted. Finally, he picked a bag of chips. He looked up at the machine and saw his reflection. He was crying, and he now realized it.

"Why?" he said out loud. "I don't understand why she has to go."

He looked up with tears rolling down his face. He wiped them away with his arm. He was talking to God now.

"I know that there's a reason for this. I know there is. Why can't I know, though? Why does she have to go? I'm in love with her. I might be selfish, but I don't want her to go."

John slid against the wall and sat down. He continued to sob. No longer was he wiping the tears away. He gave up on that. People were walking by, but they didn't bother to come in. He wasn't sure if they could hear him or not. If they did, they weren't going to see what was wrong. John was now thinking if God wanted him to be by himself. Maybe God wanted John to have someone on one time with Him.

"Father," he said to God, as he looked up again. This time, wiping the tears away. "Please don't let her suffer when she goes. Make it painless as possible. I don't want her to suffer. I know she will hurt every now and then, but don't let her hurt when it's her time. Please, let me spend a bit more time with her. Just a little while longer. As much as I can."

John sat there for a few more minutes and then got up to get the chips. He ate them and threw the bag away. Then, he wiped whatever tears were left and went back to Katherine's room. As soon as he laid down, he fell asleep.

Relax

It was around nine in the morning and the doctor was getting the discharge papers ready. John didn't have a good night's sleep last night, he kept worrying about Katherine. He must have only gotten about three or four hours of sleep. When John woke up around seven-thirty, he sat there staring at Katherine while she was sleeping.

She looked so gorgeous, even in a hospital gown. So peaceful. John remembered the good times they had together. He remembered the first day they talked to each other and hung out. It was when church was over. Katherine, John, and his dad went fishing. Everyone had a great time.

"I love you so much," John whispered to her.

Now John and Katherine were about to leave the hospital. The nurse came in to take the IV out of Katherine's arm. It scared her that it would hurt like it did when it went in. Even though the nurse told her it wouldn't, Katherine still wanted to hold John's hand. She squeezed his hand tight when the nurse took the needle out, but it didn't hurt one bit.

Katherine changed back into her normal clothes and did everything else that had to be done. Another nurse came in with a wheelchair, telling Katherine to hop on.

"Oh, goodie!" Katherine said with excitement. "I get to ride in the chair again. Are we going in the elevator?"

"Yes," the nurse smiled.

Katherine cheered and got in the wheelchair. *She's so cute.* John thought. Seeing her smile made John happy. They rode the elevator and got off at the lobby. Mary was there waiting for them. Michael was in the car in front of the hospital.

"Hey there," Mary said. "How are you feeling?"

"I'm fine," Katherine replied. "The doctor is setting me free."

"Well, that's good," Mary chuckled. "How about some breakfast?"

"No thanks. I'm fine."

"Are you sure? You can have anything you want!"

"I'm sure. I'm not really hungry."

She's not hungry? The only thing she ate last night was a small salad. Why doesn't she want to eat? It must be the cancer. Is that what's making her not as hungry? Still, I think she should eat something. Even if it's small. John thought.

It was cold and quiet in the lobby. When John's stomach growled, Mary and Katherine looked at him with a grin. He wished that this hospital had a gift shop. Some hospitals have them, but this one didn't. He wanted to buy something for Katherine. Like a balloon or a stuffed animal.

Another woman wearing scrubs came and pushed Katherine to the truck. The lady asked if Katherine needed any help. She told the woman no. The nurse then told them to have a nice day and walked back into the hospital.

"So," Michael said. "I called some people yesterday evening after we left the hospital. We're going to have the graduation celebration today around eleven. Is that alright?"

"Sounds good," John replied.

Katherine said nothing. She just nodded.

Later that day, some people showed up for the cookout. Three of John and Katherine's teachers came, along with a handful of students from their school. Most of the students were the ones who graduated with them. There were one or two students from the eleventh grade that showed up just for the food. Still, it was nice to have people over.

It was another hot day. The sun was bright as ever and there wasn't a cloud in the sky. Not even a breeze. Luckily though, there were some cold drinks: sweet tea, water, and some sodas. The guests mainly went for the water. John was sweating. He went inside and changed into shorts and a sleeveless shirt. *That's better.*

After a few minutes of the guests' arrival, John could smell the burgers and hotdogs from the grill. He could hear his dad humming every now and then, and a <u>Casting Crowns</u> cd was playing on the stereo. Michael was humming along to the music, and Mary was singing the actual words.

John's mother told everyone she had baked cookies and a cake, but they can't have any until they eat a burger or a hotdog.

The food smelled delicious, and John's stomach was growling. He had a big breakfast earlier that morning. He had two sausages and biscuits, a small bowl of grits, bacon, and a small piece of cooked ham.

Everyone was having an enjoyable time. Some people talked to John and asked how everything was going. He would tell them that everything was going alright. He wasn't going to tell them he was worried about Katherine. He didn't feel like crying again.

The food was cooked, and everyone grabbed a paper plate and fixed their food. A few feet from the grill was a small table with chips on it. Katherine, however, didn't get herself a plate. She sat in the chair and drank her water.

"You're not going to eat?" John asked as he sat down next to her.

"I'm not hungry," She said.

"Are you sure? The food is great."

"I'm sure. Right now, I'm just enjoying the sun. I'm going to try to go see Holly after the cookout."

John took her hand. "You need to relax. Please."

"I want to work, John. I don't want to relax."

"At least relax for the rest of the weekend. Can you please do that for me?"

Katherine sighed, "Yeah. For you."

"Thank you. I love you."

"I love you too."

At least she'll relax for the rest of the weekend. Maybe Holly won't make her work full time. Katherine doesn't need to wear herself out. I don't want her to end up getting hurt. She needs to rest.

John will officially work at his dad's store on Monday morning. He would work full time, but his dad is letting him only work part-time, so John will have more time with Katherine. Since he has more time with her, he can find out when the best time to go camping is. It's something that Katherine has wanted to do, and John is planning on making that wish come true. His dad has a couple of tents in the garage, and maybe Michael will let him borrow the tents and other camping equipment one day.

John walked over to his dad and talked about the whole camping idea. His dad told him he can take whatever he liked as long as he tells him when they will leave for the camping trip.

"How's Katherine doing?" Michael asked his son.

"She's not eating. I wish she would at least eat a little."

"I know. She'll be alright, son. Jesus is with her."

"I know."

"Enjoy the rest of your weekend. We both will get up early Monday morning for work. So, relax."

***

It was now two in the afternoon. Everyone left an hour ago, and they all said they had a wonderful time. The food smelt delicious, but Katherine wasn't hungry. She didn't know why she knew that her stomach wanted nothing to eat. So, she just enjoyed the sun shining on her. John wanted her to relax for the rest of the weekend. She agreed. She knows that he's worried about her. However, she doesn't just want to sit around and relax. She wants to work, at least a little.

Katherine wanted to at least go to the flower shop and talk to Holly about working there. She doesn't have to work full time, but she still wants to work a couple of hours every now and then. She went to Mary and Michael's bedroom. She knocked on the door and walked in when Mary told her to come in.

"Hey dear," Mary said with a smile on her face. "How are you? Is everything okay?"

"Yes, ma'am. Um. I was wondering if you could take me to the flower shop. I would like to talk to Holly to see if I can still work there."

"Oh, you can just take the truck. Michael wouldn't mind since I gave you permission. The keys are by the front door."

"I-I don't know how to drive."

"Your parents never taught you how to drive?"

"No, ma'am."

Katherine was a little embarrassed by that. Her mom or dad never bothered to teach her how to drive a vehicle. She always walked to get to her destination. Her parents were too busy with themselves. They never spent time with their daughter and never tried to teach her to become an adult. They never taught her how to be responsible or anything. Her dad would just drink, and her mom would do drugs and pass out in front of the TV.

"Well, you will learn today," Mary told her.

"W-What?"

"It'll be fun! Michael taught John how to drive, and I always wanted to teach someone. Now I get to teach you. How exciting!"

"Are you sure? What if I wreck it or something?"

"Oh, you'll be fine."

I'm scared and excited at the same time. Katherine told herself. *I have been wanting to learn how to drive for a while. I am worried though. What if I wreck it? I don't want Mary and her husband to get mad at me. What if they yell? I should know by now they don't yell. They'll be disappointed though.*

Katherine grabbed the keys and got in the driver's seat. Mary got in the passenger seat beside her. Katherine already knew to put the key into the ignition and turn it. After watching the Williams, she also knew to put the seat belt on first. She buckled up, put the key in the ignition, and cranked the truck.

"Good!" Mary said with excitement.

"Now you put it in reverse with this." She pointed to where the gear was. "Make sure you look behind you to make sure that no one is coming. Also, don't go too fast."

Katherine did as she was told and looked both ways behind her. No one was coming. She then put the truck in reverse and barely pressed the gas pedal. Mary continued to tell her what to do. Katherine did exactly what Mary said.

So far so good. Mary told her the speed limit. She didn't have to tell Katherine where to go; she already knew how to get to the flower shop. Even though the speed limit was forty, Katherine went thirty.

Her heart was racing. She was now in control of a moving vehicle. She never thought she would actually drive one. She took a few deep breaths, trying to stay calm. Mary told her to slowly press down on the brake at certain areas. The first two times, Mary told her when to use the brakes. After that, Katherine knew what to do.

Katherine got used to driving quickly. She was comfortable by the time they got to the flower shop.

"You did great!" Mary told her. "You learn quickly."

"Thank you," Katherine said proudly.

"I never go in the shop that much. I might go in this time and see what they have."

Katherine turned off the ignition and the two of them got out. When they got to the front door of the shop, Katherine saw a sign that said 'Hiring'. She was sad now; Holly was already looking for someone else. Katherine wanted to cry but held back the tears. *Maybe she will still let me work a little. I have to try. I love working here!*

They walked in and saw how many people were there. The flower shop was busy today. There must have been at least ten customers. *Man, she's busy today!*

She spotted Holly and walked over to her. Holly was talking to a customer, so she waited until she was done. When Holly finished, Katherine caught her attention.

"Hey, Holly," Katherine said.

"Oh, hey Katherine." Holly greeted back. "What's going on?"

"I-I saw that sign at the window."

"Oh. Michael told me you were sick. I'm sorry, sweetie."

"Does this mean I'm fired?" Katherine mumbled.

"I'm not sure. I mean, I don't want you to do too much and pass out or something while at work." A customer asked Holly over for some help. "Coming, sir! Walk with me. This place is packed today, and I can't stay still for two seconds."

She walked with Holly and waited for her to finish with the customer. As soon as she was done, another customer asked for some lilies.

"I should have more lilies in the back." She told the woman with blonde hair. "I'll go get some for you. How many do you want, a dozen?" The woman with the blonde hair nodded. "Coming right up," Holly said.

Holly and Katherine walked to the back where the rest of the flowers were at.

"Could I just work a couple of hours every now and then?" Katherine begged Holly. "I love working here."

"I don't know."

Holly snipped a dozen lilies and wrapped them up.

"Please, Holly. I need this job. Even if it's just a few hours a week."

"Oh, alright. I'm doing this for you."

"Thank you!" Katherine hugged her as tight as she could. "Can I come on Monday?"

"Sure. Now I have a lot more customers to help. Get some rest. Relax, okay?"

"Okay. I'll see you on Monday. Bye, Holly. Thanks again."

"You're welcome."

Katherine waved goodbye to Holly and got in the truck. Mary joined her a few minutes later. Katherine told her that Holly will let her keep working at the shop.

"That's good," Mary responded.

Katherine's stomach growled, and it was loud. Mary looked at her and chuckled.

"It's about time you're hungry! When was the last time you ate?"

"Last night at the hospital. I had a small salad."

"How about we go to the Drive-In? It's a couple of miles out of town? My treat."

"That sounds good. I heard that chili dogs are amazing. So are milkshakes."

"They most certainly are!"

They drove to The Drive-In and Katherine finally ate. The food was amazing, and she had a chocolate milkshake. Now, she can relax.

Rehab

Aweek has passed since graduation. John didn't like the fact that Katherine was still working part-time at the flower shop, but as long as she's happy, then John would not try to stop her. Katherine works only a couple of hours every now and then. She worked twice in the past week. Once on Monday and again on Wednesday. She worked three hours on both days. While she was at the flower shop, John worked on those days at this dad's store.

Also, Katherine and he began to read the Bible together every night. They would read two chapters. He would read one out loud, and then Katherine would read the next chapter. After they would read to each other, John would pray for both of them.

Katherine still wasn't eating much. She would only eat a big meal once a day now. Every now and then John would see her eating a small snack, but that's it. Just a snack, like an apple or something small like that. John wanted her to eat more, but he can't force food in her mouth. He begged her to eat more, but that was it. He didn't ask again. He didn't want her mad at him.

He also wanted to help her with the chores, but again, she wouldn't allow him to help. He could see her struggling when she would carry the laundry basket full of clothes. She would take breaks when she would wash the dishes. Mary and Michael told her not to worry about the chores, but she insisted. She didn't want to be a burden to them. She enjoyed helping around the house.

Now it was Friday, and John was at the store with his dad. Katherine wasn't working, but Michael wanted John to come and help, anyway. There were a lot of shelves that needed to be stacked and a lot of inventory in the back that needed to be moved around, to make room to walk. John knew that he had to help because his dad was getting older, and Michael couldn't do as much heavy lifting like he used to.

"How are you and Katherine doing?" Michael asked.

"We're doing good," John replied.

"When are you planning on taking her camping?"

"I'm not sure yet. I'm still trying to find the right time."

Just about every day, Michael would ask his son if everything is alright between John and Katherine. John knew that he was just checking up on them. Especially, since last week. Michael told the pastor about Katherine and her tumor last Sunday at church. Near the end of the service, Pastor Bill motioned Katherine to come to the front, and he prayed for her.

"You know," Michael said, quietly. "I think of her as a daughter I never had."

"Really?"

His dad nodded. "I care about her as if she was my own child. I do, however, wish that her dad was there for her, instead of drinking all the time."

"Me too. Shouldn't her dad be out of jail by now?"

"Well, it turned out he had a ton of warrants. So, he'll be in there for a while."

"Oh. I'll pray for him. For her mom too."

Working at the shop that day was hot and difficult. John was stacking a bunch of heavy equipment onto the shelves or bringing them out onto the floor. First, he moved the chainsaws. They weren't that heavy, so he moved them with ease. Then were the lawnmowers and the sledgehammers. Next were pipes and a few boxes of paint.

With the air conditioner broken, it was hot in the store. Michael could fix it because the store was extremely busy that day. A repairman was called, but he couldn't come that day. John had to take a couple of water breaks, so he wouldn't get too hot.

John understood why the store was so busy. With the hot weather, people are wanting projects to be done. Building sheds and dog houses, making a garden and painting the outside of houses. There was also yard work like mowing the grass. There was even a rumor that there would be a new bank in town this year, and some men volunteered to help if they could.

After five o'clock, the store died down some, so that was John's chance to work in the back. He would have done it earlier, but he had to help his dad with the customers. The back of the store was even hotter than the front. John had until closing to move a ton of boxes. They will be closing soon, so he didn't have much time.

He moved all the toolboxes and the extra sledgehammers to one corner. They had leftover paint, so he put those, along with brushes and rollers, in another corner. He stopped and chugged a water bottle down. The water was cold and refreshing, making John want another one. He moved more stuff around until he thought there was plenty of room to walk. Two hours had passed while he was in the back. When he was done, John walked back up to the front.

A man walked in with a blue button-down shirt and khaki pants; he looked like he was in his forties. He walked up to the counter.

"Oh, hey Jack," Michael greeted the man.

"Hey, Michael," Jack greeted back. "Is your son around?"

"Sure is. Here he comes now."

Jack turned to face John. "Hey there, John. How is it going?"

"Fine," John answered."

"I heard what happened with your girlfriend, Katherine, is it? I'm sorry to hear that she has cancer. How is she doing?"

"She's feeling a little weak and not eating much, but besides that, she's fine."

"Bless her heart. Well, I wanted to tell you that I found where her mother is at."

"Where?"

"A rehabilitation center, about an hour away from here."

"How did you find that out?"

"My sister is there. I go there every now and then to check up on her. When I heard about Katherine and her parents, I asked my sister if she knew a Lee that's there. She knew exactly the woman I was talking about. They became friends."

"Could you write down the directions, please?"

"I sure can. You can take that young lady up there to see her mother."

"Thank you."

I wonder how Katherine will react. John thought. *Is she going to want to go up there to see her mother? IF she does, I'll be there for her. Her mother needs to see Katherine, anyway. She needs to know that her daughter is sick.*

The man wrote the directions and handed them to John. After the man left, John folded up the piece of paper and put it in his front pocket.

"That was nice of him to find out about Katherine's mother," Michael said out loud.

167

"Sure was. I'll tell Katherine about her mom when we get home."

"You think she'll go?"

"I don't know."

⸺

Katherine wasn't working at the flower shop today, so she decided to help Mary bake cookies and help her with a little yard work. The baking was easy, but planting flowers made Katherine tired. Midway through, she had to stop and take a break. She ended up sitting in the recliner in the living room for a good hour or so.

Mary tried to get Katherine to eat a sandwich for lunch, but she refused it. *I'm just not hungry.* Katherine thought. *I know that the Williams are trying to take care of me, but I wish they would slow down some. I'm not hungry. I do eat every day, even when I'm not hungry. They don't want me to do any chores either, but I keep telling them I want to. I enjoy it.*

When John and his dad walked in from work, they brought her and Mary into the living room.

"What's going on?" Mary asked.

John told Katherine about the guy that came into the store and told him about her mom.

"Do you want to go up there and see her?" John asked Katherine.

"I- I don't know," Katherine replied.

Do I want to see her? She and my dad treated me badly. I still remember how she would call me names and that one time when she pushed me outside and made me clean up the yard while it was dark out. On the other hand, though, she is my mother. She gave birth to me. She needs to know that I graduated and that I'm sick. Maybe I can talk to her about Christ. I know what I can do. I can give her a Bible. That's it. I'm going.

"Alright," Katherine said. "I'll go. Will you come with me? Please."

"Of course," John said. "When do you want to go?"

"Tomorrow morning. Can we stop somewhere so I can get her a Bible?"

"We sure can."

Katherine and John left around nine in the morning the next day. Katherine was so nervous about meeting her mother; she had to take a few deep breaths even before they left the house.

"Good luck." Mary and Michael told her.

"Thanks. I'm going to need it."

The weather was warm, of course. Instead of having the a/c on, Katherine had the window rolled down, enjoying the weather. The sun was shining and beaming down on the truck.

"How do I look?" she asked John. "Do I look okay? Should I have changed into something nicer?"

"You look amazing!" he said with a smile.

She was wearing a sky-blue dress and white flip-flops. She's been wearing more dresses than t-shirts and blue jeans. She would wear stretchy shorts and a tank top as pajamas when she would go to bed though. Her hair was in a ponytail, and she took her new orange purse with her. John bought it for her the other day and she fell in love with it.

Even though the rehab center was only an hour away, it felt like it took forever to get there. Before they went to the rehab center, they stopped by a Christian bookstore and bought a New Testament Bible for her mother.

I hope that she'll read it. I know that she didn't believe in Jesus before, but maybe she'll change her mind after reading this. I want her to get saved. She needs Jesus in her life. He can help turn her life around.

The rehabilitation center was large and white, with a large entrance. John parked and asked if she wanted him to come in with her.

"No," she said. "I feel that I should go in by myself."

She kissed him on the cheek and walked into the building. When she walked in, a woman immediately walked toward her with a smile. She had medium brown hair and was quite tall. She looked like she could be in her early thirties.

"Hello there!" the woman said. "How can I help you today?"

"I-I came to visit my mother. Her name is Sarah Lee."

"Oh, yeah, I know her. Come over here and sign the sheet. Then I can take you to her."

Katherine signed the guest sheet and followed the woman. There were windows in the hallway, so Katherine was able to see the activities that were allowed. They had a basketball court, tennis court, and even a pool. There was even a small park with benches where the patients could walk and enjoy the weather. There was also a room where people could paint and a lounge to chat and watch TV.

"What do you do here?" Katherine asked the woman.

"We help people get off drugs and try to help them to not want that stuff anymore. We have group therapy and activities."

Katherine didn't ask the woman anything else. They walked quietly to her mother's room.

The woman told Sarah that she had a visitor and left. Katherine walked in and saw her mother sitting by the window. When her mother saw it was her daughter, it shocked her.

"I didn't think you would ever come and see me," Sarah said, sounding surprised.

"Y-You're my mother. I had to see how you were doing. Are you doing alright?"

Sarah nodded. "I'm fine. Well, I'm better than I was. The first week was rough, but I made it."

"When can you leave here?"

"When they think I'm ready. That could be today or in a few months. How have you been?"

"I graduated high school, and I got saved."

Her mother looked confused. "Saved?"

"Yes. I'm a Christian now."

"Oh."

Her mother looked back at the window when Katherine said she was a Christian. Katherine could tell that her mother still didn't believe in Jesus. She handed her mom the Bible that she had bought for her.

"Why are you giving me this?" Sarah asked.

"Because you're lost. You may not know it now, but you will. I'm not sure if you will read it or not, but I'm hoping that you will."

Sarah sat the Bible down to the side and sighed.

"You know I don't believe in that stuff."

"I know."

"What else is going on?"

Katherine looked at her mother in the eyes. She didn't know how to tell her own mother that she's dying. She took a deep breath and told her.

"I'm dying," Katherine said. "I have cancer and the doctors said the tumor is too deep in my brain to get it out."

"Oh."

Sarah didn't say anything else. Katherine tried to talk to her some more, but her mother would just look out the window. She wouldn't say anything back. After about half an hour, Katherine told her mother goodbye and left.

Confession

It's been two weeks since Katherine went to see her mother in rehab. Katherine's eating habits haven't changed. She was still eating one meal a day with a small snack here and there. Mary and Michael began to pay her for doing chores every week. She would get twenty dollars every Friday. She tried to give the money back to them, but they wouldn't allow her to do so. Katherine gave up after the second week.

She has worked four days in the past two weeks. After working one morning, she ran into Holly's new worker. Her name is Amanda. She has medium length blonde hair and wears glasses. She is about Katherine's height and is working at the flower shop while she is home from college during the summer.

At first, it upset Katherine that Holly hired someone full time instead of Katherine. She didn't stay upset for too long though. Katherine knew that Holly had to find someone else.

One day, Katherine took Amanda out for lunch. She wasn't mad at her and wasn't going to call her bad names or anything. She just wanted to see what Amanda was like, and what she thought of Holly.

They went to The Drive-In restaurant that's out of town. It was only a couple of minutes away, so Amanda won't be late when she went back to the shop. Katherine ordered a simple hamburger with fries and a milkshake. Amanda ordered some boneless wings and a soda.

"How do you like working at the shop so far?" Katherine asked her.

"I love it!" Amanda said with a smile. "I love working with flowers. I'm hoping that I will have my own flower shop one day."

"I'm sure you will. How old are you?"

"Twenty."

"Do you go to church?"

"Definitely. I don't go to the one in your town though. I go to the one in the town next over."

"What do you think of Holly?"

"Oh, she's nice!"

"Yes, she is. She's a good friend of mine. She's still letting me work there every now and then."

"That's cool."

After talking some, Katherine began to really like Amanda. They both like the same singers and TV shows. Amanda liked to read Christian fiction novels. Mary and Michael bought Katherine a cell phone as a graduation present, so she was able to ask Amanda for her cell phone number. Katherine made a new friend that day.

Katherine paid for their lunch and Amanda dropped her at the Williams house before she went back to work. *That girl was nice.* Katherine thought. *She's cool, too. Maybe one day we can hang out and she could show me some books she likes to read.*

In the past two weeks, John had only worked five times at his dad's store. Four of those days were when Katherine worked at the flower shop. The fifth day was when Michael had a truckload of equipment that he needed help to unload. When John got paid, he bought Katherine a dozen roses and some chocolate. There wasn't a special occasion. He just wanted to buy her something.

Her face glowed when he handed her the roses. It was like she had received the greatest gift she had ever gotten. She kissed his cheek and thanked him.

"They are so beautiful!" she told him.

"Like you," He grinned.

It was now Wednesday, and it was Katherine's turn to pick what everyone would watch that night on tv. They decided that once or twice a week, someone would pick what to watch together. This week was Katherine's turn. She wanted to watch cop tv shows. Michael ordered two pizzas for everyone: pepperoni for Katherine and John and cheese pizza for himself and Mary.

I wonder how my mom is doing. Katherine thought to herself. *I haven't seen her in two weeks. I hope she's getting better. Hopefully, she's reading the Bible that John and I got for her. Does she talk to people about me when she's in group therapy? If so, then what does she say? Does she call me worthless and no good? I hope not, but that sounds like something she would say. Maybe reading about Jesus will help her have more positive thoughts.*

172

"I hope that my mom is doing better," Katherine said out loud.

"I'm sure she is," Mary said.

The pizza was delicious. Katherine didn't want to eat, but she forced herself to eat a couple of pieces to amuse the Williams. She knew that John would beg her to eat something. Just about every day, he would ask her if she was okay. She knew that he was just checking up on her to see if she had gotten any worse.

He's so caring and wonderful. I love him so much. He wrapped his arm around her while they watched tv. She loved having him cuddle her. It made her feel loved and safe.

Lord, thank You for bringing John into my life. He makes me so happy. He makes me laugh, too. Again, thank You. I'm blessed.

After a couple of episodes, Katherine was talking about the night that her parents were arrested. She was wondering how the police knew to come to her house. *Did someone call them?*

"Hey, John," She said to him. "How do you think the police knew to come to my parents' house?"

"I-I'm not sure," He mumbled.

"I mean, someone had to tell them what they were doing. About my dad beating me and my mom doing drugs."

"Probably. Do you want something to drink?"

"Yes, please. Sweet tea."

"One glass of sweet tea, coming right up."

"Let's not worry about the past," Mary told Katherine. "God sent those officers because He knew that you were in trouble. Let's enjoy the rest of the night."

"You're right. I'm sorry."

"No need to be sorry, dear. How are you feeling?"

"Fine."

She wasn't fine. Suddenly she felt like she had to vomit. When John came back with her drink, Katherine went upstairs to puke. She felt better afterward and drank her glass of tea. *Mary makes the best tea ever. I had some from the country restaurant and at the Drive-In. They weren't as good as Mary's.*

Everyone continued to watch the crime shows. The lights were now cut off and everyone was cuddling someone. Michael was holding his wife and John was holding Katherine. She didn't want that moment to end.

"You know," Katherine said as she looked at John. "Ever since my parents were arrested, I've been liking crime shows a lot."

"Why is that?" John asked.

"I'm not sure. Maybe I should go to the police station to see how they found out about my parents. I really want to know, John. Will you come with me?"

John had a worried look on his face. She could tell by his eyes that he wanted to tell her something but didn't know how.

She wants to go to the police station to find out how they knew about her folks. John said to himself. He was getting nervous now. *How do I tell her I'm the one who called the police? How would she react? Would she get mad at me? I only did what I thought God wanted me to do.*

"Katherine," he mumbled. "There's something-"

That's when Mary got the text message.

Before he could tell Katherine that it was he who called the police, his mother had received the text.

"Oh, no," Mary said. "Katherine, your old house is being torn down."

"What?" Katherine said with a confused look. "Why?"

"Apparently your folks owed a lot of money to the bank. They never paid anything. All they did was put loans on the house. They never paid the bank back. Now that your dad is in jail and your mom isn't there to take care of the place, the bank took the house back. They're going to tear it down and use the land for something else. I'm not sure what."

"Who told you that?" Michael asked her.

"Ashlyn. You know her from church. She sings a couple of songs to everyone once in a while."

"Oh yeah. I remember her now. Doesn't she have a little girl now?"

"Yep," She faced Katherine. "Anyway, I'm sorry."

"I-It's okay," Katherine said, looking down. "Do you know when they're supposed to knock it down?"

"They supposed to start this weekend."

"Do you want to go over there tomorrow and look at it one more time?" John asked her.

"I'm not sure," She replied in a quiet voice. "I had a lot of bad memories there. However, I lived there through most of my childhood. Sure, why not? Let's go tomorrow and see it one last time."

John gave her a hug, and she leaned her head on his shoulder. They watched one more crime show and went to bed.

Everyone was up early the next morning. It was around eight in the morning. Michael was almost done with his breakfast and was finishing his coffee before going to work. Mary was now cooking hers, Katherine's, and John's. The food smelled amazing, and John's stomach was growling as if he could eat a horse.

"Breakfast smells great, mom," He told his mother.

"I hope it tastes as good as it smells," She chuckled.

"It always does."

He already put on his short-sleeve red button-down shirt and blue jeans. The only thing left to do was to put on his tennis shoes. Katherine came down and was wearing a yellow dress with yellow flip-flops.

"Hey, sunshine," John told her. "You look lovely as always."

"Thanks," She said with a small grin.

"Are you ready?"

"I guess."

She made herself a cup of orange juice. Usually, she wouldn't eat breakfast, but today was different. Today she ate half of her plate. It surprised everyone that she ate at all, but they were glad she did.

Michael kissed Mary goodbye and left for work. Mary then washed the dishes after everyone finished eating. Then she walked upstairs to get ready for her job. John went upstairs and put on his shoes. He grabbed the truck keys and he and Katherine got into the truck and drove to her old house.

There was a small cloud in the distance, but it looked like it wasn't coming toward them. John parked the truck when they got there and opened the door for Katherine to get out.

The ground was dry, and the grass was tall as if it had not been mowed in months. John should have known since no one has lived there in a while. John and Katherine walked toward the house, holding each other's hands. She was squeezing his hand a little tight, but he didn't mind.

There was a storm last week that had strong winds. At one point there was a tornado warning. Everyone was alright though. No one was harmed.

Looking at the yard, there were beer bottles and cans spread all over. John figured that the storm blew them all over the place.

"I put all of those bottles and cans in a pile," Katherine told him. "I guess the storm blew them all over. I piled them all up in one night."

"Why?" he asked.

"My mom made me. She pushed me to the ground and made me clean the yard up."

"That's terrible!"

"Yeah. Then my dad drove in and hit my back with a belt."

"I'm so sorry."

"It's alright. It is in the past."

They walked into the house and the place looked disgusting. The police took most of the drugs, but they must have overlooked some because you could see a little bit lying around. There were beer bottles in most of the rooms, except for Katherine's. John could see where pieces of the ceiling fell onto the floor and formed a cross.

"God was watching over you." He said to her.

"Yes, He was. I'm so grateful."

The house smelt bad. No one was there to clean the place up. John was wondering if it was ever cleaned.

Has she lived in this filth her whole life? How long was it like this? The smell is horrific and there's dust all over the place. Bottles and needles all over the floor. I can't believe that she would sleep in this house.

After looking around, they walked outside.

"Katherine," John got her attention. "I have a confession."

"What is it, John? Is everything alright?"

He looked her straight in the eyes and gulped. "I-It was me. I'm the one who called the police."

She looked puzzled. "You?"

"Yes. I don't know why, but I had a feeling that I should call them. I believed it was God that told me to call the police. Please, don't be mad at me."

Katherine didn't look away or yell at him. She put her hand on his face and took a deep breath.

"I'm not mad, John. I understand. I'm glad you called them. I'm not sure if I would have made it through that night if you hadn't called the police. My dad was shooting a gun that night. He was super drunk. Thank you, John. This helps put my mind at ease."

"I love you so much."

"I love you too."

Suddenly, Katherine collapsed to the ground. She was drooling and was having uncontrollable muscle spasms. John could tell that she couldn't control what she was doing. She couldn't stop it.

John got down onto his knees and cried. He forgot that he had a cell phone with him. Tears were rolling down his cheeks like a waterfall. He knew what was going on. Katherine was having a seizure. Shortly after Katherine left the hospital, He looked up what could happen when someone had brain cancer. He also looked up what to do if someone were to have a seizure.

"K-Katherine," he sobbed. "S-Sweetie, if you can hear me, you're having a seizure. I-I'm going to roll you over onto your side, okay?"

Luckily, he put a tank top on under his button-down shirt that morning. He took off his shirt and folded it up, then laid it under Katherine's head.

There was nothing John could do, except watch. He continued to cry and prayed out loud.

"Father, please help her. She needs Your help. Help her get through this. Please, Lord. She needs You."

John wanted to put his hands on her head but was afraid to touch her. Dirt was covering her back and her arms and hands. John's tears were falling onto her face. He wanted her seizure to end. He wanted her to feel better. All he wanted to do right now, was to hold her, but he knew that he couldn't. It could hurt her.

"It'll be over soon," he told her. "Just hang in there. God is watching over you. Everything will be alright. I'm not leaving. I'm right here."

What felt like an eternity, was only two-and-a-half minutes. After her seizure, Katherine told him she felt tired and had a headache. John made her sit there on the ground and rest for a few minutes. Katherine wiped his tears away. He took her home and tucked her into bed.

After watching her sleep for a few minutes, he went downstairs and into the kitchen. *She is so beautiful. It was like watching an angel sleep. So peaceful. The thing is … I don't know when I will see her breathing for the last time.*

Tears ran down his face as he slammed his fist onto the kitchen table. He sat down and continued to cry. When his mom walked in, she saw her son crying and came over and wrapped her arms around him and gave him a hug.

A manager had come in to take her place for the day. They wanted some overtime; so, Mary left work early.

"I-I'm losing her," John sobbed.

"It's okay, dear," Mary told him in a soft tone. "Everything is going to be okay."

He wiped the tears away. "She had a seizure today. I had to watch her go through that."

"Shhh. Everything is alright. God has everything under control. She's in God's hands."

"There's nothing I can do, mom. Nothing, except to watch her struggle."

Mary put her hands on John's face and looked straight in his eyes. "There is something you can do. You can pray and be there for her. Do you understand? That's the best thing you can do. Take care of her. Help her around the house. Don't you love her?"

John nodded as more tears rolled down his face. "I'm in love with her so much."

"Then be there for her and pray for her."

Mary gave him another hug and left the room.

She's right. I'm going to slow down with the store, so I can be around Katherine more. Every now and then I can mow someone's yard for a little cash.

Visitation

I t's been about two weeks since Katherine's seizure. It was early July, and the weather was hotter than ever.

Since Katherine had her seizure, John noticed that she hadn't been eating much. She's still eating one full meal a day, but she has slowed down on the snacks. Katherine has been sleeping more and letting John help her with the chores, which worried him.

She's getting worse. He told himself. *She never allowed me to help her with the chores before. After that seizure, she's been resting more and not eating as much. After doing something like the laundry, she would go and sit down for an hour or so, saying she's tired and feeling weak.*

He also noticed that she hasn't been going to the flower shop as much. Out of the two weeks since her seizure, she has only gone to the shop twice. That's including today. Today is Thursday and John just got done mowing the neighbor's yard. He too had not been working at his dad's shop much. Since Katherine has been at home more, John has been spending more time with her. Every couple of days he would go around and mow someone's yard to earn a little money.

A couple of days ago he bought Katherine a stuffed panda. Her eyes grew with excitement. She told him she would jump for joy, but she wasn't feeling too well. She gave him a hug though and thanked him. John has also been asking about five times a day if she's feeling alright. Every time he would ask, she would tell him she's okay. Mary and Michael have been asking her the same question every day, too.

He remembered shortly after her seizure, she said she had a headache and was feeling exhausted. John read that someone would usually feel that way after they had a seizure.

Why is she not terrified? She seems perfectly calm about this whole thing. I know that if I had a seizure, I would have been scared and crying. It hurt me to watch her go through that. There was nothing I could have done.

For the next two Sundays, while at church, John and Katherine would go up at the end and pray with the pastor. For John, it felt like they were stronger when they would pray together. They were still reading the Bible together every night.

Once during church, John thought about how brave Katherine was. *I could never be as brave as her. If I was going through what she is going through, I would have a breakdown. Actually, I would have multiple breakdowns. Look at her! So calm. She knows that Jesus is with her, so she has nothing to worry about. Bless her.*

About now, everyone in town knew about Katherine's sickness. Everyone at church has been giving her hugs and saying they were praying for her. Every now and then someone would come by the house and bring Katherine some cookies or something. She would thank them every time.

John just finished mowing his neighbor's yard and after resting for a few minutes, John put the mower up and the neighbor paid him.

"Thank you, sir," He told the man.

"Tell Katherine that I'm praying for her," The neighbor said.

John went into the house and sat in front of the air conditioner. *I don't know how much time Katherine has left, and I still haven't taken her camping. You know what? I'm going to plan that right now! She said she has always wanted to go camping, and I'm going to make her wish come true.*

Some people would rather travel the world, or go skydiving, or even go scuba diving. Not Katherine, though. She just wanted to go camping. John got on to the computer and browsed around for some camping spots close to home.

After about an hour, he believed that he found the perfect place. He wrote the directions down and went to the garage to make sure that his dad had everything they would need. He did. *I will make sure that Katherine will have the best time of her life!*

When Katherine got home from the shop, John gave her a tight hug and told her he loved her.

"I love you too," She said back. "What's going on?"

"Well," John said with a smile on his face. "We are going to go camping next month. How does that sound?"

"Oh wow! Really?"

"Yep. I found the perfect place. It's about a few minutes east of where your mom is at. We can go fishing and swimming. We can roast marshmallows and hotdogs too."

Watching Katherine's face light up brought happiness to John. She gave him a hug as tight as she could, which wasn't much. He hugged her back and kissed her on the cheek.

"I want you to have the best time of your life next month."

"Any time I spend with you is a wonderful time." She told John.

"Oh, and we can lie under the stars as well. So, it'll be romantic."

I just now remembered something. She went to see her mom. What about her dad? Doesn't she want to go visit him? Maybe I should ask, but before he could ask her about her dad, she asked him first.

"Could you drive me to go see my dad?" she asked him.

"Of course. Anything for you."

○

It was Thursday, and the sun was beaming down. She couldn't explain it, but the hot July weather was making Katherine more tired. It has been a couple of weeks since her seizure, and since then, she hasn't been eating as much. She knows that John notices, too. She would just tell him that she is not as hungry anymore. Sure, she would still eat one large meal a day, but she no longer was eating snacks. She also has been more tired. After her seizure, John took her home and let her sleep. She ended up sleeping through the rest of the day and all night. Now she is even letting John help her with the chores. Katherine didn't like it, but she was getting tired and weak too easily and she couldn't do everything by herself now.

With her being more tired, she doesn't show up at the flower shop as much. Thankfully, Holly is still letting her work there when she does show up. Most of the time now, she's sitting in the recliner and watching tv or reading. She's happy that John and her are still reading the Bible together every night. Reading the Bible together before going to bed puts her at ease.

Katherine wasn't terrified when she had the seizure. She was, however, confused. She didn't know what was going on with her body. On the way home, John told her what happened to her. He told her everything that he knew about seizures. Everything was clear now. If it happened again, she would know what it was.

John bought her a stuffed animal the other day, and she sleeps with it every night. It was a little childish, but that didn't matter to her.

Now she was in the green room, taking care of the flowers. Holly wouldn't allow her to help up front with the customers. She said it would be too stressful, and Katherine wouldn't be able to handle it. Katherine knew that Holly was just looking out for her.

An hour before Katherine was supposed to get off work, Amanda came in. Instead of telling Katherine that she could go ahead and leave, Amanda gave her a hand. Work wasn't boring anymore. Now Katherine had someone to talk to. Amanda wouldn't stay in the back for long though since Holly wanted her to help with the customers.

The flowers smelled nice, and it helped Katherine relax. When Amanda would come back to the greenhouse, she and Katherine would talk. Usually about movies or music.

"How are you feeling?" Amanda asked.

"I'm alright, I guess," Katherine answered.

Everyone would keep asking Katherine how she was feeling. She knew that they were just worried and being nice, but sometimes she wished they wouldn't ask her that five times a day. She wasn't going to ask them to stop, though. They were just concerned and keeping an eye out for her.

With half an hour left before Katherine would clock out, she sat down and rested. Now she was wondering about her dad. She went to see her mom but hasn't thought about her dad in a while.

Should I go see him? She asked herself. *He beat me until I bled, and he always scared me. I should still go visit him though. He is my dad. Maybe he changed after being away from so much alcohol.*

"Katherine?" Holly said as she sat down next to her. "Is everything alright?"

"Yes. I was just thinking about my dad. I went to see how my mom was doing, but never visited my dad."

"Oh. Well, maybe you should go to see him. I'm sure he's wondering what happened with his daughter."

"I don't know. Maybe. Shouldn't he be out of jail by now?"

"My friend told me he had a good bit of warrants, so he'll be in there for a while. Maybe the rest of the year."

Katherine continued working until it was her time to leave. Amanda volunteered to take her home.

Before she left the store, she could hear Holly behind her. "See you later! Good luck with your dad!"

Katherine waved her goodbye. On the way home, Amanda told her she had fun working with her. Katherine agreed. She thanked Amanda for the ride and went inside.

What would I say to my dad? How would I tell him I have cancer? I guess I'll find out when I go see him. Hopefully, John will take me there.

John told her they were going camping next week, and that made her so excited that she forgot about her dad for a brief moment. When she remembered, she asked him if he could take her to go see her dad and he agreed.

The next day, Katherine put on a short-sleeve shirt and blue jeans. Most of the time she would wear a dress, but every now and then she would wear something different. Today she wanted to wear her orange shirt that had a Bible verse on it. It was her favorite.

'Live by faith, not by sight.'

She walked downstairs and saw that John was already waiting for her.

"Are you ready beautiful?" he asked.

"Not really, but I know that I have to do this."

They got in the truck and drove to the jailhouse. It was between their town and the next one over. It wasn't that large because both towns had small populations. He parked when they got there, and Katherine said she wanted to go in by herself.

She followed the procedure and walked to one of the glass windows that had holes in them. A couple of minutes passed by and then she saw her dad. He came over and sat down on the other side of the window. He looked different. He had a beard and was wearing glasses.

"Look who it is." He said in a deep voice. "My daughter. What are you doing here?"

She didn't know what to say at first, but eventually mumbled, "Hi dad."

"Speak up, I can't hear that well anymore."

She spoke louder. "Hi, dad. How are you doing?"

"I'm in jail and I have to wear glasses now. What does that tell you? What are you doing here?"

"I wanted to come and see you."

"Why? I don't want to see you. I have nothing to say."

Even without alcohol, he is still mean. I guess he will never change. At least he looks healthier. I never knew that he needed glasses. He actually looks better with them. Even though he's still his same mean self, I will still talk to him.

"I just wanted to see how you were doing. You are my dad after all. Plus, I wanted to say that I forgive you, after all the stuff you did to me. Beating with the belt."

"Oh," he mumbled. "Okay. Is that all?"

"I'm saved now. I have Christ in my life now."

He chuckled. "Now you're one of those Christians? You're not going to preach me a sermon, are you?"

"No."

He still doesn't like Christians. Why? I don't know. I should ask, but not going to. No. I want to know.

"Why do you hate Christians, dad? Do you hate God?"

"What has God ever done for me? He gave me a horrible wife and a useless daughter."

She wanted to cry but held back the tears. Katherine took a deep breath.

"I also wanted to tell you that I'm dying."

Kenny sighed. "With what?"

"Cancer. I have a tumor in my brain. The doctors can't take it out though, because it's too deep."

"Well, I suggest you go party as much as you can. What am I thinking? Go pray to your God. Are we done now?"

"I-I mailed you a present."

"A present? What is it?"

"It's a surprise. Well, I guess I'll go." Katherine got up and faced her dad one last time, with a tear running down her cheek. "I love you, dad."

"Whatever," He mumbled.

Katherine walked out, never to see her dad again.

Another Great Sunday

I t was Sunday morning in the middle of August. John was wearing his white button-down shirt with blue jeans. It was the same outfit he wore on the day he and Katherine became friends. He combed his hair and put on his church shoes. He got them polished yesterday. As usual, he had the curtains pulled open. The sun was shining and once again, not a cloud in the sky.

John woke up a little early so he could shower and shave. With a little extra time to spare, he sat down at this desk and wrote in his journal. He hasn't written in it in a while.

Today is the day I'm going to take Katherine camping. She said that's the one thing she has always wanted to do, so today I'm making that wish come true. It looks beautiful outside and since it's August, I'm sure it will be hot. Church comes first though. I wonder what the pastor will preach about today. I'm not going to write much more. I hope that Katherine will enjoy her day today and have a blast.

After he finished writing, he put his journal and pen up. Then he walked downstairs and waited for Katherine to finish getting ready. He took a sausage and biscuit that his mother made and ate it. It was delicious, as always. Sometimes he would put jelly on it, but not today.

Katherine walked downstairs, and John couldn't believe how amazing she looked. She was wearing a white dress with white heels. Her hair was in a ponytail and she was wearing red lipstick. Even without the lipstick, she would have looked stunning.

"Wow!" John said. "You look unbelievable."

Katherine blushed. "Thank you."

Everyone got in the truck and drove off. Michael was playing <u>Mercy Me</u> on the way to church again. Everything seemed familiar that morning. John and his parents were wearing the exact same clothes they wore on the day that Katherine came into their lives. The same band and song were being played too. Today, however, the weather was hotter and this time Katherine would be coming along with them, instead of running into the church.

He turned his head and looked at her. She seemed energetic that morning. He couldn't explain why though. Maybe she was just excited about camping. Who knows? Either way, John was glad she had so much energy. It's been a while since he saw her like that. She's been smiling ever since he saw her walking down the stairs. It's a nice change. John wanted her to be like that for a while. Ever since graduation, it seems like everyone was gloomy. Today everyone, including John and Katherine, are happy and in a terrific mood.

"Are you excited about today?" John asked Katherine.

"Sure am!" she said with an excited tone. Almost like a shriek. Her eyes went wide and even a bigger smile formed.

He took her hand and held it until they got to the church. He still loves holding her hand. It makes him feel more connected to her. Katherine sang along to the music. Once she started, everyone else joined her. Mary and Katherine did a small dance in the car. John just watched and smiled.

When they got to the church, everyone greeted them with a smile and a handshake. The Williams and Katherine weren't the only ones in a great mood. It seemed like everyone that came to church was having a pleasant morning as well. So many people were laughing and being cheerful. Joy was in the air and it was about to get even better.

Church has now started, and the pastor was preaching about negativity and positivity.

"Don't worry about the negativity in your life!" Pastor Bill preached. "Satan is trying to bring you down with negativity! He's trying to bring you to his level. Instead, enjoy what God has blessed you with. Be thankful for what you have received! Inhale the positive and exhale the negative. Don't let evil ruin your life. Be happy. Be joyful. Be thankful."

He's right. John said to himself. *Instead of worrying about Katherine's sickness, I should enjoy the time that I have left with her. Instead of worrying about when she's going to leave, I should be thankful that I can still spend time with her. I shouldn't focus on her cancer. I should focus on making her happy and smile.*

He turned his head and looked at her again. *Look at her! She's still smiling. She's not worried about her tumor. She's just glad she came to church,*

186

and she's enjoying this beautiful day. I need to be like that. You know what? I am! I'm not going to worry about her sickness. Today, I'm just going to be thankful that I can spend time with her and enjoy the rest of the day.

He looked up and whispered. "Thank You, Father."

Once church was over, everyone went back to the house and got changed. John was now wearing a red short-sleeve shirt with black stretchy shorts. Katherine changed into blue jeans shorts and a purple short-sleeve shirt. They both put on flip-flops.

Now John was loading everything in the back of the truck. First were the tents. One for him and one for Katherine. Katherine called dibs on the orange tent so that means John would have to sleep in the green one. Then there was the fishing poles and the food. His mother bought them marshmallows and hotdogs to roast. Then there was the cooler filled with drinks. John and Katherine stocked up on sodas and bottles of water and made sure there was plenty of ice in the cooler. Katherine made sure she brought sunscreen, bug spray, and blankets. Michael made sure they brought sleeping bags and lawn chairs. Everything was now ready to go.

"You kids have fun now," Mary said as she hugged both of them.

"We will." They said.

Katherine gave Michael a hug and got into the truck. Mary made them sandwiches to eat before they left, but Katherine was ready to go. She was so excited that she made John wait to eat his lunch until they would get to the lake. John told his parents goodbye one more time and then drove off.

Instead of having the air conditioner on, John and Katherine rolled down the windows. They were enjoying the weather and the small road trip.

The sun was beaming down on them and John was already sweating. He still couldn't believe that Katherine was still energetic. She was playing the radio in the truck and dancing along with the music. *Today sure is a blessing. I love seeing her like this. Dancing. Smiling. Happy. It's nice. Thank You, Lord, for this day. I pray that we get to the lake safely and that we will enjoy the rest of the day. Amen.*

"I liked today's sermon," Katherine said while she was jamming to the radio.

"Me too," he looked at her and grinned. "You are so cute."

"Even though I'm enjoying this sunshine, I hope that we will have a bit of shade."

"I'm sure we will."

"We didn't forget anything did we?"

"Not that I know of."

Katherine looked over to John with a large smile. "I love you."

"I love you too." He smiled back.

—⊙—

They got to the campsite and saw that there weren't many people around. In the distance, a good bit away across the lake, you could see a small boat with people in it. Besides that, John and Katherine were the only ones there.

Before unloading the truck, John and Katherine ate the lunch that Mary made for them. They pulled the tailgate down and sat on it, enjoying the sandwiches and the weather. They had a little shade, so they wouldn't have to be in the heat all day and get too hot.

"This place is beautiful!" Katherine said out loud.

She looked around, observing the area. The water in the lake was as calm as it could be. If she looked hard enough, she could see small bubbles forming on the surface of the water. *That must be the fish,* she thought. Trees surrounded the area, along with a few bushes. However, there was shade only on one side. That was enough, though. At the edge of the lake, there was grass that was almost knee-high.

They finished their lunch and unloaded the truck. While John took out the big stuff like the cooler and the tents, Katherine handled the small load. She sat the lawn chairs in the shade for now and put the bag of sunscreen and such beside the chairs. They both put up the tents. It wasn't that difficult, but Katherine gave John a hand, anyway.

The tents were of average size. Enough for one person to sleep in each of them. Katherine grabbed the sleeping bags and put them in each of their tents. She inhaled the fresh air.

"I'm loving camping already!" she said with a cheer. "We just got here too."

John chuckled. "Well, I'm glad that you are."

"Let's go swimming! Please, please, please!"

"Alright. Sounds like a good idea to me."

They changed clothes in their tents and ran straight toward the lake. John jumped in first, and then Katherine. The water was a little cold, but she got used to it quickly. She looked to see if the boat was still around, but it wasn't.

Katherine could feel the fish nibbling at her toes. It didn't hurt, but it sure tickled. She giggled and dove under the water to see if she could see the fish. They swam away once she was underwater.

When she rose, she splashed John.

"Oh, it's going to be like that, huh?" he said while laughing.

He splashed her back, and she laughed. After splashing each other for a few minutes, they got out and grabbed two blankets from the truck. They laid them down near the lake and laid down, enjoying the rays.

It sure is peaceful out here. Katherine thought. *Quiet.* Every now and then, she would hear birds chirping in the distance. She dozed off for a couple of minutes before John woke her up. *I sure was relaxed. So far, camping is so much fun! I wonder what we're going to do next.*

"Are you having fun so far?" she asked John.

"Of course." He replied. "We need to put sunscreen on before we turn into lobsters."

Katherine laughed and went to grab the sunscreen. They put some on, along with bug spray. After about a half an hour, they got up and sat in the lawn chairs that were in the shade.

"What's next on the camping to-do list?" she asked.

"Fishing."

"I haven't done that since the day I went with you and your dad."

"Yea, it's been a while. Do you remember how to fish?"

"I think so, but I may need to be reminded."

"No problem. I'll show you after we sit here for a while. The weather is extra hot today. I think it's supposed to reach one hundred degrees today."

"I'm fine with that."

They talked for another two hours and then John went to get the fishing poles. Luckily, he remembered to stop by a store on the way to the lake and bought bait. He put the line on each fishing rod and showed her how to put the bait on the hook. She got it on the first try. Then they moved the chairs closer to the lake but made sure they were still under the shade. John carried the cooler and put it between the two of them.

He then showed her how to cast the line into the water. Again, she got it on her first try. Now they waited for a bite. Katherine grabbed a soda from the cooler and enjoyed the refreshing drink. After a few minutes, Katherine's fishing pole tugged.

She stood up and reeled the fish in. It was a decent size, and John congratulated her on the catch. John caught a good size fish as well.

"Are you ready to have fish for supper?" he asked.

"I don't have to watch do I?"

John chuckled. "No, you don't have too."

John told her that his dad taught him how to gut a fish a week before the camping date. While John gutted the fish, Katherine read a chapter of her Bible. She hasn't gone a day without reading it ever since John bought it for her.

After reading a chapter or two, she smelt John cooking the fish on the grill he brought. It smelt delicious, and it was making her stomach growl. *I can't believe that I'm hungry. I also can't believe that I have so much energy today. Usually, I'm tired and would have to rest a few times, but today is different. Today I feel good and not exhausted. I don't feel weak. God has truly blessed this day.*

Katherine stared at the clear blue sky and said, "Thank You, Lord."

Fish wasn't the only thing they had that day. Mary and Michael made food for them too, just in case they didn't catch anything. Along with the fish, they had coleslaw and egg salad. All of it tasted amazing.

"You sure can cook fish," She told him.

"Thank you. My dad can sure make some great egg salad."

"He sure can."

"Tonight, we can build a campfire and roast some marshmallows. How does that sound?"

"Sounds like a plan! I never had roasted marshmallows before."

"Never? Well, you're in for a treat."

They watched the sunset, and John made themselves a campfire. The stars were popping out in the night sky and so was the moon. John grabbed some pitchforks and showed her what to do. Katherine burned the first marshmallow but got the second one just right. After having some marshmallows, they roasted a few hotdogs.

After they ate, John put the small fire out and they laid on their blankets, staring at the bright night sky. The stars were shining as bright as ever, along with the moon.

"The night sky is beautiful tonight, don't you think?" Katherine asked.

"Sure is. Did you enjoy today?"

"Yes, I did. I had a wonderful time. Not just fishing and all the other stuff, but that I could do all of it with you. Thank you, John. Today was perfect."

"Anything for you. I'm glad you had an exciting time."

"So, what's next?"

"Next, we just lay here and relax. Enjoy the night sky and then we can do our nightly Bible reading."

"Sounds like a plan."

I had such a fun day today. I went fishing, swimming, and had fish that John cooked. Church was good, too. I agree with the pastor. We shouldn't worry about the negative and evil things that go on. We should just focus on the stuff that God has blessed us with.

"Today was a good Sunday," John said randomly.

"No," Katherine told him with a huge smile on her face. "Today was a great Sunday."

Peace

I t's been a few days since the camping trip. Katherine had a blast. One of the best times of her life. She could have stayed up all night to look at the stars. Eventually, she went to sleep in her tent.

Now it was a sunny afternoon and Katherine was at the pond. The pond where she fished for the first time with John and his dad. The pond she would bathe in when she used to live with her parents. She saw bubbles forming from the surface of the pond a few feet away.

Everything was quiet around her. Every few minutes or so, she would hear birds chirping or a chipmunk talking to one of its friends. Once she even heard a woodpecker. No one else was around. No screaming. No machinery. Just silence, with a noise coming from nature every now and then.

Katherine was sitting on the grass with a white dress on and white flip-flops. There wasn't a breeze, so the water was as calm as ever. She watched a grasshopper for a few minutes until it was so far that she couldn't see it anymore.

For John, the heat would have been too much for him. However, for Katherine, it felt nice against her skin. For her, it wasn't too hot. It felt just right. She looked up, and like most of the time, there wasn't a cloud in the sky. Just an ocean of blue with a sun bearing down on her.

Such a beautiful day today. She thought. *So calm and peaceful. I could sit here all day with no worries.*

She wondered how her dad was doing, and if he enjoyed the gift she sent him. *Maybe I should go see him again. No. Everyone has been so busy lately and I don't think he would even talk to me. I know that he was mean to me, but I forgive him, and I hope that one day, he will find Christ.*

Her mom has been in rehab for quite some time now. She hasn't seen her in a while either. Hopefully, Sarah was reading the Bible that Katherine got for her. *I hope that she's doing okay.* Katherine thought about going to visit her again, but the trip was far and lately Katherine has been feeling more tired as usual.

Now, she was thinking of what everyone was doing today. Michael and John were at the shop. Michael had a new truckload he needed help with. They finally got someone to fix the air conditioner in the store.

Mary has been doing great with her job. She just got a raise. *Maybe she could let me come by one day and show me what she does. That would be cool. Mary is such a nice lady. Maybe after my mother gets out, she and Mary could talk. Maybe even convince my mom to come to church one Sunday.*

She thought Michael could even try to get her dad to come to church, but that seemed highly unlikely. *I pray that one day he will change.*

Katherine didn't know how long she was out there. She knew that she left shortly after lunchtime. Her phone was beside her on the ground, but she didn't want to touch it. She didn't want to be around any technology. She wanted to enjoy the plants and animals that God created. Eventually, there was a small breeze, and it felt nice.

Katherine had left the flower shop. Left as in no longer working there. She enjoyed working there, but it was time to go. Holly didn't fire her or anything. Katherine left on her own. After trying to work Tuesday, she realized that she couldn't keep up the pace anymore. She was too tired and had to sit down longer than usual. That evening she told Holly that she had to quit the job at the shop.

"Are you sure?" Holly asked her. "I know that you love working here."

"I'm sure. I just can't keep up anymore."

"Well, alright. How about this? I can give you a fifty percent off discount."

Katherine knew that Holly was just feeling bad for her.

"No, thanks," Katherine answered. "That's generous of you though. I hope that you will continue to do great with the shop."

"Thank you. It was nice to have you working here, Katherine. Don't tell Amanda, but you're the best worker I've ever had."

Katherine chuckled. "Thanks. Bye."

Katherine then went to the back and gave Amanda a hug. After telling her she was leaving, Amanda told her she would be missed.

"I heard that college has started again this year," Katherine told her. "Good luck with that."

"Thank you."

Katherine waved goodbye and walked out of the shop. She couldn't work anymore, and now she couldn't even do chores. When she would try to do them, she would have to stop and take a breather three or four times. Carrying the laundry basket alone took her five or ten minutes to get from the laundry room upstairs. Eventually, after watching her take too long with the other chores, Mary and Michael made her stop. They told her to rest and to take it easy.

At the house, she would now just watch tv or read. She even had time to think about John's problem. She knew that he was searching for his gift, but now she thought he was taking a break from it. After a few days, she finally figured out what he should do with his life. However, with John being busier at the hardware store, she didn't have time to tell him.

Before leaving the house to go to the pond, she grabbed her Bible. She figured that since it's so peaceful there, she could read a chapter or two. The Bible was the only book she would read now. She read one or two detective books that Amanda let her borrow, but that was about it.

Katherine remembered when John told about the sky being God's canvas. Now she figured that everything is His canvas, not just the sky. Everything from the galaxies to the plants and animals, to the tiny grains of sand that you see on the beach. He painted all of it. He created all of it. So beautiful. So amazing.

I wonder what Heaven is like. Is it anything as beautiful as the view I have right now? What am I saying? Of course, it is! The best part is that Jesus will be there.

It was so quiet that when her cell phone rang, it made her jump. She was so relaxed and was having such a peaceful time. The caller ID said it was John who was calling.

John. I miss him. I know that he's been around, but it seems like he's been at the store more now than before.

She answered the phone. "Hello?"

John was on the other line. "Hey there! Where are you?"

"I'm at the pond. Why?"

"I was able to come home early, and you weren't here. I hoped that we could spend some time together. I miss you."

She missed him, too. Katherine just now realized that there was a sunset. It was gorgeous. The sky turned pink and orange. Only an artist could make a sight so beautiful.

"I miss you too," Katherine replied.

"I thought we could go to that country restaurant. If that's okay."

"Sounds good to me."

While watching the sunset, she had a feeling she didn't have much time left. She wasn't going to be around much longer, and she wanted to spend as much time with John as she could. Katherine couldn't explain it, she just knew. She took a deep breath and watched as the sun disappeared behind the horizon.

"Hey, John," Katherine said.

"Yeah?"

"I love you so much. I thank God that He brought you into my life."

"I thank Him for bringing YOU into my life. I love you too. Do you want me to come and pick you up?"

She tried to picture heaven one last time but failed. No matter what she thought, she knew that it would be even better than that.

"No. I'm coming home."

GoodBye

It was September first, and Katherine woke up from a good night's sleep that morning. It was eight in the morning. Something was different about today than most days. Today was her birthday. She turned eighteen that day. However, her birthday is no big deal to her. Her parents never celebrated her birthday before. Not once has she had a birthday party or presents or even one person to tell her a happy birthday. Eventually, she got used to the fact that no one cared about her birthday. She told John and his parents, but she doubted they would do or say anything about it.

Katherine got up and walked over to the window like she does every day. After pulling the curtains, a ray of sunshine came through the window. In the distance, you could see a small cloud or two. However, it's supposed to be sunny all day, so she wouldn't be seeing many clouds. The two she saw that morning will probably be the only ones out that day.

She wasn't feeling weak, but she also wasn't feeling energetic either. She wasn't sure how she was feeling. Normal, she guessed.

It looks lovely outside today. She said to herself. *What do I want to do today? Hang out at the pond again? Go check up on Holly and the shop? I'm not sure.*

Katherine didn't bother changing her pajamas with rabbits on them. She went ahead and walked down the stairs and into the kitchen. The food smelled amazing, like always. She wasn't hungry, but she'll eat something, anyway. After making herself a cup of orange juice, she sat down at the kitchen table.

Mary was still wearing her pajamas, just like Katherine. Mary was wearing pink pajama pants with a pink short-sleeve shirt to go with it. Her cooking is the best cooking that Katherine has ever had. Mary's hair was combed nicely, and she had a smile on her face. Of course, Mary usually smiles all the time. Why wouldn't she? She has a great husband and a caring son.

Then there was Michael. He was sitting at the end of the table, reading the newspaper while drinking his coffee. He liked his coffee black. No sugar or cream, which Katherine wouldn't be able to drink. She would have to have both for her to drink coffee. His hair was already slicked back, and he was already dressed for work. He was wearing blue jeans and a blue button-down shirt that was tucked in. He was a terrific man. He was tough, but when you needed him, he would turn into the most caring person on the planet. He's also the spiritual leader of the family. He would always pray for them and when things get tough, he would pray to God for guidance, no matter where he was at.

John walked in a few minutes after Katherine. He was wearing the same clothing that his dad was wearing. That would happen every now and then. John and Michael would wear the same clothes on the same day. It doesn't always happen. They don't do it on purpose either. It happens randomly.

John was looking handsome as ever. He had his hair combed, and his shirt was also tucked in. Katherine loved John very much. She was in love with him. If it wasn't for him, she would probably never have found Jesus. He was the one who invited her to go fishing with him and his dad on that one Sunday morning. He gave her a Bible and eventually they became boyfriend and girlfriend. He's so caring and kind. She never met a person like him. When they read the Bible every night together, she would feel closer to him. Like they were growing stronger together. Katherine couldn't have asked for a better boyfriend.

John fixed a plate for her like he does every morning. Most of the time she wouldn't eat it, but she ate that morning. Mary cooked eggs, bacon, pancakes, and ham. It was delicious, of course. It surprised everyone when she ate breakfast.

"Are you feeling alright?" Michael asked. "You never eat breakfast."

"I'm fine," Katherine replied.

Was she fine? She wasn't sure. Something was telling her she had to spend the day with John and his parents. She couldn't explain it.

They're like family. Forget that, they are my family. Michael is like the dad I never had. He's always been there for me and looking out for me. I could always talk to Mary about girl stuff, especially when I wasn't comfortable talking to Holly about it. Mary is like a mother to me. Michael didn't drink, and Mary never laid a finger on drugs. They're like the parents I have always wanted and needed.

Holly is like a cousin or a sister. I'm not sure which. I don't think it matters though. Maybe I should go talk to her someday and see how she's doing with the shop. I text her every now and then, but I want to see her in person. She's cool to hang around with.

Would Michael, Mary, and John even take a day off from work for me? I doubt it, but it wouldn't hurt to ask. I feel like I should spend one whole day with them. Or at least a dinner or something.

"Um …" Katherine mumbled. "C-Could you guys take the day off?"

All three looked up at her.

"Why's that?" Mary asked.

"I can't explain it, but I feel like we all should spend some time together. You don't have to. I just think it's important and I understand if you can't."

They looked at each other and then back to her.

John grinned. "Sure! We can do that. What are you wanting to do?"

"I'm not sure. Maybe we could go out to eat or play some games."

"Sounds like a good idea to me," Michael said without hesitation.

"Me too," Mary answered.

"Me three," John agreed.

I can't believe that they will actually take the day off for me! They always seem to surprise me in some way or another. Why are they all smiling though? It's like they're up to something.

"How does that country restaurant sound?" John asked. "I've been craving their food for the past few days."

"Sounds great," Katherine replied.

Before they left for lunch at the restaurant, Katherine picked out what to wear. The white dress has become her favorite, and she wore it that day. It was that or the polka-dotted dress. She then braided her hair and put on the white heels she wears a lot when she goes out of the house.

There was a knock at the door. "Can I come in?" John asked.

"Yes, you can."

John walked in. "We're ready when you are, gorgeous."

"Yeah, I guess I'm ready. Thank you for taking the day off."

"No problem. We haven't hung out all together like this in a while. I'm glad you suggested it."

Katherine was in for a surprise.

It was Katherine's birthday today, and John and his parents had planned a dinner party. They have been planning it for the past week and have tried to decide on what presents to get her. The day ended up being better than John expected. Katherine suggested that they should spend all day together. He didn't know what made her want to do it, but it was easier than having him and his parents try to come up with a reason to get her out to celebrate her birthday.

The weather was supposed to be sunny all day, which was happy weather for John. Sure, there was a cloud or two in the distance, but that should be alright. Just as long as they don't block the sun. There wasn't a breeze, and the sun was beaming down on him. The warm air was comfortable and made him feel relaxed.

Katherine, surprisingly, ate breakfast that morning. It shocked him and his parents, but they were glad she was finally eating something. For the past week or so, it seemed like she wasn't eating at all.

John hid her gift under the seat at the kitchen table the other day. Getting it out without her noticing would be a challenge, but he knew that he could hide it from her. They went to the country restaurant for lunch and when they got there, Michael pretended that he wanted to talk to John in private, so they let Mary and Katherine go to the restaurant. John covered the gift with his jacket and they walked in and sat down across the table. Michael and John were sitting on one side, and the girls were sitting on the other.

"Why did you bring your jacket?" Katherine asked curiously.

"It gets cold in here sometimes," John replied.

He was trying to stay calm. He didn't want her to suspect anything out of the ordinary.

Mary ordered herself some pork chops, with mashed potatoes and macaroni and cheese. Her food smelt so good that it made everyone's mouth water. She had water with lemon as her drink.

Michael had a soda. He was craving a thick juicy steak with a baked potato. The steak was well done, and he had to have a lot of butter with his potato. John and Mary thought it was too much, but that didn't stop Michael. The steak was his favorite thing to eat at that restaurant. He would always order it, and nothing else.

Katherine had a normal cheeseburger with fries. She wanted extra pickles on her burger. She had a sweet tea with lemon. John heard her stomach growl a few times before her food finally got there.

"Someone's hungry," he said as he looked at her with a smile.

"A little," She replied.

Lastly, John ordered his catfish with fries. Nothing too special. He also had a sweet tea.

I can't wait to see the look on her face when we surprise her. He said to himself. I love watching her face glow.

Michael prayed for the food and they dug in. Everyone was enjoying their food. Especially Katherine, even though she was taking longer than everyone else to eat.

"So, Katherine, I understand that you turn eighteen today," Michael said to her.

"Y-Yes, sir," She answered.

"Well, we all have something to say to you about that."

"W-What?"

Everyone stared at her with huge grins and yelled, "HAPPY BIRTHDAY!"

Katherine covered up her mouth with her hands, looking shocked.

"What's going on?" she asked, sounding confused.

"We've been planning your birthday for the past week," Mary told her.

"Really?"

"Yep! We already had the day off today. We couldn't come up with a story, so you wouldn't get suspicious. We care about you, dear. You're like the daughter that Michael and I never had."

"I-I don't know what to say."

John grabbed the box and handed it to her. "I bought you a present."

"Thank you!" Katherine said with a tear running down her cheek.

The present was a hoodie that had her favorite Bible verse on it.

"I had it specially made for you," John said. "I hope you like it."

"I love it!"

She ended up telling them how no one has ever celebrated her birthday before. Not a present or dinner, no one even told her a simple 'happy birthday'. Katherine ended up crying with tears of joy. John never enjoyed seeing her cry, even if they were tears of joy. At that moment, though, he was just glad to see her so happy.

Lunch started at eleven and ended at twelve-thirty. Katherine had a great time. He could see it in her eyes she enjoyed her birthday surprise. Since it was her birthday, they let her choose the next activity. All she wanted was to watch a movie together as a family.

She didn't last five minutes through the movie until she told John that she was feeling tired and would take a nap.

"Can you wake me up when the movie is over?" she asked.

"Sure."

"I'm sorry."

"It's okay. I know that you're not feeling well. I'll miss you."

He gave her a hug and a kiss on the forehead.

I still can't believe that she never had her birthday celebrated. Well, I'm glad I was able to help her feel what it's like to have a birthday. I love her so much. If I could, I would just hold her all day and never let her go. She is truly amazing.

When the movie was over, John walked upstairs and knocked on her door. When she didn't answer, he knocked harder again, but still no answer.

"Katherine?" he said as he knocked one more time.

When she failed to answer the third time, he opened her door and walked right in. He rarely does that, but he had a bad feeling that something wasn't right.

"Katherine?" he said again. "The movie's over."

He nudged her, but she still wouldn't wake up. Then, he shook her a little harder. She still didn't wake up.

"Katherine? Wake up, hun."

He tapped her cheek, but no response. He could barely tell that she was breathing.

"Come on! Wake up. P-Please wake up!"

When he heard footsteps walking up the stairs, he turned his head and yelled for his parents to get the truck started. He heard one pair of feet running down the stairs. He figured they didn't have to ask questions about what was going on. They already know.

John carried her to the truck, and they drove Katherine to the hospital.

Katherine woke up a few minutes after arriving at the hospital. She didn't realize where she was at first or what was going on. After looking around, she knew that she was in the hospital. No one bothered to change her into a gown, so she was still wearing her normal clothes.

She felt the tube being attached from the IV to her arm. She didn't like having a needle in her arm, but she knew that she had to have it.

It was quiet. John and his parents weren't around. Katherine didn't hear any traffic outside, or any doctors or nurses talking in the hallway. She couldn't even tell if John and his folks were out in the hall. It was that quiet.

The last thing she remembered was lying in her bed to take a nap. She asked John to wake her up in a bit. *I guess when I didn't wake up; he drove me here.* She thought. *I hope they're alright. The doctor may be speaking to them or something. They'll be here soon. I miss them.*

A minute or two passed by when a nurse walked in. It was the nurse with the white hair. Katherine hasn't seen her in a couple of months. It must have been May when she saw her last. The nurse walked over and checked Katherine's IV. At first, the nurse didn't say a thing. Katherine was tired of the silence, so she spoke first.

"What's going on?" Katherine asked.

"You already know, Katherine," the nurse responded.

"Yeah, I guess I do. Where is everyone?"

"They will be here shortly. How would you like to speak to them, dear? One at a time or all together?"

Katherine knew what was going on. She was feeling different. The feeling was indescribable. Her voice was soft, and she couldn't speak up loudly. She tried to get up twice, but that wore her out.

"I guess one at a time," Katherine said.

"Very well." The nurse walked over and put her hand on Katherine's head. "Everything will be alright. God will take care of everything."

"I know," Katherine whispered.

The nurse walked out, leaving Katherine alone for about a minute. Katherine wasn't really scared. She knew what would happen to her, and she knew where she was going. She looked at her hands. *This body is only temporary. These hands. These legs. This brain of mine. All of it. Heaven is an eternity. Talking to everyone will be rough, especially for them. I know that I want to speak to John last.*

She could hear her heartbeat. Usually, she never could hear it beat before. This time is different. She didn't have to put her hand on her chest to feel it beat either. Katherine took a few deep breaths.

"I'm ready," she said out loud.

Mary was the first one that walked in. Katherine could tell that she had been crying. Her eyes were red and filled with tears. When she walked in, she covered her mouth with one of her hands. Mary couldn't believe what was happening. She was scared, and Katherine could tell.

"H-Hey sweetie," Mary choked. She walked over to Katherine's right side of the bed and sat down beside her. "T-They said ... They said ..."

Mary couldn't say the rest. Katherine knew what she was trying to say though.

Katherine put her hand on Mary's arm. "I know."

More tears rolled down on Mary's face, as she wrapped her arms around Katherine, squeezing her tight. Katherine gave her a light squeeze. She was feeling too tired to give her a bigger hug. Mary didn't want to let go, and neither did Katherine.

For the next few minutes, neither one of them said anything. Mary just cried as Katherine rubbed her hand on Mary's back.

"Y-You're like a daughter to me," Mary sobbed, still holding on to Katherine.

"And you are like a mother to me. I love you."

"I-I love you too, dear."

"Your cooking is the best I have ever eaten."

Mary chuckled at that. "Thank you. I will always remember you. You're such a sweet girl. You make John so happy."

John ...

After a few more minutes of hugging each other, Mary got up and left the room.

Next was Michael. He walked in with a soft look on his face. She knew that he wasn't going to act all tough. There was no need for it, and he wasn't heartless.

Michael grabbed the chair in the corner and sat it next to her. He sat down and took her right hand. Then he gave it a small squeeze and looked at her. A tear rolled down his cheek, and he sighed.

"I-I know that I'm not your real dad ..." He mumbled. "But it sure feels like I am."

Katherine gave him a smile. "I know. I love you as if you were my dad."

"And I loved you as if you were my own child."

Katherine let go of his hand and wiped the tear off of his cheek. He put his hand on hers as he continued to look into her eyes.

"I know that you're John's dad and that it's your job to watch out for him, but can you keep an eye on him for me? I love him so much and I want him to stay safe."

"Of course. Anything for you."

It got quiet for a while. Michael stayed in the room a few more minutes longer than Mary could. They said nothing else to each other.

The nurse with the white hair came in after Michael left.

"Where's John?" Katherine asked, concerned.

"He'll be in shortly," She said.

"Oh, okay."

"They are such a caring family. You're very lucky to have them take care of you after your parents' arrest."

Katherine figured that the nurse knew about her parents because small towns like to spread gossip. So, she understood that the news about her parents would have spread into a few towns close by.

The nurse put her hand onto Katherine's. Her hand was warm and comforting.

"John is very gifted," The nurse said.

"Yes, I know. He has no idea how talented he is."

"God will watch over him and his parents."

"I know. Can I see him now? Please."

"Of course."

John was terrified when he carried Katherine into the truck and drove her to the hospital. He put her in the front seat, so his parents sat in the back. They didn't care; they wanted to get Katherine to the hospital. He was able to keep himself calm while driving there. Every minute or so, he would take a deep breath.

When they got inside, a nurse and a doctor put her onto a bed and rolled her away. The doctor told them to stay in the lobby until further notice.

A half-hour went by until the nurse with the white hair came toward them. John and his parents stood up when she was a foot or two away from them. Before saying anything, she looked at all three.

"Katherine is surely blessed to have all of you to care for her," she told them.

"How is she?" John asked. He didn't want to wait. He just wanted to know how Katherine was doing; if she was alright.

The nurse looked at them. "She ... have little time left."

"No ..." John sobbed.

"She wants to see you one at a time."

"I'll go first," Mary said. Tears were rolling down her face.

"Very well. Michael and John and can wait outside of her door if they like."

While Mary went into Katherine's room and Michael waited outside the door, John walked down the hall and stopped around the corner. He slammed his fist into the wall. He wanted to punch it straight through the wall. He wanted to scream and throw everything around. He didn't though. Instead, he cried.

The nurse with the white hair appeared behind him.

"John?" she said. "What's wrong?"

"I-I don't want to lose her."

"I know. It's her time though."

She put her hand on his shoulder. It felt warm and comforting. He felt like he could tell her anything.

"I love her so much," He sobbed.

"I know you do, John. She'll be alright. God has everything under control."

"I don't want her to go, though. I want her to stay."

He wiped some of his tears away, but more kept coming.

"John." The nurse said as she turned him around. "Let me ask you something. Are you glad you were able to spend the time you had with her?"

"Of course!" he said as he looked at her straight in the eyes.

"Are you thankful and blessed she came into your life?"

"Yes."

"Do you trust your Lord God?"

"Yes."

"Everything will be alright, John. Trust me. Trust God."

"A-Alright."

"It's your turn. She wants you to be the last person she sees before God takes her home. When you go in there, don't leave her side. Hold her hand and never let it go."

John nodded as he wiped more tears away. The nurse put both of her hands on his shoulders.

"Go say goodbye," She breathed as John looked down.

When he looked up, she was gone.

John took a few deep breaths and walked toward Katherine's room. He saw his dad holding his mother, letting her cry into his chest.

Father. John prayed before he walked in. *I know that You have your reasons for everything. I just ask that You make it as painless as possible for her. Please, Lord. I cherish the moments I had with her. I will always have the memories of the months I spent with her. I will never forget her. I love her, Father. I know that You do too, just like you love all Your children.*

John turned the doorknob and walked in. Immediately, he noticed the IV and the needle in her arm. Her eyes were closed, and she was barely breathing. Another tear ran down his cheek as he sat down in the chair that was right next to her. He moved it closer toward her.

When he sat down, she opened her eyes. She turned her head and looked at him. She smiled and reached out her hand. He held it lightly as if she would break if he held it any tighter.

"Hey there," She mumbled.

Her voice was soft and quiet. He could tell that she couldn't talk any louder than that. He didn't know if it hurt her or what, but that was okay.

She smiled, and he smiled back.

"Hey, beautiful," he said. "How are you feeling?"

"Tired, I guess would be the word. I dozed off while I waited for you. I hope that was okay."

"That's fine," Another tear ran down his face. "I love you so much."

"I love you too. Everything will be okay. God is watching over me."

"I-I know."

"I wrote you a letter. I put it on my dresser in my bedroom. You can read it when you're ready."

"I will."

She closed her eyes for a moment. She gave his hand a little squeeze before she opened her eyes again. They didn't say anything for a couple of minutes.

"Can you do something for me?" she asked.

It was getting more difficult for her to speak.

"Anything," He answered, still crying.

"Can you tell me a poem?"

"I-I don't know any."

"Make one up."

"I'll try," He took a deep breath and told her a poem.

"There's a sun,
It neither rises nor sets,
Making the sky beautiful,
It's always there/ so you'll never forget.
There's a never-ending ocean,
So calm that it never makes a sound,
Every now and then you can see doves,
Flying in the background.
Under your feet,
There are unlimited miles of sand,
Jesus is in front of you,
He says 'Come child and take My hand.'"

"That was beautiful." Katherine breathed. "What is it called?"
John couldn't stop crying now. "Heaven."
She took a deep breath. "Thank you."
"You're welcome, sweetie."
He leaned over and kissed her forehead. "I'll never forget you."
She hasn't left yet, but John's heart was already feeling like it had a piece missing. She looked at him one last time and gave him the most gorgeous smile he has ever seen. She then closed her eyes, never to open them again. Katherine passed away at that moment.

Funeral

It has been three days since Katherine passed away. Since then, all John has been doing is lying in bed, crying. He didn't get up to go to work or do any chores. He also wouldn't spend time with his mom and dad. Every now and then they would come to his room to check up on him. When they asked if he was alright, he would just lay there, staring at the wall with tears rolling down his face.

His eating habits drastically changed. He wasn't eating that much. Maybe late at night, he would go downstairs to drink a glass of water and snack on some chips. That was it, though. He would ignore his stomach, growling. John didn't care what his stomach wanted, or anything, or anyone else for that matter.

He hasn't touched his Bible or done any Bible studies with his family, nor has he written in his journal. He wouldn't even know what to write. That his heart was hurting? That it felt like there was a hole in his heart like someone shot through it? Or that it felt like someone reached inside his chest and squeezed inside it? No. He didn't want to write. He didn't want to do anything.

Today is the funeral, and he hasn't been out in a month since Katherine died. *Do I even remember what the outside world looks like?* He asked himself. *I'm not sure. I haven't been outside in a while.*

He also hasn't showered in the past couple of days. When he got up, he picked out his funeral clothes. Black suit and tie. Black pants and socks. Black shoes. All of his clothing was black. He laid them on the bed, spreading them all out.

After staring at them for a minute, he walked over and opened the curtains. It was cloudy. The clouds were thick and dark enough that the sun couldn't shine through them. It was as if it were night. It was like the sky was covered with charcoal.

I guess it's supposed to storm today. Oh, well. John used to love the sunshine and warm weather, but now all of that has changed. Now he doesn't care about the sun being covered and not shining through his window.

He took his shower and got dressed. When he walked out of his room, before heading downstairs, he stared at Katherine's bedroom door. It hasn't been opened since Katherine last slept in it. After a couple of minutes, he walked downstairs.

His parents were already in the truck, waiting on him. He got in, not saying a word. Michael didn't play music on the way to the church. Neither he nor Mary said a word to each other or to John all the way there. It was quiet.

John looked out the window. Dark black clouds went out for miles and miles. It was as if they never ended. John let out a sigh as a tear rolled down his cheek.

When they got to the church, few people were there. No one knew Katherine that well. They parked and got out of the truck. As soon as John walked into the church, everyone came up to him and shook his hand, telling him they were very sorry for his loss.

Holly and Amanda were there. So was the pastor, but he was supposed to be there. The rest of the people were ones that went to church. *That's nice of them to come, even though they didn't know her that well.* The only people that Katherine knew, but didn't show, were her parents. He knew that her dad was in jail, but he didn't know about her mother. *Is she still in rehab or did she get out? I'm not even sure if she knew her daughter passed away.*

John didn't say much. The only time he talked was when the people came and spoke to him. When they said they were sorry, all John would say was 'thank you'. He only said that once or twice. The rest he nodded. He didn't feel like talking.

All the people that Katherine knew sat in the front row. Pastor Bill spoke first.

"When I first met Katherine," he started. "I didn't know her. She was just a random girl who ran into church one Sunday morning during a sermon. She seemed confused and lost. Not lost as in, didn't know where she was, but lost as in, she didn't have Jesus in her life. Well, from what was a lost and confused girl, became a happy, loving, caring, saved young woman. I'm glad I got to know Katherine Lee."

He finished up and walked down, allowing other people to get up there and talk. It was a closed casket, so no one saw her face or anything.

However, there was a picture of her with the Williams that was taken on her birthday, sitting beside her casket.

John's parents took care of the funeral arrangements. John couldn't do them. He was emotionally wrecked. A white casket was picked. It was white on the inside as well.

Michael and Mary went up first. They talked about how they took Katherine in and treated her as if she was one of their own children. She was like a daughter to them. They also said they know that she is having the best time in the Kingdom of Heaven with Jesus.

"When she left," Michael said. "it was like I lost my own child. It felt like a piece of me died, along with her."

After they finished, it was Holly's turn.

"I offered Katherine a job at my flower shop," Holly said, sobbing. "She was the best worker I have ever had. Katherine loved working there. It made her so happy and smile. It was as if she was a small child at a playground. She wasn't just my employee, she was also my friend. I'm going to change my shop's name, to Katherine's Flower Shop. May she rest in peace."

When she was done, it was John's turn. He knew that getting up there and talking about her would hurt. It was going to hurt bad, but he knew that he had to do it.

Suddenly, there was loud thunder. Rain poured down, hitting the roof as if it was hail. A tear rolled down his cheek, and it landed on the carpet floor. He closed his eyes and took a long, deep breath. He then got up and walked to the front.

"Once Katherine ran into this church a few months ago," John said. "My life changed. She didn't know who Jesus was, but she was looking for Him. I sat her down and told her about God, Jesus, and everything I knew about being a Christian. Then I bought her a Bible. She lived in a home, where her dad would beat her until she bled, and her mother would scream and talk down to her. That didn't stop her though. Even though she was living in a bad home, she continued to read the Bible and she continued to grow in her faith."

John gave a quick scan and then continued. "Eventually, we began to date. We weren't married, but we grew together through Christ. We ended up falling in love. She meant the world to me." He wiped a tear away. "After her parents were arrested, she came to live with us. We would play games, have Bible studies together, and watch movies like one big happy family. She turned eighteen last month, on the day she died.

"The last time I saw her, she was lying in a hospital bed. She wasn't scared. She didn't cry. She wasn't angry. Katherine knew that she would join God in His wonderful Kingdom. She was my first love and my best friend. I will always cherish the memories I have of her. She came to this life as a girl who was broken and left this life as a woman of God who was full of joy."

It thundered again, and this time it lasted longer than the first one. He read the poem he made up for her at the hospital. He gave another quick glance around the church and saw that everyone was crying. They had a Kleenex or a handkerchief out. John too was crying. He wiped away his tears and finished what he wanted to say.

"As I finish this up, I want you to remember what I have said. I want you to remember what Holly and my parents have said. I want you to remember what Pastor Bill has said. Because, you may not have known her in person, but you can know her in memory."

John walked down, and the pastor finished it up with a prayer. Michael was one of the pallbearers. It was pouring down rain, but he didn't care. She was his daughter in some way, and he would make sure he played his part as a father and watch her get buried.

The rain slowed down some, but most of the people that were at the church left. When they got to the cemetery, the casket was lowered into the ground. John stood there along with his parents as the dirt was piling up on the casket. Mary cried on Michael's shoulder, while Michael wrapped his arm around his son. They cried together as they watched Katherine being buried.

Michael and Mary walked away with the umbrella. John didn't follow them. He stared at the pile of dirt in front of him.

"Are you coming, son?" Michael asked.

When John didn't answer, Michael handed him the umbrella and walked off with Mary. They sat in the truck until John finished.

He didn't care about the umbrella. He let it fall out of his hands. The rain was getting him soaked, but that didn't stop him from standing there. John didn't care about getting soaked from the rain. He didn't care that the raindrops were freezing cold, making him shiver. John fell to his knees and cried.

Closure

J ohn was doing better after the funeral. He was eating normal now. Instead of lying in his bed all day, he was actually getting up and moving around, doing activities. He has been writing in his journal as well.

I've been getting up and spending time with the family now. The funeral really helped me out. I felt better after I spoke to everyone and cried in the rain. I guess I just had to let it all out. However, there is still one problem. Katherine's room. I want to go in there and look at all her stuff. I want to get in and read the letter she said she has left me. But I can't get myself to even touch the doorknob. I'm not sure how long it will take for me to go inside. Mom and dad said they will not go in there to do anything until I go in first. Anyway, that's all that I have to say for right now.

John has even been opening the curtains, hoping for the sun to shine through his window. The sun felt warm and comforting. It felt natural.

He also has been spending more time with his parents again. He's doing Bible study again with them and playing games and watching movies. He missed doing that with his family. Especially, being a part of Bible study. John also went back to eating with them as a family. At first, it was quiet, but after a few days, it got a lot better. Now they were talking about how their days went and what they could do together.

John was able to get his sleep back to normal. He's able to sleep through the whole night and is no longer staying awake, crying. His eyes went back to normal. They were no longer red and sore.

After a few days, he was able to go back to work at his dad's hardware store. For about two weeks, he would stay in the back. People would keep asking if he was okay. John knew that they were just checking up on him to see if he was alright, but he wanted to be alone for a while. He did breakdown and cry about twice, but that was alright. He was holding his emotions in and had to let them go occasionally.

Then he could work up front in the store. Moving items around and stacking the counters. Michael even let him run the cash register a couple of times. It was new for him, but he got used to it quickly.

"Maybe I should make you a manager," Michael told him one day.

"No thanks, dad. I don't think I'm supposed to be a manager."

I'm pretty sure that God doesn't want me to be a manager of a hardware store. He told himself. *I'm sure He doesn't want me to be any kind of manager.*

"Let me at least give you a raise," His dad said.

"Sure, dad."

It took him a few weeks, but John was back to working at the store full time. He went slow at the beginning. He worked part-time, trying to get used to everything again.

One day, John was standing in front of Katherine's bedroom door. He reached for the doorknob slowly. When he got a half an inch away from the doorknob, he pulled his hand away. It still wasn't the right time.

He leaned his head against the door, taking a couple of deep breaths. Then he closed his eyes, thinking about her and how much he loved her. He didn't want to go inside and have a mental breakdown. He didn't want all of those sad memories of seeing her in the hospital to come back. He remembered how she suffered before she passed away. The headaches, the seizure, and how she was feeling tired all the time.

John felt a hand touching his shoulder. It was strong and had a grip on it. It was his dad's hand.

"It's okay, son," Michael told him.

"It's so hard," John mumbled. He was trying not to cry.

"I know. Her room isn't going anywhere. I promise you. Take your time. Go inside when you're ready."

"I-I miss her so much," That was it. Tears were rolling down his cheek.

"I know. Me and your mother miss her too. It'll be okay."

Lord God. I beg of You, please give me the strength to do this. I need Your help. I can't do this on my own. I made it through the sleepless nights, and the crying non-stop and avoiding going outside. I passed all of it. I fought through it all. Now help me, Father, to get through this. Please. This is the last one.

Near the end of September, John finally went to Holly's flower shop. He hasn't been there in a while because he was trying to avoid seeing the store's new name. He was happy that Holly changed it, but he couldn't handle seeing it. Not for a while at least.

When he got to the shop, the first thing he saw was 'Katherine's Flower Shop' in bright orange letters. He took a deep breath and walked right in. The place has been busy for the past month, and Holly was able to hire herself a new employee. She was in her early thirties and needed the job. Amanda would still work there after school as a part-time employee.

"Well, hey there, John!" Holly yelled with a smile on her face. "I haven't seen you in a while."

She was at the cash register, just finishing up with a customer.

"Same to you," He replied.

"Do you like what I've done with the place?"

Holly was able to remodel the shop. The shelves had a wooden look to them, and she put in solid wood floors. It was a terrific look for the shop. It definitely gave the place a country style to it.

"Looks fantastic."

"Thanks! What can I do for you?"

"A dozen roses, please."

"Coming right up. So how are you holding up?"

"I'm getting there, I guess."

"That's good," She handed him the roses, and he paid her.

"Keep the change."

"Thanks, John. I hope that you get to feeling better."

John waved her goodbye and left the shop. He knew that Holly wouldn't be able to work full time at the shop for too much longer. It usually slows down a lot during the winter. That's when Holly would only work at the shop part-time, and another place full time. For the last year or so, he would see her at the post office. So, that's probably where she'll be at this winter.

John drove to the cemetery where Katherine was buried. When he got there, he got out and walked over to her tombstone. There, he laid the roses down, along with the other flowers that were there. Holly had laid some lilies down, and his parents had laid down orange looking flowers the other day.

He didn't sit down or anything. He stood there looking where her name was. The sun was beaming down on him. It may be fall, but since he was down south, the weather was maybe in the high sixties or low seventies. After a while, he left and drove home.

Now it was the first of November, and John was once again standing in front of Katherine's bedroom door. It was time. He grabbed the doorknob and slowly turned it. When it opened, he walked in and turned the light switch on.

The entire room was covered in dust. She had a desk and a computer against one wall. She didn't use the computer much. Maybe once or twice a week she would get on it to look up a music group or a movie. That's pretty much it though.

Then there was her bed. It hasn't been touched since she was taken to the hospital. The bed was not made. Not even changed, for that matter. So, the same sheets and quilt were still on there, along with her stuffed animal.

John took a deep breath, trying not to cry again. *I can do this. I know I can.*

Lastly, there was her dresser. Her clothes were still inside the drawers, untouched. In the middle of the dresser was a letter covered in dust. John picked it up and shook the dust off it. He then opened it up and read it.

John,

If you're reading this, then it must mean that I have gone to a better place. First off, I wanted to tell you I couldn't have been happier than the last few months I was with you. You made me laugh, smile, and made me feel loved. I have never done any of that when I used to live with my parents. Since you came into my life, I have found Jesus Christ and let Him into my mind, heart, and soul. I was free. I was at peace. You don't have to do this, but I ask if you could check up on my parents, Sarah and Kenny. Kenny is probably still in jail, and I have no idea where my mom could be. I know that Michael and Mary are your parents, but I ask that you keep an eye out on them. They weren't my parents, but they treated me as if they were. I thank them for that. They were there for me and treated me with such kindness and love. One more thing. I may have figured out what you should do in life. You've told me just about everything you have thought of; architecture, school teacher, scientist. Even a professional motorcyclist. However, there was one thing you left out. John, I think you should be a writer! You could write books, or poems, or even songs. I might even try to test my theory out and get you to come up with something like a poem one day. You also have an amazing singing voice, so that's a bonus if you ever chose to write songs. So, there you go. I hope that you will pray about my suggestions. Does that sound right? It sounds weird, but I'm going with it. Anyway, I am leaning toward the songwriting (and maybe even a singer) idea. So, you should try that. I love you with all my heart.

Katherine.

Starting Over

A few days went by and John was driving to the rehab center to see Katherine's mother, Sarah. He packed up some of Katherine's clothes and put them in a box. He figured that Sarah would want something that was her daughter's. It would be difficult to get rid of most of her stuff, but he knew that it had to be done. He also would give Sarah Katherine's computer.

John didn't even know if Katherine's mother was still at rehab or not. He must try though. *What if she isn't there though?* He asked himself. *Maybe the people that work there could tell me where she would have gone. Hopefully, she is willing to talk to me. I never actually got to meet Sarah.*

Katherine has told me stories about her though. How she would cuss at Katherine and talk badly to her. Like saying she does nothing, or that she was worthless. She also told me that her mother was a giant drug addict. That's why she went to rehab. Maybe she's changed by now. Who knows, though? Katherine wanted me to check up on her parents, and that's what I'm going to do.

When he got there, he didn't bother to get the box of clothes or the computer out of the truck. He wanted to see if Sarah was still there first. He walked to the front counter and got the woman's attention.

"I'm looking for Sarah Lee," John told her. "Is she still here?"

"I'm sorry, sir, she isn't," the woman said.

"She got better?"

I can't give out that kind of information. However, I can tell you where she said she would be staying."

"Please. Thank you."

"Here you go. You're welcome and have a great day."

Sarah might be living in the town that's right next to Bruce. Before he would try to find her, he decided to eat lunch. His stomach was growling.

He stopped by at a drive-in fast food place. He ordered himself a chili cheese dog with tater tots and a milkshake. Instead of eating in the truck as most people do, he got outside and sat down on one of the blue metal tables. John enjoyed eating outside, it was calm and relaxing.

It was partly cloudy. The sun was out most of the time. However, every few minutes or so, it would get covered up by a small cloud. *Hopefully, it won't rain. I enjoy the sun.*

When he finished his lunch, he drove to the town that Sarah said she would be living in. He asked people in grocery stores, a bank, and even a gas station, but no one knew where she lived at. An owner of a restaurant knew who John was talking about and where she lived, but he didn't want to give out her information.

John finally asked around at an apartment building. He found out she was living there and went inside the building with the box of clothes and the computer. He sat the box down and knocked on the door. The building had an old style to it. Hardwood floors and it had a few spots where old wired telephones used to be. The doors were also wood and the one he knocked on still had the smell of new paint around it.

A woman opened the door and asked if she could help him.

"I'm looking for Sarah Lee," He said.

"I'm her. Who are you?"

"I'm John William. I dated your daughter."

"Oh. Come in, come in."

She motioned him to come in. So far, she seemed like a nice lady. Her hair was short, and she was wearing a blue skirt with a thin long sleeve shirt tucked in it. Sarah kindly told him to have a seat, and he sat the box and computer down in front of him. So far, so good.

"How did you find me?" she asked with a puzzled look.

"It wasn't easy. I had to ask around."

"Oh, okay. I didn't hear about Katherine's death until I got out of rehab. That was a couple of days after the funeral. When I heard, I cried my eyes out. I wanted to see her again."

"I'm sorry."

"I went to her grave and sat some flowers on her tombstone yesterday. I still can't believe that she's gone."

John didn't know what to say next.

"She told me some stories about you," John said.

"Bad ones, right?" she sighed. "I-I was a terrible mother. I would call her names and make her do hard work late at night while I would go do drugs. I even pushed her around a few times." Sarah was crying now and grabbed a tissue to wipe her eyes. "I should have been a better mother. I wouldn't even do anything when her dad beat her with that belt of his."

"She forgave you."

"I don't know why she would. I was horrible. She came to visit me in rehab once and gave me a Bible. I began to read it, and I changed after that. Every morning I would get up to read it. Once I left rehab, I moved here and went to church every Sunday. I made one or two friends there. Kind people. They let me join their book club they have once a month."

"That's good. I'm glad you started going to church."

"I was saved last week. It was a remarkable experience. I'll never forget it."

She told him about the day she got saved, and some other stories. She's now working at a restaurant where she's a cook and makes decent money. Not once has she written to Kenny or even tried to visit him since she got out of rehab.

"I'm going to get a divorce. I don't want to be married to a man like that. I'm not sure how's he doing, but I know that if I want to be with someone, I want them to be a Godly man."

"That's good to hear. He's still in jail, I believe. Should be getting out soon."

"I noticed that you brought a box and a computer. Why did you bring it?"

"Well, I kind of figured that you would want some of Katherine's belongings."

"Oh, why thank you!"

John handed her the box and watched her go through it.

"I packed some of her clothes. Skirts, dresses, t-shirts, and one or two pairs of shoes. I also brought you her computer."

A tear rolled down Sarah's cheek. "T-Thank you, dear. You don't know how much this means to me."

"I also wanted to give you a picture of her we took on her birthday."

He handed her a picture of Katherine, with him and his folks. John put it in a frame for Sarah.

"Oh, how lovely," Sarah smiled. "Look at her smiling. Thank you."

"You're welcome."

"Would you like something to drink? How about some water?"

"Sure, that sounds nice."

While Sarah went into the kitchen, John looked around the room. She didn't have many pictures on the walls. There was one picture of some mountains, and another one with a painting of a cat hanging out with a dog. The coffee table between the two couches had a puzzle on it. John figured that she liked puzzles. It wasn't finished though.

That's good, she's better and follows Christ now. If only she was like this around Katherine. I wish Katherine could see her mother now. A woman of God who has a job and no longer on drugs.

Sarah came back and handed him a bottle of water. "Here you go."

"Thank you. There's one more thing I wanted to give you."

"Hmm?"

John handed her a piece of paper that had words written on it. Sarah didn't understand until she read what was on it. She cried and wiped more tears away from her eyes.

She looked up at him. "Did you write this?"

"Yes, ma'am. I wrote it, in memory of Katherine."

"It's beautiful. Thank you. I'm going to frame it once I get paid."

"You're welcome. Well, I better get going. I'm glad you're doing much better."

"Goodbye, John," She said as she walked him to the door.

"Goodbye."

Next was Katherine's dad, Kenny Lee. He was still in jail for the warrants he had. However, he would be getting out in a couple of weeks. John figured that he should go ahead and visit him, in case the man leaves town.

I know that he's in jail and won't be able to hurt me, but I am still a little scared to meet the man. He's the one that beat on Katherine with a belt. From what she told me, he would drink a lot and fight with Sarah. When that didn't satisfy him, he would go to Katherine's room and hit her on the back with a belt. Sometimes making her bleed. Kenny was a violent man, and I'm about to give him a visit. Katherine told me she mailed him a Bible. Hopefully, he read it and changed as Sarah did.

An hour later, John was sitting down on one side of the glass window. It was the glass between him and Katherine's dad. John was shaking a bit and was nervous. He gulped as Kenny sat down on the other side.

He was clean shaved and had short hair. His eyes didn't read evil or angry. They read hurt and ashamed.

"Who are you?" Kenny asked in a calm, soft voice.

"I-I'm John William," John replied. His voice was a little shaky. "I dated Katherine."

"Oh. Nice to meet you."

Nice to meet me? This isn't the man that Katherine told me about. What's going on? Has he changed?

"How are you doing?"

"I'm getting better. I've been reading the Bible that Katherine mailed me. I didn't read it at first, but after a couple of days, I finally gave in. After I read the first chapter of Matthew, I couldn't stop reading it. It changed me. Jesus has changed me."

"T-That's good to hear," John was calming down.

"I used to be an alcoholic. I would use up all the money I had and buy beer and liquor. Now the thought of that stuff makes me want to hurl. I don't want to touch that garbage ever again. I would get so drunk I would hit Katherine and her mother." Water was forming in his eyes. "I-I would get my belt and beat my own daughter until she bled. I would see her struggle when she would move."

"She forgave you."

Kenny continued talking like he didn't even hear John. "When she came to visit me, I mocked her for believing in God. When she told me that she loved me, all I said was 'whatever'. That's all I said. I should have told her that I loved her too."

"Jesus forgives you."

Kenny kept talking with tears falling off his face. "I was a horrible, horrible dad, and I was a terrible husband. I shouldn't have done any of that stuff."

"Kenny, ask for forgiveness. Let Jesus into your life."

"I'm working on that. Slowly, but surely. I'm understanding the Bible more."

"That's good. Umm. I wrote something in memory of Katherine. The officer said I can hand it to you personally."

Kenny read what was on the paper. When he finished, more tears ran down his cheeks.

"You wrote this?" he asked John.

"Yes, sir."

"Katherine would have loved it. Thank you. I'll make sure I keep it safe. I might get it framed for when I get myself a new place to live."

"Good luck."

"Do you know what really made me pick up that Bible? When I saw in the newspaper that my daughter had died. I cried in disbelief. I should have treated her better. I cut out the part from the newspaper about her and I keep it under my pillow."

"Everything will be okay. I have to go now, but you take care. Keep reading the Bible and hopefully one day, you will let Jesus into your heart, mind, and soul. Have a good day."

"You too, and God bless you."

Memories

"**A**re you sure you want to do this, son?" Michael asked John.

"Yes."

"You can wait if you need to. No need to rush anything. Just say the word, and we can stop right now."

"No. I want to do this."

It was now Friday, and John was about to clean up Katherine's old room. John and Mary bagged up the rest of Katherine's clothes. Mary will donate them to a charity. Michael and one of his friends will take the bed, dresser, and the desk down the stairs to put them in the yard sale today.

"Alright," Michael said. "Let's do it."

While Mary left, John went inside the room and pulled the curtains, allowing the sun to shine through the window. First, he shook the sheets and quilt. Dust flew, floating everywhere. He balled up the sheets and quilt, and threw them out of the room, along with the pillows. On the bed was Katherine's stuff animal. He set it down and grabbed a rag.

While he dusted off the desk, he remembered some memories he had with Katherine.

One night, while they were reading the Bible together, they thought of a game. One would ask about what they just read, and if the other person gets it wrong, then they will have to pay the consequences. The person that got the answer wrong would have something written on them with a washable marker.

It was a fun way to memorize the Scripture verses. Surprisingly, John got the first question wrong. Katherine grabbed a marker and drew 'CUTIE' on his forehead. She had a handheld mirror, so he could see.

"Oh, I'm so going to pay you back for this," he chuckled.

"Best two out of three?" Katherine asked.

"You're on!"

Katherine ended up wrong next, and John wrote the word 'PUMPKIN' on her forehead.

When she saw what he wrote, she said, "Oh, this means war!"

John ended up losing that night. Katherine drew a giant smiley face on his hand, and a rabbit's face on his other hand.

John smiled at the memory. *That was a fun night.* He said to himself.

Michael came up with his friend and they took the bed away. It took two trips to do it. John sighed and opened the window, letting air in. He looked out the window and felt a cool breeze blowing against his face. He looked up and there wasn't a cloud in the sky, just pure sunshine.

Next, he dusted the dresser, and another memory of Katherine came to mind.

Katherine, John, and his folks couldn't decide on what to do one day as a family. So, they had a pie-eating contest. Mary had a few pies that she bought from the grocery store and warmed them up. Once they cooled, they began the contest.

All the pies were blueberry, which everyone loved. It was a close one, but Katherine ended up winning. Pie was covering everyone's faces. Mary had pie up her nose, which felt strange. Michael somehow had gotten pie on the back of his neck, and John had pie in his ears.

"Alright, Katherine," Michael said with a big grin. "You won, so you choose what we do today."

Katherine looked around, thinking. Then after a few seconds, she grabbed a handful of pie that was left over.

She shouted, "Food fight!" and threw the pie in John's face.

"You're in for it now!" John laughed.

Everyone grabbed something and threw food at each other. Mary tossed flour at Michael. Katherine shoved some mashed potatoes in Mary's face. John took some green beans and poured them down Michael's shirt. It was a mess after they were done, but they all had a terrific time. They blasted some music while cleaning up.

Good times. He thought.

Michael and his friend came in and picked up the dresser. It was too heavy, so they took out all the drawers. After that, it was easier. They came back and grabbed all the drawers.

John then grabbed the broom and dustpan. He slowly swept up the dust and dirt. He started in the corner where the stuffed animal was. The stuffed animal and Katherine's Bible were the only two things that John wanted to keep. Those and the letter she wrote to him.

Once half of the room had been swept, one last memory came to his mind.

One day, while Katherine was working at the flower shop, John stopped by and gave her some candy.

"What's this for?" Katherine asked as she opened the candy up.

"I just wanted to buy you something." He replied. "Also, to get you off work so I can take you out to eat."

"Wait, what? I'm working, John."

"I already talked to Holly, and she said it'll be alright."

"Oh, really? Well, I guess if she's alright with it."

John didn't expect that a few days later, Katherine would do the same thing. She took John from the hardware store an hour before closing. She did something better, though. John was surprised by what she did. Katherine had set up a picnic for the two. There were also candles. The flame was inside of a glass, so they wouldn't have to worry about it catching something on fire.

Mary taught her how to cook. She ended up making lasagna, and it tasted incredible.

"I hope it was okay," Katherine said.

"It was amazing. I even want seconds!"

After dinner, they laid down and watched the clouds. They were thin and moving fast. It was beautiful since the moon was shining through them. It sure was a gorgeous sight to see.

He took her hand and held it.

"Isn't this romantic?" She asked him.

"Sure is. I wish it wouldn't have to end."

"Me either."

That memory is one of my favorites. Of course, all of them are fantastic. I miss her so much. Her smile. Her giggles. Her hands holding mine. I miss it all. However, I know that she's having the best time up there with Jesus.

"Is this the last one?" Michael's friend said as they came in.

"Yep," John's dad said.

They picked up the desk and carried it downstairs. John then swept the rest of the floor up. The room looked different. It was bigger now. It was empty.

He picked up the stuffed animal and brought it to his room. He sat it on his desk, right beside Katherine's Bible. John sat down in the chair and picked up the picture of her with him and his parents.

A tear rolled down his cheek.

"I miss you so much," He said out loud.

John wiped the tear away and walked downstairs. His mom was still in town, and his dad was now in the garage. The garage door was opened, showing the desk, bed, and dresser.

It didn't take long for people to show up. There was a huge sign beside the mailbox that said, 'Furniture for sale'. Within five minutes after it was all set up, people came rushing in.

A man bought the dresser for his daughter. He figured that she would like it. Michael didn't charge much for it. The guy came back with a buddy and they loaded it up in his pickup truck.

Next, an elderly woman stopped by and bought the bed. She said her old one is giving her trouble, and she was looking for a new one. After talking to John and Michael about her back trouble, she ended up buying the bed. Even though she knew it was used, anything was better than the bed she had now. She also loved the headboard.

Finally, a woman came by and bought the desk. She said it was for her teenage son, who loved to write. He asked for a computer desk for his birthday, and the desk that John and Michael were selling would be perfect. She didn't have a problem loading it up into her truck.

All the furniture from Katherine's room was now gone. John and Michael stood there for a while, staring in the distance. It felt strange, now knowing that Katherine's old room was now empty. Most of her stuff was officially gone.

John took a deep breath and exhaled slowly. "That's it. That's all of it."

"Are you going to be okay, son?" Michael asked.

"Yeah, I will be."

Mary came back with a bag of groceries.

"Hey, I had an idea," She said. "I bought all of us some bread that is a foot long each. How about we make ourselves some giant sandwiches? John, how much do you want to bet that your dad will make his sandwich so thick, that he wouldn't even be able to fit a small piece in his mouth?"

John laughed. "Ten bucks says he can!"

"Deal!"

"Wait, a minute," Michael laughed. "Do I get a say in this?"

John and Mary looked at him and said, "No."

Later that night, John was having dinner with his parents. Mary cooked chicken spaghetti. John looked across the table where there was an empty chair. It was the spot where Katherine would always sit. John had already finished his food but continued to stare across the table.

He took a deep breath and sighed. "I miss her so much." He mumbled.

Michael and Mary stopped what they were doing and sat their forks down. Then they put their hands on John's shoulders.

"It's okay," Mary said softly.

"I'm going to sing at church this Sunday," John told them.

"Sing?"

"Yeah. I wrote a song, in memory of Katherine. I gave a copy to her parents."

"That's great, John. I guess you found your gift, huh?"

"Yeah. Katherine is the one who figured it all out."

Michael looked at his son. "I'm looking forward to hearing it. What's the song called?"

John wiped away a tear. "Singing with Angels."

Singing with Angels

It was Saturday morning and John woke up early. It was seven in the morning, and he went downstairs to make himself a cup of coffee. John liked his coffee black with just a teaspoon of sugar. After making his drink, he sat down at the table.

He couldn't figure out why he woke up so early. He had his alarm set for eight-thirty. The sun was beaming through the windows, but the weather wasn't supposed to be that warm today. It would be in the low sixties.

John drank his coffee and put on some clothes for work. Then he opened his window as usual and let the sunshine into his room. Since it would be cool today, it didn't warm up his room. However, the sky was as blue as ever and without a cloud in sight.

He read a few chapters of his Bible and then went downstairs once he heard his mom singing to herself in the kitchen. The house was quiet that day, so if someone said anything, you could hear it no matter where you were in the house. He headed downstairs and told his mother a good morning.

Mary was making a simple breakfast. Sausage and biscuits, with scrambled eggs and toast. Nothing fancy. It was still good, though. Michael came down and made himself a plate and a cup of coffee. He was already dressed for work. Once he and John finished their breakfast, they headed to the hardware store.

John was wearing a thin long sleeve shirt while his dad was wearing a short sleeve one.

"It sure feels great this morning," Michael said.

"What are you talking about?" replied John. "It's a little chilly."

They opened the store and worked. Michael opened the cash register and turned on all the lights. Then he flipped the 'Closed' sign to 'Open'.

John went to the back and moved around some boxes. A truck was supposed to come by today, so he had to move stuff around for room. When the truck came, John unloaded the truck, along with his dad. A customer hasn't shown up for the past hour, so Michael figured that it wouldn't hurt to leave the counter.

There wasn't that much to unload. A couple of boxes of paint, some toolboxes, a few chainsaws, and some hammers along with a few boxes of nails and screws.

Michael heard the door open and ran to the front. After John finished unloading the truck, he went to the front to see if the customer needed any help. The man wanted to fill out an application for a job.

"I never had anyone wanting to come and work for me before," Michael said. "However, I do keep one or two applications around, just in case. Here you go."

He handed the man an application. The guy must have been in his mid-twenties and had short black hair and was wearing glasses.

He looked up at John and said, "Hey, I heard that you're going to sing at the church tomorrow morning. Is that true?"

"Yeah. Who told you that?"

The guy pointed to Michael.

"Really dad?" John said.

Before Michael could say something back, the guy continued talking to John. "Is it going to be a gospel song, or something with a fast beat, like rock?"

"Maybe southern gospel or something like that. I'm not completely sure yet."

"Just going to go with the flow?"

"Probably. I'm going to let God handle it."

"Sounds like a plan."

He finished up his application and handed it over to Michael, then walked out. John gave his dad a look like he wanted no one to know about the song until Sunday.

His dad shrugged. "You know that I can't keep a secret. You should have known that."

John smiled and laughed. "Yeah, I should have known."

It was around ten in the morning, and by that time tomorrow, John will be singing his song in church. *I'm not even that nervous.* He thought. *At least, not right now. I may be once I get on stage. When I wrote that song, it felt right; it felt comfortable. I cried while I wrote it, but that's because it's for Katherine.*

John moved the boxes that were unloaded around the back room. It may have been cool outside, but in the back of the store, it was hot. John was sweating and had to roll his sleeves up. Michael handed him a towel and a bottle of water.

At one o'clock, Michael and John sat at a table in front of the store on the sidewalk. It was lunchtime, and both of them were starving.

Michael made them ham sandwiches and brought a couple of bags of chips and two sodas. John had extra ham and cheese on his sandwich. Once they finished their lunch, someone walked up to them. It was an older woman, maybe in her late forties.

"Hey," she greeted them. "There's a rumor going around that you're going to sing a song at church tomorrow. I'm looking forward to it."

"Thank you," John replied.

"So, are you nervous? About being in front of everyone and having them watching you?"

"Not really."

"I know I would be. I have major stage fright! Well, good luck! I'll be listening."

"Thanks."

They waved goodbye to each other and John and Michael went back to work. The store wasn't that busy today. One person came in and bought a nail gun with a few boxes of nails to go with it. Another person came in and bought themselves a table saw. The last customer bought himself some lumber and a couple of boxes of screws. John and Michael helped him load the lumber into his small trailer.

They closed the store around eight that evening and went home and ate supper, which was delicious like always. John took a shower and then went straight to his room. There, he sat down at his desk and took out a pen and wrote in his journal.

Tomorrow morning, I will be singing the song I wrote, 'Singing with Angels'. I'm not sure how the music will go. I'll probably just tell the musicians to go along with it as I sing. I was told that I have an amazing singing voice. Katherine told me that. My parents and a few people from church said the same thing before when I sang in the choir once or twice. I'm sure that my parents heard me sing while we were in the truck before. I don't know how it will go tomorrow morning, but I do know that this is what God wants me to do. He wants me to write songs and sing them to people. This feels right. People may applaud, or they may just sit there and do nothing. Either way, I have to do this.

As I write this down, I can't help but think of Katherine. She's the one who figured out I should be a writer. I thank her and God. I thank God for bringing her into my life. I thank her for figuring out what I should do in life. I am truly blessed. Katherine may be gone, but she is still in my heart and I will never forget her.

Anyway, tomorrow will be the beginning of a new era. I might cry while I'm singing, but that's okay. People may cry with me, and that's okay. This is God's plan for me. He gave me the gift of writing and I plan on using it. I just wish that Katherine was here to watch and hear me sing tomorrow at church. She would be proud of me. Tears are now falling onto the paper as I'm writing this, but that too is okay. Katherine knew that I was supposed to do something great. She believed in me. This song is for her. I don't know if she will be watching over me tomorrow morning or not, but if she is, I hope that she'll be smiling. I hope that she'll be clapping.

That's all that I have to write for now. Tomorrow morning, I will begin the first day of my career. I will put my gift into use.

John closed his journal and closed the curtains. He went to brush his teeth and came back and got on his knees. He closed his eyes and folded his hands. Then he prayed.

"Father, I thank You for this gift that You have given me and for the months You let me have with Katherine. I will cherish those moments for the rest of my life. I know that You will be watching over me as I sing tomorrow morning. I wouldn't be able to do it without You, Lord God. My king. My Savior. In Jesus's name, I pray. Amen."

John got in bed and fell asleep within seconds.

That Sunday morning, John got up and did his normal routine. He prayed, brushed his teeth, and put on his church clothes. Today he wore a white long-sleeve button-down shirt, with blue jeans and his black church shoes. He then grabbed some gel and slicked his hair back.

He looked in the mirror to make sure that everything looked alright. Everything looked good. John then opened his curtains to see if it would rain. Not a cloud in the sky. That brought a smile to his face. He didn't want it to rain on this day.

John then walked downstairs. His parents were already waiting for him in the truck. There was no need for breakfast since the church usually offers it. Every now and then Mary would cook them something, but not today.

"Do you have your lyrics with you?" Michael asked.

"Don't need them," John replied with confidence. "I memorized it. I know it word for word."

"That's good, son. You know it by heart."

"Yep."

While they drove to church, John closed his eyes and took a deep breath. He wasn't nervous, but he wanted to feel relaxed and comfortable when he would go up on stage. His heart was beating faster. He wasn't sure why. *I guess it's because of the excitement. I am excited about today. Not nervous, but excited.*

"I'm so excited!" Mary said out loud. "I get to see my son sing on the altar! This will truly be a Sunday that I will never forget!"

Michael smiled. "Calm down, dear. Don't get too excited."

They got to the church and parked. Some people were outside, talking to each other. Before John could walk into the church, someone stopped him.

"Hey there!" A man said. He could have been in his fifties. He sounded cheerful and shook John's hand. "How are you doing this beautiful morning?"

"Great," John replied.

"I was told that you will be singing this morning, after the sermon. That's nice to hear. Did you write the song yourself?"

"Yes sir, I did."

"That's great. God has blessed you with an amazing talent."

"He sure did."

John then walked into the church and grabbed himself a sausage biscuit and a cup of orange juice. When he was done, he sat down in the front row.

Everyone seemed to be cheerful and smiling. After the pastor finished his conversation with one musician, he came over and talked to John.

"Are you ready this morning?" Pastor Bill asked him.

"Yes, sir," John nodded. "I'm looking forward to it."

"Well, I told the musicians that after the sermon, you will be singing a song. So, once you go up there, they'll follow. Do you know how you want the music to go?"

"Just tell them to go with what God tells them."

Pastor Bill smiled. "Will do! Today's sermon is about love."

There were a few minutes left before church would start, and John's parents came over and sat down next to him.

"Everyone seems to be excited about you singing this morning, John," Michael said.

"Did Holly show up?" John asked.

"Yeah, but she'll be sitting in the back. I don't think you'll be able to speak to her before church starts though. She's being eaten alive by Samantha and her husband."

John chuckled. "I hope that she'll enjoy the song."

Church began, and the pastor did his usual sermon. Once he was done, he told everyone John had something he would love to share with the church.

"He wrote a song and would like to sing it for everyone," Pastor Bill said. He then walked off the stage, allowing John and the musicians to come up.

John set the microphone to his height and spoke. "A girl name Katherine passed away not too long ago. She was an amazing young woman. She made me smile, laugh, and she had the biggest heart I had ever seen. I loved her. Then she passed away from cancer." He took a long deep breath. "This song is called 'Singing with Angels', and I wrote it in memory of Katherine Lee."

As the musicians played, John sang.

"When you saw Jesus did you fall to your knees,
When you touched His hand did He cure your disease,
Did He take all of your pain away,
Are you able to sing to Him every day,
I hope you're singing with angels,
I hope you're feeling free,
I hope when you close your eyes you can still see,
I hope you're singing with angels,
Are you able to dance while you sing,
Are you able to bow down to your king,
Can you raise your arms to worship God Almighty,
Do you feel at peace when you walk in the Kingdom of Heaven,
I hope you're singing with angels,
I hope you're feeling free,
I hope when you close your eyes you can still see,
I hope you're singing with angels,
I hope you're singing with angels,

Do you no longer fall,
Do you run instead of crawl,
Do tears of joy run down your face,
Can you feel the Lord's grace,
I hope you're singing with angels,
I hope you're feeling free,
I hope when you close your eyes you can still see,
I hope you're singing with angels,
I hope you're singing with angels …"

Everyone stood up with tears in their eyes and applauded.

In Memory of
Alberta Jane Orr
December 18, 2017

Acknowledgments

I would like to thank God for giving me the gift of writing. Without Him, this wouldn't have been possible. I would also like to thank my wife for being by my side and believing in me. She was there for me when my stepmother passed away. I also would like to thank my readers! I hope that you have enjoyed this book as it is my first novel. Don't worry! There are more books to come.

Follow me on social media!
Facebook @writeroutcast
Twitter @AuthorOrr

CPSIA information can be obtained
at www.ICGtesting.com
Printed in the USA
BVHW050909120922
646800BV00005B/82